CITY
AT
BAY

CITY AT BAY

A NOVEL BY

DAVID THOREAU

ARBOR HOUSE New York

The author wishes to thank the following members of the San Francisco Police Department for their time and the benefit of their knowledge and experience: Officer Tom Deltorre, Officer Eddie Rodriguez, Officer Bob Barry, Inspector Paul Morse; and special thanks to Officer Phil Dito.
I would also like to thank Dudley Frasier, Bernard Wolfe, M.T. Caen, Pennfield Jensen and John Dodds for their consistent support and editorial guidance.

To Margaret and H.D.

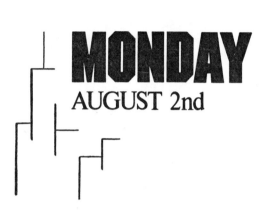

MONDAY
AUGUST 2nd

1

THE limousine moved noiselessly toward the crest of Nob Hill. The morning sun peeled away the shadowed streets as it crept above the victorian rooftops. The sky was slow with haze and the bay flat like a pale blue stain.

"Another hot one," the mayor thought to himself. The city wilted in the heat. She always had. San Francisco was too pretty, too delicate for the summer sun.

His driver-bodyguard, Mike Spivac, picked his way through the double-parked trucks at the top of Mason Street. It was Monday morning and it seemed as if every produce, linen, meat, and bakery company in the city was making deliveries to the elegant hotels and apartments at the top of the hill. Petrini, Gianini Bros., New French, Huey Sing—he knew the names and many of the faces. San Francisco names—families, like his own, who for generations had been making the same deliveries to the same addresses.

The air smelled rich and slightly decayed like the people who lived there. He knew those faces too. After sixteen years as mayor of San Francisco there were very few Nob Hill apartments and townhouses that he hadn't been invited to. Naturally he'd turned most of them down, but once or twice a year, especially a campaign year, he'd let Bryce

3

Stevens talk him into accepting an invitation from San Francisco's finest. Usually he would go alone, Constance had never felt comfortable around "society people." Inevitably the conversation would begin with the arts; the latest success of the opera, ballet, or symphony. Then some gin-laden matron would start in about his vulgar modernization of the city. He would patiently explain that he wanted to make the city livable for all its citizens, not just a repository for the gentle memories of a few. She would then airily dismiss his arguments with a wave of her fleshy arm and her husband would ask him about the rating of the latest city bond offering, which both of them knew was slipping.

The limousine turned right on California Street falling in behind a cable car. There was a mayor right after the war who wanted to do away with the cable cars because they were too dangerous and too expensive. Needless to say he was a one-term mayor. Sam Belardi might be the son of an immigrant Italian baker and unused to the ways of patrician San Francisco, but he wasn't stupid. Politics to him was business. He'd spent much of his adult life at it and the first thing he'd learned was never to trade for something you can't replace. It was one thing to tear down a rotten pier and replace it with a far more lucrative and attractive restaurant or parking lot. It was another to turn the historic waterfront into a shopping center.

They passed beneath the gothic shadow of Grace Cathedral and began the long descent down the back of the hill into Polk Gulch. Spivac tried to bring him to work a different way each morning, partly for security reasons but also because he liked to take different routes through the city, often stopping to see old friends and political allies. Or at least he used to. The past few months he could barely remember looking out the window.

Ever since Constance's death it all looked the same. Nothing seemed to matter any more. Not the job, not the

4

people, not the politics, not even the city itself. His wife had given him more strength than he ever realized. That was the cruelest legacy of death. All his life he'd seen himself as a self-sufficient entity. A man who was a husband, a father, a lawyer, a Democrat, an Italian-American, a mayor, and some would believe almost a vice-president. It was only after his wife's death the previous winter that he understood how for forty-three years of that life he'd had a silent partner, a full partner whose silence had given him love, approval, encouragement and faith. Now she was gone and he wasn't the man he'd always presumed to be.

The press blamed his uncharacteristic apathy on the fact that he was a lame-duck mayor with nowhere to go. They said that at sixty-three he was too old to run for statewide office and too proud to run for anything else. One columnist, with whom he'd been at odds for more years than either would admit, said that after the upcoming November election Sam Belardi would become a political "gill," or as the columnist explained "a fish out of water, lying on the river bank, wriggling and gasping for the mire of city politics."

His attitude toward the press in general had deteriorated to the point that when he announced his decision to step aside at the end of his fourth term, the only reporters he invited were the publisher of the North Beach Italian weekly and the two San Francisco bureau chiefs of *Time* and *Newsweek*. Of course, he knew better than to think he could escape the press. All any politician could ever hope for was to inconvenience them. . .

A police patrol car crossed in front of them at Larkin. The patrolman on the passenger side frowned at the black limousine.

"Michael, do you think the cops will strike if the City Council doesn't give them their raise?" he asked his driver, who worked for the sheriff's office.

5

"You can make book on it, Mr. Mayor. The guys I know are pissed. They think Zimmerman is jackin' them around, makin' them look like chumps so he can be the next mayor."

"That's what he's doing all right," the mayor agreed, referring to City Council President Fred Zimmerman.

"The way the cops figure it, he won't look so good when the animals take over. People won't be safe in their own homes much less on the street."

The mayor reflected on what the sheriff just said. There had been other police strikes across the country in the last few years, some more violent than others. Every city was different. Every police department was different. There had always been a certain camaraderie between San Francisco and her police, a much different relationship than, say, existed in cities like Los Angeles or San Diego where the police were more like an occupying army. He wondered how much of that camaraderie still existed or if it would make any difference if it did.

Spivac turned south on Polk Street when they got to the bottom of the hill. A male prostitute cased the car as they drove by. The man was wearing a leather jacket studded with silver stars, jack boots and a pair of skin-tight pants. His eyes were made up with sequins and he wore a small goatee. He reminded the mayor of a repulsive little satyr, ready to perform any act imaginable or unimaginable for the price of a cheap bottle of booze or a piece of junk jewelry. He winked at the mayor when Spivac stopped for a pedestrian and then made an obscene gesture when the mayor disgustedly turned away.

"Get me away from these faggots, Spivac," he yelled suddenly at the startled driver, who quickly wheeled the car onto a side street.

The mayor shuddered at the thought of the queer, not that it had been the first time. The city had changed so much over the past few years. It had gotten dirtier and dirtier. He

6

remembered, not so long ago either, when Polk Street had been a working-class neighborhood. Now it was known as the gay ghetto. It was as though a disease had come into the city. He wasn't sure what started it. Maybe it was true of all cities in the country, after financial rot sets in moral rot follows.

The tragedy was that nobody knew. To most people San Francisco was still their favorite city. They came from all over the country to climb its romantic hills and stare at its beautiful bridges. He wondered how long the facade would last. He wondered how long she could keep fooling everyone, including her own residents who thought they knew her so well.

One thing was sure. He wasn't going to save her. Not this time. San Francisco didn't need him anymore. That's what the private poll he'd commissioned said. It was time for a change. A new face. Not that he believed in polls. He'd been in politics for too many years to think that polls taken six months prior to an election were good for anything more than to raise money (provided you were ahead). But the interviews had hurt him. He'd read many of them himself. Even in districts where his support was strongest: the white, blue-collar areas of the Sunset and Portals districts; the black, Latin and Pacific Island communities of the Fillmore and the Mission; Chinatown; even his own home district of North Beach. They wanted someone younger, prettier, someone who wasn't identified with the Catholic, Irish and Italian machine which had run city politics since vigilante days. If they only knew how rusted and run-down that machine was.

They drove past the marble columned automobile show-rooms on Van Ness Avenue. During the depression, on Sundays after Mass, he and his father would walk from North Beach, through Aquatic Park and up Van Ness Avenue to stare at the luxurious Packards in the showroom of Earle C. Anthony and the equally wonderful Cadillacs of Don Lee. In those days there were two things that counted in the world of an Italian merchant; getting to heaven and owning a Packard. Dominic Belardi was always much closer to the Pearly Gates than he was to the driver's seat of a Packard.

"Isn't that going to be another one of Mr. Stevens's hotels?" Spivac asked, nodding toward a huge excavation site.

"The man never stops," the mayor answered. "Last year he bought a shipping company, this year he's building three new hotels. From what I hear, this one is costing twenty million dollars."

Spivac whistled softly. There was no denying Bryce Stevens thought big, and the older he got the bigger he thought.

Twenty years ago, he and Stevens formed a political alliance that would rule San Francisco politics for the next generation. He had been the fire-eating city attorney who served Stevens's father with an injunction to integrate his hotel or the city would close it down. Bryce Stevens, Sr., died three weeks after refusing to comply with the court order. His son, Bryce Jr., carried out the injunction in less than a week's time. It seemed only natural that the rich, liberal hotel man and the populist city attorney team up to take on the old guard in the next mayoral election.

But Bryce was never satisfied with city politics, just as he wasn't satisfied to own one hotel. Over the next two decades the mayor had seen Stevens's hotel chain grow to over thirty in seven countries and had watched his political influence spread nearly as far. His latest protégé, Governor William Moffat, was said to be a serious contender for the White House two years hence; meanwhile, Stevens's son-in-law, Fred Zimmerman, was the favorite to be the next mayor. Over the preceding weekend it had occurred to Sam Belardi

8

more than once that the tension surrounding the stalemate between the City Council and the Police Officers Association was more political than monetary. It had also occurred to him that certain individuals had more to gain than others and he didn't mean the police.

The mayor had little regard for William Moffat. The arrogant, ambitious young governor had only been elected because in the post-Watergate California gubernatorial election no one else had been clean enough or rich enough to run against him. Because his father had once been a Democratic National Committeeman and had also served as Ambassador to Venezuela in the Kennedy Administration, Bryce had been able to finance the campaign through a series of interest-free loans based on the father's name and the son's lack of competition. Left alone, Moffat couldn't get near the White House but with the brilliant, aquisitive mind of Bryce Stevens behind him anything was possible.

Although he was loath to show it, the mayor felt an uncomfortable pulling on his insides as Spivac approached the Italian Renaissance dome of the city hall. He had a premonition that after his many years of serving her, his city wasn't going to let him go without a fight.

2

THE mayor reached across the oak tabletop for his humidor and gently picked out a long, thick Havana cigar. He offered the jar to Ken Topham, the city's chief administrative officer, expecting his number-one political operative to refuse, which he did. It was just one of the many things he liked about working with Topham.

Slowly, carefully, he licked the fragrant tobacco leaves, savoring the rich taste and smell as if it were hundred-year-old brandy. The Havanas were one of the few pleasures he allowed himself. Or, to put it more truthfully, one of the few pleasures society and his doctor allowed him at his age. Biting off the tip he completed the ritual by lighting the cigar and taking a deep, satisfying draw.

"Chief Murphy will be here shortly," Topham said, characteristically getting down to business. "I think we should go over this before he gets here."

"What's to go over? I'm not granting another extension. The contract officially expires tonight at six P.M.

"Yes, but you know there's little chance of a compromise by then."

"I know both the City Council and the Police Officers Association have had three months to settle this goddamn thing and nothing's been done."

"You also know the cops deserve the twelve percent raise they're asking for."

Topham's remark surprised the mayor. It was true. He did think the police deserved the twelve percent raise called for by the traditional wage formula: parity with Los Angeles, the highest-paid police department in the state. And he also thought Fred Zimmerman was playing politics by offering the cops a token five percent raise. What surprised him was that Topham, who had no love for the police department, would bring up the mayor's personal opinion as opposed to his official position. That wasn't like Ken Topham.

"So what do you suggest?"

"Give them another month."

Before he could answer, his secretary announced Police Chief Murphy. Both men watched the large man come into the room. Unlike most of the police chiefs in the United States, Charles "Pinch" Murphy liked to wear his uniform. He nodded formally to both men, his face creased with anxiety. It was not an expression that suited such a marvelous Irish face.

"What are we going to do, Sam?" Murphy asked despondently before he had a chance to sit down.

Although he and the chief were contemporaries, Murphy looked ten years older. The difference amounted to over a pint of scotch a day for the past twenty years.

"If I were you, chief, I'd get on the phone to my supervising captain and my nine district commanders," Topham suggested.

"I'm talking about my *men,*" Murphy said impatiently, his faded blue eyes fixed on the mayor. Since the possibility of a police strike had first presented itself the previous Thursday, when the Police Officers Association president, Clint Wallace, made public a POA survey indicating that over seventy percent of the POA would go out on strike if the twelve percent raise was not approved, the mayor had constantly maintained the position that all striking law-enforcement officials would be fired. He knew, as did Murphy, that the City Charter specified a mayor could dismiss a policeman only with the police chief's approval.

"You don't think I could ask you to fire them, do you, Pinch?" he asked softly.

Murphy's face relaxed only slightly. Pinch Murphy, like Sam Belardi, was of the old school. He was a throwback to the days when all a police chief needed to know was how to look honest, be able to give a five-minute speech at Academy graduations, and remember to kiss the archbishop's ring. He was a relic of the days when law enforcement was discussed in terms of cops and beats, not grids and computer printouts.

"I think we should start talking about the men who will be staying, not deserting," Topham said matter-of-factly.

The chief looked sharply at the smaller man sitting next to him. Like most high-level civil servants in the city, Pinch had no love for Ken Topham, or "Mayor Topham," as he was known in the corridors of City Hall.

"Hold on a minute," the mayor said. "I think both of you are putting the cart before the horse. We're not even sure there's going to be a strike. Once the council realizes that I'm not granting another extension, they might break ranks with Zimmerman. I don't think there's a politician in this city who would want to be responsible for the consequences of a police strike."

"With the election coming up in November, there's not a politician in this city who wants to be responsible for a jump in the property tax rate, that's for sure." Topham said. "Proposition Thirteen was no fluke, gentlemen. The political reality of the situation is that Wallace and the cops couldn't have picked a worse time to try and bluff the council."

"What do you mean, the cops couldn't have picked a worse time? The police have been paid the parity wage formula for the last twenty-three years. The City Council are the ones changing the rules. You know as well as I do that the budget analyst's five percent recommendation is a crock. Zimmerman and the others put him up to it to cover their asses."

"I don't have to remind you, Chief Murphy, that if your man, Neilsen, had won the last POA election like you said he would, this whole mess could probably have been worked out long ago."

"Listen, you little weasel!" Murphy suddenly burst out, taking a step in Ken Topham's direction, "I've taken all the crap I'm going to . . ."

The mayor leaned over the desk and caught Pinch by the arm before he could reach Topham.

"God dammit, Pinch, you've made me drop my cigar," he swore, still hanging onto the big Irishman.

Topham, temporarily confused, stood behind his chair. He was half Murphy's size at best.

"All I said was . . ."

"Do me a favor, Ken, don't say anything," the mayor told him.

Murphy looked at the mayor like a circus bear who'd just scratched his trainer.

"I'm sorry, Sam, I don't know what got into me," he said, shaking his large gray head apologetically.

"Mother of God, the strike hasn't even begun and a free-for-all breaks out in my own office," the mayor said with some amusement.

"I'll be down the hall if you want me," Topham said, quickly moving to the door, at the same time keeping a nervous eye on Murphy.

"Where are you going?"

"To work on your statement."

"How can you work on my statement when we haven't even discussed it?"

"If you're not going to grant an extension and if you're not going to fire the strikers, the only thing left is to institute the chief's contingency plan providing emergency police services with supervisory personnel. The press is going to want to know how many men that means, how much protection that gives, what crimes will be given priority, and so forth. That information is in my office."

The mayor looked at Murphy who didn't seem to care.

"Call me when you finish it. There's no reason to say what we're going to do before we have to. Something might give yet."

Topham nodded and disappeared into the hall.

"Well, Pinch, I know it's still morning, but I could use a drink. All this excitement is getting to me."

The mayor looked down at the crushed end of his Havana, the first casualty.

"I'm sorry about your cigar, Sam. My temper got the best of me before I had a chance to tell the saints from the sinners."

"Don't apologize to me about that Irish temper of yours. If it hadn't been for that raw streak down on the docks a few years back my head would be held together with clamps today."

He put an arm around Murphy and they walked to the bar. He could feel both of them shaking slightly.

"That was more than a few years, Sam," the chief said fondly.

"So it was," the mayor smiled, his recollection of the school books incident fresher in his memory than yesterday.

He was the assistant city attorney then, in the days before anyone had ever heard of a wop kid from North Beach named Sam Belardi. The head of the longshoremen had closed the port after the major shipping lines and a "downtown" mayor refused to improve certain safety standards on the wharf. One of the ships involved in the lockout was a freighter from the East Coast carrying textbooks for the city schools. After obtaining an injunction from a sympathetic judge, he and two policemen, one of them a strapping rookie patrolman from the Sunset District by the name of Pinch Murphy, marched onto the ship and began unloading the books by hand. A few longshoremen took exception and a brawl ensued. Pinch single-handedly put four stevedores into the emergency ward. The books were delivered and Sam Belardi first found out what it was like to have his picture on the front page.

"Sam, I've never liked that man."

"He's not so bad, Pinch, maybe a little officious."

"Officious isn't the word," Murphy said, hoisting a two-ounce shot glass of Black Label to his lips.

"You know, I better be getting back to the Hall of Justice," he said, wiping his mouth with satisfaction before pouring himself another, "I just wanted to check in with you before I went ahead."

The men stood staring at one another. Belardi could sense his friend's apprehension, and worse, his disappointment. But there was nothing he could do. Not this time.

"How many men do you think will go out?"

"The POA represents over ninety-five percent of the patrolmen in the city. That's some fifteen-hundred men. From what my people tell me, over half will walk. None of them wants to but they don't have a choice."

"How about your supervisory personnel?"

"There aren't many sergeants still in the Association. Most of them drop out when they become eligible for their pension."

"But you don't expect any trouble with them?"

"Well, a lot are in sympathy with the strike. So are a lot of captains and lieutenants. But I talked with all the station commanders over the weekend and they say the emergency support is solid. They know there's nobody else."

"How about the inspectors?"

Murphy looked pained. The mayor knew the chief's opinion of most detectives. Pinch Murphy was a beat cop.

"As long as they get their time and a half there'll be no problem. They have no love for Clint Wallace."

"So how long do you think we have?"

"Before you can't walk down the street without a gun?"

"Before the people begin to panic."

"If this heat keeps up, two days, maybe three. I've been checking with some other chiefs around the country. I talked to Lloyd Walkup in Detroit this morning before I came over. There was a strike there a few summers ago and he said it took a few days before the dirt floats to the top. But once it does . . ."

"It's going to be critical that we keep a high profile with the manpower we do have. We have to keep people thinking the six- or seven-hundred men we do have are enough."

"There's not a hell of a lot more we can do," Murphy lamented.

"What do you think is the lowest compromise figure Wallace will accept?"

"Two weeks ago I would have said nine, but after the council refused to negotiate I doubt if he'll take anything less than the full twelve percent. Hell, he doesn't have to. It's a matter of departmental pride now."

"Clint Wallace is an overweight, low-brow demagogue who doesn't have the imagination to appreciate how much trouble he's causing."

"You're wrong, Sam. Just like I was. He may look like a slob and talk like a farmer but he's a dangerous man. He's a liar and a manipulator who'll do anything to get power. He poisoned the men against Al Neilsen and he's trying to

16

poison them against both of us. He and his little group of supporters, 'Officers for Equal Justice' they call themselves, have been telling the men for months that Los Angeles is paying its starting patrolmen fifteen hundred dollars a month and giving them double time for anything over eight hours."

"That's a bald-faced lie!" Belardi bellowed. "We've had parity with LA on everything until now."

"Yeah, but it isn't a lie that a bus driver or a street cleaner makes as much as a cop. I told you when the council passed that city workers' pay increase at the beginning of the year it wasn't going to sit well with the men. I have half a mind Zimmerman set this whole thing up as a campaign stunt from the start. Our pay formula is no secret. He knew how large our pay increase should be this year."

The chief downed another shooter. His broad features were flushed with frustration and anger. The more Murphy talked the angrier he became.

"It should never have come this far, Sam. You know it and I know it. There was a time when we'd have taken punks like Fred Zimmerman and Clint Wallace out in the street and spanked them if they tried to pull a stunt like this."

"What do you want me to do, Pinch?" Belardi demanded. "You do remember it's the council that approves the police wage contracts, not the mayor."

"I'm not blaming you, Sam. I blame myself more than anyone. If I'd been spending less time down at OHara's with this," he said, holding up his glass, "and more time with the POA Executive Committee, Wallace would be sweeping cells at Taraval Station."

Murphy tried to smile but couldn't. He looked old and tired, but Belardi knew he wouldn't fold. A police chief with no policemen—Murphy would still patrol the streets himself.

The mayor of San Francisco heaved a sigh of exasperation. His stomach was acting up again and he didn't feel like arguing. He wished his own conscience were as clear as his police chief's.

"I know it's been hard for you, Sam," Murphy said gently. "Connie was a fine woman. The finest."

"Too good for me."

"Mary and I light a candle for her every morning. For you, too."

"I appreciate that, Pinch. Tell Mary I'm grateful for her prayers."

"I've got to be getting back now. The reporters will be all over the Hall of Justice. What I was thinking, Sam, was maybe you could talk to Zimmerman. See if there's a chance of his reconsidering before anyone gets hurt. I could try and talk to Wallace."

The mayor nodded. His enmity toward Zimmerman was no secret.

"I don't think it's going to do any good but I'll try—after the meeting, of course."

"Of course," Murphy said.

Sam put his hand on his friend's broad shoulder and walked him to the door.

After the chief left, he felt restless but didn't want to see anyone. He looked around his large, high-ceilinged office. On the walls and in the bookcases were the mementos and memorabilia of nearly thirty years of public service. There were plaques and awards from every section of the city: Chamber of Commerce, Knights of Columbus, Sons of Italy, Sun Church of Samoa, La Raza Republica, Temple Beth Israel, Black Brotherhood, Son Lee Tong, Nippon Business Alliance, and even a scroll from the Gay Activist League that Topham finally badgered him into accepting before the last election.

There were pictures, too. Pictures with the Kennedys, one with Jack at a black-tie dinner at the Fairmont in 'sixty-two and one with Bobby in the Mission barrio the spring before his death. He'd always liked Bobby more. With Jack he'd had the feeling politics was the means to an end but he wasn't sure what the end was. Bobby knew politics meant power and power meant change. There was an exhilaration, a hope. After that night in the Ambassador Hotel the exhilaration was gone; only the power had remained.

More pictures. One with his wife and Lyndon Johnson at Bryce Stevens's Woodside home. LBJ didn't like San Francisco, said it had too many hills and not enough money. "Not bad for a Texan," Connie said later. As usual she was right. The last picture of her was at William Moffat's inauguration. There were four of them in the Capital rotunda: Constance, Charles Moffat, his son the new governor, and himself. Looking at the picture you didn't have to be a doctor to know that both Charles Moffat and Connie didn't have long to live, yet the expression on his own face was more funereal than either of theirs. Only the young governor seemed oblivious.

3

THE dispatcher's voice made its way through the crackle of the police radio. Frank Parker had hated the radio his first months on car patrol. He could never sift the numbers out of the incessant static and had always been slightly surprised when he and his partner arrived at the scene of a crime. It had been the most frustrating part of the job—that and filling out arrest reports. The reports were still a headache, but after four and a half years of patrol duty the radio seemed to filter itself out, giving him time to think of other things while cruising the streets of North Beach and Chinatown.

The past six months his thoughts had been painfully similar, the break-up of his marriage. What an ass he'd been to think he was different from any other cop. He remembered the hours spent listening to various partners talk about their marital problems, thinking to himself what a cliché their experiences were—the gradual alienation, the lack of communication, the sexual problems, the wife's increasing anxiety, the cop's deepening cynicism, the drinking, other women, the inevitable divorce. How many times had he promised himself the job would never come between Kathy and, him?

But that was all before the Mickey Wong trial. After the

trial everyone in the city knew who the two cops were who sent the Kum Hon gang leader to San Quentin for armed robbery. Of course, he and his partner, Barney Schultz, knew better than to think the gang would go after them. They understood that neither of the two rival Chinese youth gangs, the Kum Hon (the so-called inside gang, made up predominantly of American-born Chinese) or the Wah-Chung (the outside gang, made up predominantly of foreign-born Chinese) could afford to kill a cop. A dead cop meant that Chinatown would have no tourists, and with no tourists the shops and clubs would go out of business, and that would leave no one for the two street gangs to extort and terrorize. It would also displease the elders of the Son Lee Tong, the secret society of Chinese businessmen who directly or indirectly controlled all of Chinatown crime including the two juvenile gangs.

He had been trying to explain that to Kathy for months. She wouldn't listen. She said she was sick of hearing about Chinatown. "Next you'll have yourself a little Chinese girl friend. You spend enough time there."

That was three weeks ago. Since then he'd only seen Rita Chan once—to end it. Not only because of Kathy. He had other reasons too, good ones.

"I love afternoons like this," Barney said, loosening the collar around his muscular size-eighteen neck. Barney's face wasn't much but he was the only guy in the department who couldn't fit in the uniform shirt. "You can feel the city breathe on a day like this. Makes you want to grab hold of a feisty cunt and throw her in the back seat."

"You find the cunt, I'll do the driving," Frank offered.

"How about that little number we ran into at the Doggie Diner the other night? I thought she was going to jump inside your pants!"

"You keep forgetting I'm a married man."

"Not for long." Schultz laughed.

"Fuck you," Frank replied.

"I bet you say that to all your partners, cutie," Schultz said with a lisp.

"Only the ones who aren't married."

Schultz grinned. Like half the men on the force he was the self-avowed master of any and all sexual techniques. He was also crazy and the best partner Frank ever had. Unlike the other cops he'd worked with, Barney didn't give a shit about how many more years he had to work before he could retire and buy that dream condo in the mountains, or how many "eating places" he could cultivate, or how many of his academy classmates had been promoted above him. Barney was a mover, he was in perpetual motion. When he and Frank patrolled together they looked for action. They didn't try to avoid it like a lot of other cops Frank had worked with, who spent half the night in one of San Francisco's thousands of neighborhood bars.

The patrol car drove slowly along upper Grant Avenue, passing the famous haunts of the beatnik era. He had never read any of Allen Ginsburg or Jack Kerouac but he knew from what Kathy had told him that they used to live and work in North Beach. That was one of the reasons she wanted him to go back to college, "to learn about people, not perverts." It was hard for him to believe that any of the derelicts he saw along the street each night were working poets and writers. They had enough trouble walking. Being an artist was a kind of life he had never been able to fathom. Kathy was always trying to drag him to poetry readings and art exhibits but he usually got out of it. He'd seen too many bloodied heads and heard too many tormented cries to believe in the romance of the North Beach artist.

Schultz stopped the car in front of the Dead Whale Saloon. Three scruffy black men and a white hooker were camped out in the doorway passing the warm afternoon waiting for business hours to start.

"Would you just look at this lovely integrated gathering? Just like 'Streets,' isn't it?"

"Just like Streets" was Barney Schultz's favorite line, referring to the "Streets of San Francisco" television show, which was a standing joke to almost every cop in the SFPD. He used it at least once an hour, applying it to anything from a homicide to a parking violation.

"Do you know you're in violation on Section 119 of the Criminal Code—illegal assembly?"

"We can stand here if we want, man."

"Don't talk back to police officers," Barney scolded. The man looked as though he expected to be momentarily shot. "Shall we take him in?" he asked Frank.

"We should, but I'm getting hungry. Why don't we give him three hours to vacate the doorway?"

"Did you hear that? My partner is giving you three hours to vacate that doorway."

The black man looked at his friends. They were smiling so he smiled too. It was the kind of response Barney usually got from people who didn't know him. A mixture of relief and bewilderment.

"Fuckin' nickel pimps," he laughed, accelerating away from the Dead Whale.

He turned off Grant and headed back toward Columbus in front of St. Peter and Paul's Church. It was Monday afternoon but Washington Square was full of people. Old Italian men sitting on park benches talking about wars and bocce ball. Old hippies playing Frisbee. Strippers, waiters, and musicians lying on the grass drinking wine before they had to go to work. The clock on the left-hand spire of the church said it was 4:30 P.M.

"What time are we supposed to meet De Angelo and Carr?"

"I told 'em five-thirty down at Aquatic Park. The council meeting should be over by then."

23

"Let's go by Gino's first."

"What should I tell the dispatcher?"

"Shit, I don't care. Tell him we're goin' fishing."

The raw, steamy odor of Dungeness crab was unmistakable as they approached the wharf. Gino, wearing a full-length rubber apron, was standing in his usual place behind the big metal vats. When he saw the patrol car coming he bent over the wooden bucket to find them the best of the day's catch.

He pulled a large crab out of the boiling water. With effortless precision he dissected and cracked the orange-pink crab. Barney, as usual, couldn't wait and almost lost his thumb and index finger reaching for a claw.

"You got no patience, Schultz, it makes you a good cop and a lousy person," Gino scolded.

"Are you going to get my partner one of those ugly things or keep on giving me grief?" Barney said putting a five-dollar bill down on the brick counter.

"Keep your money, Schultz," the bald man said, pushing the five back towards Schultz with his hammer, "all I hear today on the radio is cops cryin' about how much money they don't have."

"Wait till tonight if you really want to hear some cryin'. After we're gone then we'll see who's cryin'," Barney said.

"You go on strike, Schultz, and I get robbed, I'll come after you with this," Gino said, holding up the twenty-pound hammer as if it were plastic.

"If you get robbed, Gino, call a street cleaner, they make more than we do," Barney said pushing the money away. Gino grabbed it this time.

"How about a coupla cold ones?" Barney asked when they got back to the car. Frank didn't object.

He and Barney climbed the old concrete bleachers behind the Maritime Museum. There were more people than usual on the promenade because of the warm weather. Ordinarily

24

they wouldn't have opened the beer cans in public but there was a satisfaction in making the gesture that seemed to answer the hostile looks they were getting.

A puffy-chested sea gull strutted toward them, arrogantly demanding food.

"Get outta here, you winged rat," Schultz swore at the uninvited guest.

They ate in silence. The crab was delicious. Both men gorged themselves on the fresh white meat.

"He was pissed, wasn't he?" Schultz said breaking open a claw.

"A lot of people are going to be pissed," Frank said, taking a long pull on the cold beer. "All you gotta do is look around."

"Screw them. Screw 'em all. If they're going to pay us like garbage men, screw 'em."

"Does that mean you're going out?"

"You heard what those assholes said today down at City Hall. Saying we lied to them about our demands. That we have the slowest reaction time in the state. I'd like to see that bastard Zimmerman's reaction time if I met him in a dark alley."

"You know Mike's going out. When I talked to him this afternoon he said he was. Skip probably will too."

"Carr would catch the scabies if De Angelo scratched his balls," Schultz said contemptuously.

A light westerly breeze came around Black Point. The shadows were lengthening but still soft from the heat. The Maritime Museum sat above the little curved beach like a shipwrecked boat. He watched the couples walking out on the Municipal Pier.

He and Kathy used to go fishing out on the pier when they were first married. They used to go out with Mike De Angelo and his wife Janis. Kathy and Janis had been friends in high school. Frank remembered how uptight he'd been when Kathy first told him her friend was married to a cop. Less than six months later he was taking the Police Academy entrance examination. A beginning patrolman made twice what he was making working in his uncle's sporting-goods store. It was typical that over half the force was about to walk out because of money when he knew the main reason most of them had joined was because the pay was so good.

"You're staying, no matter what, aren't you?" Schultz asked him.

Frank hesitated.

They'd talked a lot about the possibility of a strike the last few days. Most of the other young cops at Central Station were gung ho about walking out. They'd bought the package of the Police Officer Association's president Clint Wallace without opening the box. But both he and Schultz knew it wasn't that simple. They didn't trust the power-hungry sergeant any more than they trusted the City Council president, Fred Zimmerman. But it had happened so quickly. Wallace had taken over the POA leadership from Al Neilsen almost without a struggle. Wallace and his men were moving fast. There would be a strike vote by the POA Executive Committee that night if the City Council didn't vote to approve the raise, and in his mind there was little doubt as to the outcome of either.

"There's gonna be a lot of guys who want to kick my butt if I don't."

"Big football star like you can take care of yourself."

Frank smiled. There was something incongruous about Barney Schultz telling anyone else they could take care of themselves. Although it was true that at six feet two inches and two hundred and twenty pounds Frank was a little taller and possibly a little heavier than his partner, Schultz's physique was so imposing that it made him appear the larger of the two.

"The thing about you, Frank, is that you can't stand to do

26

what other people do. If I said the sky was blue you'd say it was green. Know what I mean? You're contrary."

"You're not much different."

"Maybe not, but I'm going to be on that picket line if the council screws us over. I hate that fat-ass greaseball Clint Wallace more than you do, but if there's gonna be a strike we've gotta stick together. It's no good having a thousand men walking and another thousand staying. Somebody's gonna get fucked."

"And it's not going to be you?"

"I'm talking about the old blues. The guys who need six months for their thirty years. If they get fired it's straight to the glue factory and all those guys got are their pensions. They're scared shitless now. If the five- and ten-year men don't stick together, the old farts are gonna belly up. You can bet on it. They didn't want this strike. They wanted to wait for Chief Murphy to work out a deal with the mayor."

"So did we. Remember?"

"I remember. But things have changed. Murphy and Belardi don't have the clout they used to. You heard what Captain Brady said, Murphy's drunk more than he's sober. And Belardi . . . who knows what that bastard is up to.

"You and I, we've got lots of open sky. I'm single and you're . . . and you don't have any kids. We've got no overhead, you know? We're young, we can take a punch. But the old guys, Ballante, Kendall, Orme, they can't do it alone. Someone's got to look out for them."

Frank took another pull on his beer. He'd guessed they might come down on opposite sides like this. He'd suspected it when they reported for work that afternoon and Barney had hung around the locker room talking to the older day-shift men. They all liked Barney, they respected him just as the younger cops feared him. Their respect was important to Barney. Much more important than the principle or the money.

With Frank it was different. He felt no obligation to the other cops on the force, nor did he respect many of them. His obligation was to the people he took an oath to protect, the citizens he was paid to serve. Most cops he knew held the public in contempt. After a few years on the job it was hard not to develop a certain bias. No one knew better than a cop that the world was full of assholes. But that didn't mean that everytime you saw a black man park in a red zone you wrote him up a parking ticket, tearing up the original so the poor sucker didn't even know he was tagged until the warrant was issued. That didn't mean you took your best shot at every junkie or car booster once they had the cuffs on, or every drunk who thought he could take you in the booking cage.

He had the reputation around the department as a red-hot. Cops didn't like red-hots because they made them look bad. Before he teamed up with Schultz, De Angelo told him no one in the company had wanted him as a partner . . . "you're too straight, Frank, you gotta loosen up." With most cops the longer they were in the more cynical, the more give-a-damn they became. With him it was the opposite.

Since he'd been with Schultz his relations with the other men had gotten better. As Barney said "they figure anyone who can work with me and still be sane can't be all bad." But just because the men at Central tolerated him he didn't have to change his opinion of them.

"How about the Gino Machettis and the Joe Louies?" Frank asked. "What do you think's going to happen to guys like Joe when the Kum Hon and Wah Chung realize there are no baahk gwai to chase them. Every small merchant in the city will be at the mercy of the street punks."

"Then maybe they'll vote in a council that will pay us what we deserve."

"Don't give me that Clint Wallace political crap. We're talking about people, friends, not politics. You can't have it

28

both ways, if you try you're just like they are . . . using people to get power."

Schultz looked at his partner from behind his beer. There was a familiar playfulness in his eyes.

"I know you can argue better than I can. Remember, I was protecting my country while you were playing Joe College."

"I wouldn't call two years of San Francisco City College on a football scholarship a college education."

"Then I won't call what I did with those Bangkok whores protecting my country."

Frank laughed and dropped the crab shells into a paper bag. "Let's get back to the car. I told Mike we'd meet them at the Jefferson Street entrance."

"I was thinking," Schultz said, picking at the last piece of his crab, "there's no reason for us to go to this pep rally. Why don't we go over to the Kowloon and see Joe. Who knows? Your friend might be around."

"I told you, it's over."

"And I told you. Women get over. Men get off."

When he told Rita Chan he couldn't see her anymore, she just looked at him. As usual, her round lovely face was a mask. He'd met her in the Club Kowloon four months before. She'd seen him on television. "Hello, Frank Parker," the saucy voice greeted him one night from the bar as he and Schultz were making the rounds. He'd never seen a more beautiful woman. She had the delicate cream coloring of a northern Chinese with the striking features of a Pacific Islander. Lovely eyes and a wide mouth. Her black hair fell below her shoulders. She was sitting with two other girls. They all worked as cocktail waitresses at the Mandarin Palace and had just gotten off work. They were a little high and thought they'd have fun with Chinatown's two celebrity police. He and Schultz came back after work and suggested going to Japantown for a foot massage. The other two girls said they'd love to but they had to drive to Hayward. Barney said he couldn't believe any Orientals lived in Hayward and insisted on going with them. He and Rita ended up going to Japantown and spending the night at the Miyako Hotel. It cost him seventy-five dollars for the room . . .

To say he'd never known anyone like her was an understatement. Two or three nights a week for three months he'd met her in the Kowloon after work. Sometimes they'd go to a hotel, but most of the time they'd gone to her little apartment on Pine Street near the Tenderloin. He couldn't get his clothes off fast enough. Sex with her was from another world. They would stay in bed for hours, talking—he'd do most of that—touching, loving. She would lie there, black eyes devouring him like she'd never known any other man before. He'd asked her once if she'd ever been married. She laughed and told him Hong Kong girls weren't allowed to marry. The way she said it, the bitterness in her laugh made him not want to ask her what she meant. Now he wished he had.

"Two Adam five," came the call on Frank's pocket radio.

"We're five tonight, aren't we?" he asked Schultz.

"I think so. Wait and see if anyone else answers."

"Two Adam five. Two Adam five," the dispatcher repeated.

"Adam five ten-two," Frank said, picking up the radio.

"Respond to an 802 on Pier seven for possible ID. Repeat: Respond to 802 on Pier seven for possible ID."

"Adam five ten-four," Frank answered.

"They want us to go look at a stiff?" Schultz asked.

"That's what it sounds like."

"But we just ate."

4

THE covered pier smelled of stale seawater and rotting wood. It was cool and dank even in the heat. A beat-up Clark forklift near the entrance and some fifty-gallon barrels stacked along the north wall were the only evidence of activity. Frank thought it could possibly have been weeks, maybe months, since a ship had been loaded there.

"We should have driven out here," Barney said as they walked toward the group of men at the far end of the pier. Frank guessed Pier 7 was over three football fields long and a hundred yards wide.

"They should turn these old docks into something useful, like a dog track."

"How about a field house? The high schools could play here."

"Don't kid yourself, they're worth more as firewood. You know how much a building like this is insured for? Millions."

"I thought the city owned most of the piers," Parker said.

"It does." Schultz laughed.

The five men at the end of the pier looked up from the corpse as he and Schultz approached. Frank recognized two patrolmen from Central Station. The Embarcadero was their beat. He also recognized the short, stocky detective in the light tailored suit standing next to him. Most San Francisco cops knew who homicide inspector Phil Andropolus was.

"Captain Brady thought you might be interested in this," the inspector said, pointing to the body with the toe of his brown boot.

The dead man was white, in his early forties. The bay had given his clothes a needed rinse. The back of his head and neck oozed congealed clots of dark red blood onto the wooden timbers. His hands and feet were tied behind him. He hadn't been dead long. Four, five, maybe six hours, Frank thought. After five years of police work every cop became an amateur coroner.

"You guys know him?"

Frank was sure he'd never seen the weathered face before. It was a lonely, unattractive face.

"Should we?" Schultz asked.

"Brady thought you might. When Mr. Miller here found him under the south-side pilings he was wearing one of those."

Andropolus pointed to a soggy clump of white burlap near the body. Schultz picked it up and held it out. Frank had already guessed. It was a rice sack.

"I haven't seen one of these since last summer," Barney said.

"There haven't been any Chinatown gang killings since last summer," the inspector said.

Frank looked sharply at the detective, then at the dead man. He bent down and studied what was left of the head.

"Five, six small caliber bullet holes in the back of the head, hands and feet bound, unmarked rice sack," he repeated.

"Sounds familiar, doesn't it?" Andropolus said.

The pier creaked under them from the pull of the evening tide. Frank stood up to get away from the stench. "No youth gang did this, inspector," he said slowly.

"There was no ID on the body," Andropolus continued, ignoring Frank's comment. "He isn't greatly distended so I doubt he's been in the water more than a couple of hours. Whoever killed him probably moved him afterward. Damned if I know why. Maybe robbery, maybe the yellow bastards just like to keep in practice. From the looks of that nose I'd bet you his blood alcohol hasn't been under point two in the last fifteen years. A wharf rat who stumbled into the wrong boat."

"I've never seen him around here," the watchman, Miller, said shaking his head. "How about you, Les?"

The other man, who, Frank guessed, was also a watchman, shook his head.

"Could you show us exactly where you found him, Mr. Miller?" Andropolus asked.

"Sure enough," the older watchman said obligingly, leading the detective and the two uniformed cops out the shed door to the uncovered end of the pier.

They walked around to the long loading dock on the south side.

There wasn't a breath of fog or wind on the placid gray waters of the bay. Above them the sun touched the silver towers of the Bay Bridge. Behind them the financial district high-rises stood in quiet grace. It was a slow, lazy evening. All that moved were wisps of steam from the pipes on the pier and a distant stream of cars crossing the bridge.

Miller stopped a hundred feet or so from the end of the pier. He stepped to the edge of the loading dock and pointed down.

"Right down there. He was stuck right down there. "Course I didn't know what it was 'til Les and I hoisted the sack up with the baby pulley. Cut the rope and this head falls out. Damndest thing I ever saw."

Frank knelt down and looked under the pier. The pilings

were covered with mollusks and seaweed. The black water rubbed lightly between them.

"See anything?" Andropolus asked.

"Yeah," Frank scoffed, "a yellow peril."

The homicide inspector turned away, looking over at the next pier. There were several large drums sitting alongside the shed. The large side door was open but it was impossible to see inside because of the weak evening light.

"Was there a boat docked over there recently?" Andropolus asked.

"No, but there was a *ship* berthed there about five o'clock. *Riki Maru*'s her name. Jap freighter out of Kobe. Western Stevedore berths mostly Jap ships now."

"Did the body look like it had floated into the pilings or could it have been dropped?" Frank asked.

"Today's Monday, officer, ain't nobody been on Pier seven today 'cept for me and Les," Miller said with the finality of a man who knew his job and did it well.

"Don't look like you got a whole lot of Tuesday business either," Schultz said.

"It's been slow here lately," Miller admitted. "Ever since the containers come."

As he spoke, three warehousemen walked out on the loading dock of the adjacent pier. They stopped at the sight of the uniformed policemen.

"Maybe you should go over to Pier five, inspector. Ask those longshoremen if any Kum Hon warriors booked passage on that freighter."

This time the detective frowned at Frank's sarcasm.

"I didn't ask you to come down here, patrolman. Your captain thought you and your partner might be interested because you work in Chinatown. I don't need your help to close this case. I've put more murders away than you've given parking tickets."

"I know the way these tides work," Miller cut in. "That sack

34

could have come from anywhere. North, south. Hell, I wouldn't be surprised it if came from the other side of the bay. You get some mighty strong currents running out there."

The detective kept his black eyes on Frank as the watchman spoke. Homicide detectives weren't used to patrolmen giving them lip. That wasn't how the game was played.

"The coroner is here, inspector. So's the crime lab," one of the other patrolmen yelled from the end of the pier.

"It's about time," Andropolus snapped.

The detective ran his hand through his thick black hair. Again he regarded Frank.

"You two secure the area until your sergeant comes. I'm going to take a walk over to Pier five. If that's all right with you, patrolman?"

Frank didn't get a chance to answer. The watchman followed Andropolus back around to the door. Soon he and Schultz were left alone on the long boarding dock. A sea gull picked idly at a piece of garbage floating below them. Frank could feel his shirt sticking to his back.

"Why is it you're always such a kiss-ass?" Schultz smiled.

"Have you ever heard of the Chinese executing a white man?"

"No."

"So why does that asshole automatically assume some fifteen-year-old punk in Chinatown did it?"

"Because the MO for tong executions isn't a matter of public record. Rice sack murders mean Chinatown, and Chinatown violence means youth gangs."

"Barney, we know that guy was murdered in the ritualistic manner in which the tongs have executed their enemies for a hundred years. There's only one tong in San Francisco powerful enough to order and carry out the execution of a white man—the Sun Lee Tong. Not one of their street gangs. Somebody important wanted him dead, not a bunch

35

of delinquents trying to keep in practice."

"So why didn't you tell him that? Why do you think Brady sent us over here? We're supposed to help the guy. Anyway, who gives a rusty fuck about some wino who can't swim. I'm going on strike soon, partner. Let the City Council help Andropolus find the guy who did this."

Frank looked at his partner to see if he was serious. With Schultz you could never tell.

"Hey, I forgot to tell you my new joke," Schultz smiled. "What do you get when you cross a spade with a chink?"

Frank shrugged. He was in no mood for jokes, but Barney went on.

"A car thief who can't drive."

Frank tried not to laugh, but working with Barney it was impossible to stay too straight for too long.

When he turned back toward the city, his gaze moved to his right from Nob Hill, across to the high-rise apartment houses of Russian Hill. Below Russian Hill he could just make out the colorful curved rooftops of Chinatown.

For the last ten months they had managed to keep the lid on. The Kum Hon and Wah Chung gangs hadn't disappeared, but violence had become the exception rather than the rule. There had been fewer than half the number of robberies and extortions than at the same time a year before, and, more importantly, the lines of communication had finally begun to open between the police and the Chinese community. Even with the Chinatown task force discontinued, there was a chance—a slight one—that they might be able to get to the adults who Frank knew were behind the youth gangs—the elders of the Son Lee Tong.

That's what had really been bothering him the last few days. He was worried. Worried that the trust and confidence they had built up over the past year would be destroyed by the strike and would be impossible to regain. The Chinese were a suspicious people.

36

5

HARRY Carl waited in the lobby of the Marine Cooks and
Stewards Hall for the appearance of Clint Wallace. Harry
had no doubt as to the outcome of the special session of the
POA Executive Committee. After the stormy City Council
meeting half an hour earlier, Wallace and his committee had
little choice but to order the first police strike in San
Francisco history.

In the finest self-serving tradition of city politics, the
police and the council were equally to blame for the chaotic
meeting. After a unanimous vote adopting the five percent
wage increase recommended by the budget analyst, City
Council President Fred Zimmerman had refused to even
recognize Clint Wallace in the packed council chambers. A
shouting match immediately ensued between council members and off-duty police—with the police yelling "Strike!"
from the gallery. At one point a fight nearly broke out
between a black councilman, Jimmy Cleveland, and Wallace
when the POA president complained loudly to one of his
aides that "the council was controlled by sheenies and
niggers." Cleveland, a constant critic of the police department, had come after Wallace with fists clenched but was
restrained by sheriff's deputies. And it was only after a
second detachment of deputies arrived and Wallace had

37

been escorted from the chambers that order was restored.

To the practiced eye of the magazine bureau chief, there was a potential cover in what was happening that evening. He remembered the New York police strike in 1970 and how close that had been to becoming a disaster. He remembered his wife refusing to let their children walk to school, insisting that he buy a gun to protect their thirtieth-story apartment from vandals. He had thought then that if the strike lasted another day, the city could have become a stretcher case.

Of course, San Francisco wasn't New York, thank God, and Harry Carl was no longer married, for reasons neither God nor his editorial board could be thanked, but he knew that the tentative truce between urban America and her police remained as precarious as it had been then. Over the last decade there had been police strikes in Detroit, Rochester, Baltimore, Albuquerque, Cleveland, and New Orleans, as well as New York. As cities ran out of money the need for police had become more acute. Police salaries were leveling off—in some cities cops were actually being laid off—while the crime rate soared. The thorny question of collective bargaining rights for public employees remained unanswered. Although the law forbade public safety strikes in many states, including California, not one policeman had been fired in any of the previous strikes. Could the police actually kidnap a city and hold it for ransom? The recent past seemed to indicate they could. Were America's cities then no more than police states? It was an intriguing and terrifying question.

"Your lame-duck friend Belardi seems to have lost more than his wings," Buddy Mullahy of KBAY-TV said to him. They were standing in a crowd of reporters and off-duty police. Mullahy was a typical TV news reporter, pleasant to look at, pleasant to talk to, but you wouldn't want to live there.

38

"There wasn't much he could do. It was the council's decision."

"Sam Belardi has had the City Council and the police department eating out of his hand ever since he became mayor of this city. My guess is his friend Bryce Stevens told him to lay off and let Freddy-boy take a few bows before November."

"The election is eighty-seven days away. If Zimmerman can keep the streets quiet for three months without the police he deserves to be more than mayor."

"You know the strike won't last that long. Zimmerman breaks it and—he's in."

"I don't have to know anything until Thursday. That's the good thing about my job, you only have to think once a week."

Mullahy didn't like Harry's humor—not many electronic media people did—and began untangling the loose cord from around his feet. It was Harry's experience that TV reporters spent most of their time untangling themselves from loose cord.

The truth was, he *had* considered calling the mayor that afternoon after hearing Belardi had refused to grant another contract extension, but he'd decided against it. The mayor's moods had grown increasingly dark over the summer, culminating in the press conference he held the month before to announce his retirement. Only three reporters had been invited, Harry included. Ever since his wife, Constance, had died of cancer the previous February, Sam Belardi had become a changed man. He seemed older and very tired. There was a time, and not so long ago, when nothing happened in San Francisco that Belardi didn't or couldn't control. He combined a rugged, outspoken charm with an uncanny political instinct. He was usually compared to autocratic mayors like Dick Daley. His press secretary

39

liked to say about him, "Sam's not a bad sort, he always asks you if you want to do something before he tells you to do it." But Harry, who liked and admired Belardi, saw him in a different light. To Harry, Sam Belardi was more like Fiorella LaGuardia with a touch of Machiavelli thrown in.

Miranda Stone, KSFT's attractive field reporter, walked into the hall with a handsome young man in his early thirties whom Harry had first seen at the council meeting that evening.

"Buddy, who's that LA type talking with Miranda?"

"Nick Simmons. He's from the governor's office of emergency services. He's down here to keep Moffat up to date."

"He got down here pretty fast, didn't he?"

"You know the governor. He doesn't like to have anything going on he doesn't know about."

Harry knew the governor. In fact, he'd done a cover story on him the previous year. William Moffat, the nation's latest political phenomenon, at the tender age of thirty-nine supposedly on the verge of the presidency. Why? After spending five days with him Harry had found out. He hadn't written it but he knew. William Moffat embodied the seventies. He was glib, but not funny; ambitious, but not dedicated; precocious, but not intelligent; mean, but not cruel; honest, but without integrity; and most important, completely self-centered.

"I think I'll mosey over and have a talk with Mr. Simmons."

He walked up behind Miranda. The scent of "Coriandre" was familiar. Painfully so. Miranda Stone was a woman going places and Harry Carl, well, he'd been to those places and didn't particularly like them.

"Does your office possess clairvoyant powers, Mr. Simmons? Or are you in town on other business?"

The man behind the tinted glasses looked at Harry.

Uncomfortably. Miranda turned and smiled at Harry. Unpleasantly. The night she told him she was leaving for New York she'd cried. She'd cried once after that, the night he'd begged her to stay. Since then she acted like nothing had happened. Maybe nothing had.

"Harry Carl, this is Nick Simmons from the governor's office of emergency services. Nick, this is Harry Carl, San Francisco bureau chief of America's leading weekly news magazine."

Simmon's face brightened. Like any politically aware bureaucrat he was always concerned with the governor's national image.

"Actually, Mr. Carl, the governor requested I come down this morning when we found out the mayor wasn't going to extend the contract."

"The governor has good information."

"That's part of his job," Simmons beamed.

"What exactly is your function, Mr. Simmons?"

"Basically, to keep the governor apprised of the situation. Of course, there's nothing he can or would do now, but if the situation continues . . ."

"You mean if the police go out on strike?"

"Yes, that, or if the governor is asked to mediate or otherwise intercede."

"Intercede how? The National Guard?"

"That could be one possibility, yes," Simmons said with some reluctance.

Before Harry could ask another question the door of the conference room opened and Sergeant Clint Wallace came out to face the lights of the TV cameras.

Flanked by two bulky aides, the pink-faced sergeant began to read from a yellow scrap of paper in his hand:

"By a unanimous vote of five to zero, the Police Officers Association Executive Committee has voted to instruct its members to suspend their services at six P.M. tonight."

A loud cheer went up from the police officers.

"A strike committee has been formed consisting of one representative from each district and/or company. Each station will have three picket captains, one for each shift. They will be responsible for the security of the men and their behavior on the picket line . . ."

Wallace spoke in a midwestern drawl. The former desk sergeant from Taraval Station seemed an unlikely candidate for a strike leader, but it was obvious he knew what he was doing. Harry had heard rumors that Wallace and a group of conservative officers had been pushing for the strike ever since his election but there was no proof. Still, there was a determination, a sense of righteousness about Wallace that disturbed Harry and led him back to his original question: What should be the ultimate bargaining power of the police?

6

"QUIET down now, you hear?" Councilman James Cleveland shouted across the crowded bar. Less than a third of the patrons paid any attention. He had spent enough time there to expect nothing more. The Place was too hip for politics. It was a place where people went to be seen, not to be educated.

"Ain't you sick of watchin' that ugly face of yours yet, JC?" a large brown man said from one of the tables.

"Pay attention now, Styles, this might be the break you need to get your black ass out of debt. You watch how ol' JC takes care of business. Keepin' your taxes down and gettin' rid of the pig at the same time."

"I can hear that," Styles said, turning toward the television set above the bar. Jimmy had known Henry Styles since they were boys. Styles had adopted Jimmy as his big brother when they were in the Red Shield together. Now, at six feet five inches, two hundred and fifty pounds, the Vietnam veteran was no longer anyone's little brother.

Most of the customers followed Styles's lead. There was one notable exception. Jimmy could feel Kim's disapproving brown eyes watching him as he tried to concentrate on the screen. He knew he shouldn't have brought her here. The dudes that hung out in this spot weren't her type. She hated their polished leather and their digital watches and their black cool.

"... In a surprise vote this afternoon," Miranda Stone began in her efficient newswoman's voice, "the City Council unanimously approved a five percent wage increase for the San Francisco Police Department. The vote came after Mayor Sam Belardi announced this afternoon that he would not renew the contract extension in the current police–City Council wage dispute.

"Clint Wallace, newly elected president of the Police Officers Association, was not allowed to address the council and a fight almost ensued when Wallace got into a shouting match with Councilman James Cleveland inside council chambers. . . ."

"All right, JC, kick that white boy's ass!"

"... Wallace and the Police Officers Association had been asking for a twelve percent increase, which they claim is mandated by the City Charter formula. The five percent figure adopted by the council was recommended by city budget analyst Dick Thornton.

"In an impromptu press conference called on the City Hall steps, Wallace announced that the POA executive committee would meet immediately to determine what action is appropriate. It is widely presumed that Wallace will ask for a strike vote . . ."

The fleshy face of Clint Wallace came onto the screen. Jimmy had never met the sergeant until the council meeting that afternoon, but he knew the type from his Navy years. Wallace was a farm boy who saw the world as a struggle between good and evil. Good being white, country, hard work and God-fearing. Evil being nonwhite, city, welfare, drugs and crime.

"... When asked if he knew it was against the law for public safety officials to strike in the State of California,

44

Wallace replied, 'It's against the law for the council not to pay us by the formula but they're not doin' it.' "

The next face on the screen was that of Mayor Sam Belardi. Seeing his blunt Italian features and iron-gray hair reminded Jimmy of a description he once heard from the mayor. A friend said Belardi reminded him both physically and mentally of the late Vince Lombardi. Jimmy thought the description a good one, except that the mayor had never lost. His old friend was retiring undefeated. No one had to tell Jimmy how tough that was to pull off.

The mayor wasn't on screen three seconds when a special news bulletin flashed on the screen. The first police strike in the history of San Francisco had begun. Patrolmen were being called in from all over the city by the POA strike committee. Pickets were due to appear around all nine district stations within the hour.

The Place erupted in celebration.

"I sure hope you folks got your pieces greased, because those mothers ain't gonna get a hair off my ass," Jimmy said, raising his glass.

"Do it to 'em, JC," Hollis Barnes said from the other end of the bar. Jimmy saluted the big football star. He enjoyed the people who frequented the bar. Athletes with their foxy women, pimps with their prize whores, black businessmen with their company plastic.

"Things gonna be poppin' without the pig. Everybody's gonna be gettin' some," Clyde Cathings observed from behind the bar. Clyde was the "soul" proprietor of The Place.

"I think I'd better makc me out a list of the places I'm gonna be stoppin' by," Styles said, pulling out a gold pen with a flourish worthy of a tax lawyer. "Coupla those Nob Hill hotels, clip me some of them farmers with white shoes, hog eyes and heavy cakes stuffed full of ghetto cabbage."

45

"Let your string of girls take care of the farmers, Henry, you get down to the banks," Jimmy yelled to his old friend, holding up his hand as his own image flashed on the screen.

". . . The City Council isn't going to be party to some low-grade extortion effort on the part of the police department. The five percent increase adopted by the council this afternoon is in line with other public employees' raises, actually it's higher in most cases, and quite simply it's all the city can afford. As a representative of the taxpayers of this city, I would be derelict in my moral and fiscal responsibility if I gave in to the police wage demands. Strike or no strike."

The coffee-colored face was the same, but the tenor of the voice, the style of speech, the mannerisms were completely different. The man at the bar was the "uptown" JC, the man on the tube was the "downtown" councilman James Cleveland. The contrast wouldn't be lost on Kim. He didn't look over at her but kept watching the screen.

"Listen to my man talk," Styles said, slapping his thigh.

"JC knows where the juice flows," another man said.

"He knows too good for some people," Clyde said from behind the bar.

"You got a problem with me, Clyde?" Jimmy said, catching Clyde's eyes with his own.

"No problem, JC," Clyde said, freshening his drink. "Just that there's some talk goin' down about you backin' that Jew boy for mayor."

"You got somethin' against that?" Jimmy said, raising his voice.

"Not me personally, JC, but I know some people who won't be too happy to hear it."

"Since when did you become a messenger boy for the Temple, Clyde?"

"Don't go gettin' uptight on me, JC. I'm just passin' on the word."

"Hey, man. Don't give me that 'word' shit. If Ray

46

Robinson or Jamaal Muhammed, whatever he calls hisself, wants to tell me somethin', he knows where to find me."

Clyde peaceably put up his hands.

"Relax, man. What's the matter with you?"

He was a little shorter than Clyde but some forty pounds heavier. Jimmy knew Cathings had a gun behind the bar but he didn't think he'd use it. Clyde was basically a house nigger.

"Ain't nothin' the matter with me, brother, 'cept I'm sick and tired of Jamaal Muhammed and every other Muslim in the Fillmore cryin' and bitchin' behind my back. You think I don't know who looted my store over in Martin Luther King Center last week? You think I don't know who tried to break into my office over the fourth of July? Listen, messenger boy, you give Muhammed a message for me. It's gotta stop or he'll be sorry he ever heard of Allah."

"Easy, baby, take it easy," Kim was saying as she held his right arm.

He shook her hand loose, keeping it free to defend himself, but Clyde wasn't about to start anything. By now, a few brothers at the bar had come over to see what the problem was. They cleared away when Henry Styles approached. Jimmy might not be the most popular man in the bar but no one would mess with him as long as Styles was nearby.

"What's happening, my man? You don't wanna go messin' up Clyde. Kim, why don't you take this man outta here . . . get him in the fresh air."

Jimmy could feel his anger subside. He'd made his point. Clyde was frozen in place. His mustache was glistening with sweat.

"Don't forget, messenger boy," he said flashing that famous Cleveland smile. Clyde watched him carefully, his hands still cupped. Kim and Styles began moving Jimmy toward the door. Most of the patrons hadn't noticed the incident and Jimmy slapped skin all the way out the door, amid congratulations from the pimps and kisses from the whores for gettin' the pig off the street.

"What went down in there?" Styles asked when they got out on Divisidero Street. It was past six o'clock but the street was still warm.

"I almost killed that Muslim pimp, that's what happened."

"I told you, JC, you gotta be cool with 'em. They're like the Viet Cong, they don't care if ten of 'em die as long as they get you."

"Don't tell me about the Muslims, man. I know their program backward and forward. I don't give a shit how many white boys they chop up. They think they can push me around, tell me what to do in my own neighborhood, they better think again."

"Your own neighborhood!" Styles howled. "You ain't lived down here since we was in Red Shield."

Kimberly didn't join in their laughter. He wasn't surprised, although he knew she liked the top of the hill as much as he did. She talked all the time about bettering their people, about reordering black values and priorities, but when it came to the squeeze she'd rather take a car than a bus.

"Seriously, man, thanks for the help back there. I could handle Clyde with no sweat but some of those other goons might have crowded me. You don't know who to trust these days."

He lay open his palm and Styles wrapped his huge hand around it.

"Long as me and my boys is around, you're covered. You know that. You called it, they can kill as many honkies as they want but if they try to mess with the blood they gonna be sorry."

"I'll be talkin' with you man. We might do a little business this week."

48

"That's cool," the other man answered and turned back into the bar.

Kim didn't say anything as they walked down Divisidero toward the Redevelopment Agency where they'd parked. Jimmy nodded to the little Arab standing out in front of the corner liquor store on Bush Street. They packed more guns in those stores than a militia and still there were robberies all the time. Three Arabs had been killed in the last year in liquor store holdups. Yet they stayed open.

When he was a boy it had been the Jews. Then in the fifties it was the Chinese, now the Arabs. Like their predecessors he guessed the Arabs would leave the ghetto once they made their money. Move down to the peninsula and buy a supermarket or a restaurant. You pays your dues and you gets out. He had tried to explain that to Kim many times, but all she could see was what was owed. You don't get out with IOUs, baby.

He unlocked her side of the Mercedes coupe and walked around to his own. She made no motion to unlock his door from the inside.

"I couldn't have been that bad, could I, baby?" he said letting himself in.

She looked at him fiercely.

"Just when I think I'm beginning to know the real Jimmy Cleveland I get a big surprise."

"Give me a break, baby. You know that was just business back there."

"All that macho bullshit. I had to look twice to make sure that jive-ass nigger at the bar was the man I love. I'm still not sure. The man I love wants to help his people, not incite them to riot."

"Baby, you got it wrong. That was just talkin'. None of them turkeys back there could stick up a pinball machine. Those are business people. They're about as likely to rob a bank as I am."

49

"Those people back there are pimps and pushers. And Henry Styles is the worst."

She was beautiful all the time but when her milk-chocolate cheeks flushed with anger she was even more beautiful.

"Take it easy on Henry, now. If it wasn't for him I might not be pullin' city purse strings to get those kids of yours to the country every weekend. You saw what happened in there."

"The man is evil. Everything about him reeks of violence."

"Violence is part of it, baby. It's where we come from."

"But it doesn't have to be, Jimmy," she said in a familiar, pleading tone. "If the right people would set an example . . ."

"How many times do we have to go over it, baby? I didn't make the rules. You want me to let Jamaal Muhammed and those other crazy bastards destroy everything I've built up down here—the Boys' Club, the trade-technical school, the safe street program, the whole redevelopment concept. Just when the kids start to learn to deal with the white world you want me to let Muhammed and his men take them into their temple school and fill them full of hate? Teach them how to kill instead of how to read? Is that what you want?"

"No," she said, putting her head on his shoulder. He stroked her coarse black hair. That was one thing he did like about white women, their soft hair . . .

They drove up Divisidero and in a matter of blocks the neighborhood changed. There were no more condemned houses or vacant lots. Instead, the houses had fresh coats of paint, and patches of green grass. The ghetto starkness was gone. The broken bottles and faded doorsteps disappeared. A few blocks further up the hill and they would be among the mansions of Pacific Heights. It had always amazed Jimmy that the richest and poorest parts of the city were virtually next to one another. Just as it had always given him

50

a perverse sense of pride to know that part of his district included both the Fillmore tenements and the Pacific Heights mansions.

In a few minutes they would be at his apartment. He would be lying with that great body next to him. Because she had gotten mad at him now she would be forgiving. He would forgive her. Oh my, yes.

Suddenly he felt fine. His performance at the council meeting was very good and he had been meaning to call Cathings out for some time. The Muslims had been crowding him and it was time he pushed back a little. Saying he was a honky stooge was one thing, trying to elect their own candidate to the Redevelopment Agency was another. By provoking the first move, he was relatively sure he could take care of Muhammed. A lot of time had passed since they used to play roundball in St. Dominic's playground, but Jimmy always could beat Ray Robinson one on one. And if he found he couldn't now, there was always Henry Styles.

7

IT was past eleven when Frank parked the patrol car and walked down Stockton Street towards the Kowloon. There were no tourists on the street, only Chinese merchants taking out the evening trash. The air was warm and the putrid smell of rotten fish and fowl clung to his nostrils as he sidestepped the piles of garbage that lined the sidewalk. It was the favorite time for the Chinese gangs or *fei jai* (flying youth) as they were called in Cantonese. They'd wait for a merchant to come out with his trash then either follow him into an alley or back into his store and demand protection money.

Lieutenant Burns, his watch commander, had ordered him to stay on the street until Captain Brady determined how many of the night watch would be reporting. The strike had been much more effective than anyone thought. Over ninety percent of the evening watch had stayed out, including many of the sergeants who, as supervisory personnel, had been expected to remain on duty.

Earlier, when the "902" (return to station) call had gone out over the radio, Frank had driven Barney back to Central. Since then Frank had stayed away from the station, spending most of the evening checking in with bar, club, and store owners in the North Beach area. The radio was quiet but he didn't know whether it was because crimes weren't being committed or just not being reported. He'd heard that one hundred inspectors were being dispatched into the field to pick up the slack, but the only detectives he'd seen all night were two vice cops sitting in a Broadway club getting drunk.

It hadn't surprised him that so many patrolmen had walked out. Most cops were prima donnas, their feelings got hurt easily. When Zimmerman had snubbed Wallace at the council meeting that afternoon, it was all they needed.

What pissed him off was the POA really thought they were going to win. When he'd dropped Barney off at the station, De Angelo had come up to the car and told him they had the city by the balls, and it wouldn't be twenty-four hours before the council gave them everything they wanted.

Mike De Angelo and his partner, Fred Carr, were typical San Francisco cops. They were both smart enough to pass the entrance exam, but neither had the brains to think it was easy. Neither they, nor anyone else at Central, seemed to understand that it was the public, not the City Council, who would ultimately determine their worth.

He stopped in front of the Chinatown Smoke Shop. Lo Ng smiled when he recognized him. The wispy-bearded old man never forgot the time that Frank had collared a robbery suspect in front of his store. Lo attributed the fact that he hadn't been robbed since to that arrest. Whether Lo considered Frank good luck or a deterrent Frank didn't know.

"No fei jai?" Frank asked.

Lo Ng shook his head. "Where's Schultz?"

Frank wasn't in the mood to explain.

The Chinese were very curious and anything out of the ordinary was noticed. Frank knew that very little went on in

Chinatown without being seen. The trick was in finding out what they saw. It wasn't easy. To most Chinese the police were known as *baahk gwai*—white devils. Captain Brady told him the name had originated in the nineteenth century when the San Francisco police and the fighting tongs took turns squeezing the poor Chinese for every cent he had. A hundred years later the resentment and suspicions still were very much a part of the culture. So was the extortion.

Like everything in Chinatown it had taken a certain amount of luck and a lot of hard work before the police began to understand the extortion tactics used by the youth gangs. Police Intelligence had heard for years about the widespread extortion of Chinatown merchants, up to a thousand dollars a week from certain restaurants, but there were never any witnesses. The merchants would rather pay the money than go to the baahk gwai.

Ironically, it was only because the extortion rackets were so successful that the police had been able to gain a foothold in the community. The previous summer the two major Chinatown gangs began fighting over territory—the Kum Hon resented the increased activity of the Wah Chung and a bloody running battle erupted between the two. In a four-month period sixteen gang murders were committed on Chinatown streets—shootings and stabbings, many in broad daylight. Yet not one arrest had been made. Even for Chinatown that was appalling.

The media reveled in it and by September the mayor's office had set up a special police task force. Because of their Chinatown experience Frank and Schultz were assigned to the ten-man group. Captain Brady was made chief advisor because, as Central District commander for the past seven years, he knew as much about Chinatown as any *lo fan*—non-Chinese—in San Francisco.

Coincidently—or not so coincidently, as Frank later learned—the same day that the special task force took to the streets a prominent member of the Wah Chung was found floating in the bay wrapped in a rice sack. He had been shot in the head five times and his hands and feet were bound. The next day a Kum Hon leader was found in the same condition. For four straight days thereafter either a Kum Hon or a Wah Chung was found floating in the bay. After the sixth rice-sack murder, word went out that a truce had been agreed upon by the two gangs. As far as Frank knew there had not been another underworld murder in Chinatown since then—until that afternoon.

To the media and to the public, and even to the chief of police, it appeared that the youth gangs had simply fought to a bloody draw. But those who worked in Chinatown knew better. There was only one man who could have ordered the kidnapping and execution of six Kum Hon and Wah Chung members, just as there was only one organization that would carry out these executions by ritually binding the victims' hands and feet. That man was R. Y. "Mancat" Ling and the organization was the Son Lee Tong. What made the tong executions all the more sensational and effective was the fact that it was generally known throughout Chinatown that the tong had dealings with both gangs. Evidently, the president of the Son Lee Tong had become nervous when he heard a special task force was being sent into Chinatown and had decided to take matters into his own hands. The tactic eventually worked when the special task force was discontinued eight months later because of Chinatown's "exemplary crime rate."

However, it was during the tong's imposed peace that the task force began to open lines of communication with the frightened community. For the first time in San Francisco history, Chinatown residents actually started cooperating with the police, giving descriptions, even disclosing hideouts of the two gangs. It was from an informant's tip that he and Schultz were able to stake out Mickey Wong's apartment.

Wong was a notorious Kum Hon member, second in command only to the gang's leader, Sidney Yee. One night Mickey got careless and brought his girl friend home to show her some jewelry. The jewels were the property of Hop Yen Jewelry Company, and Mickey was now the property of San Quentin.

Frank turned off Stockton and walked down Jackson Street toward St. Louis Alley. He walked past the entrances of the Hotel Sam Wu, the Wong Family Benevolent Association, the Su Hon Fat Company. Most of the signs were in Chinese and English. The buildings were all two- and three-story brick—Chinatown had burned to the ground in 1906 and the Chinese learned their lesson. Many were decorated with the familiar wooden Gothic trim and had brightly painted eaves and buttresses. Tour guides said the pagoda-like roofs were curved to keep the evil spirits away. They also said the tongs were synonymous with family benevolent associations. The criminal tongs of previous eras, which had controlled gambling, prostitution and narcotics, no longer existed—so the tour books and tour guides said . . .

Frank remembered listening eight months earlier to Ben Louie, Joe Louie's nephew. Ben had been standing in front of the modern marble business offices of the Son Lee Tong on Powell Street telling a group of tourists about the many good deeds performed by the tongs. He told them how the Son Lee Tong was particularly active in civic affairs, running their own language school for Chinese immigrants from Hong Kong and Taipei who couldn't speak English. He told them about the loans made to new Chinese businesses and the paternal attitudes towards young Chinese boys who strayed from their families. The tong was like a second family, he told them.

None of those tourists were around three months later

when Ben Louie's body was found in a garbage heap in back of the Sam Wu Hotel. Cause of death: heroin overdose. Heroin that Frank and Schultz suspected was smuggled in from Hong Kong by Mancat Ling and the tong. They suspected it but were a long way from proving it. Further away, now that the mayor had discontinued the special task force.

Some people, Captain Brady for one, said that Ling had gotten to the mayor. Frank didn't know. What he did know was that Ling was untouchable. Schultz had sized it up. "You find me a Chinaman to give evidence against R. Y. Ling and I'll show you a dead Chinaman." There were times when he thought that as long as Mancat Ling controlled the Son Lee Tong and the tong controlled Chinatown crime, whatever progress he and the other cops made against the youth gangs was futile.

Joe Louie's Club Kowloon was at the end of St. Louis Alley. Frank could smell the wok-fried noodles coming from the restaurant kitchens that backed on the tiny alley. As always, there was the constant clatter of Mah-Jongg tiles from behind dark doorways. He knew of five steady games in the alley. He didn't bust the small games. Gambling was part of the Chinese culture. Old men busted one night for playing Mah-Jongg would be back the next night playing pai gow and chinese chicken dice the night after that.

As he pushed open the club's lime-colored door his elbow automatically rubbed the butt of his police issue Smith and Wesson .357 magnum. After being a cop for nearly five years he never entered a public place without checking his gun.

The Kowloon was a long dark room. The bar was on the right and tables on the left. It looked like any other Chinatown bar—complete with dragons, snakes, Buddhas, Lao Tzus and even a girlie calendar, courtesy of Ah Chuck's

57

Garage. Louie was in his usual place, one hand propped against the cash drawer. He was talking to Harry Jew, a tailor from down the alley.

Frank nodded to Joe as he walked to the other end of the bar. From there he could see the front door and most of the tables. There were about twenty customers in the dark, smoky room. Maybe half were Chinese. On a given night you could find almost anyone there; even an occasional black man had been known to wander in. They were served but not encouraged to stay. Joe Louie, like most Orientals, had no great affection for blacks . . . or whites.

Joe followed him through the club. He was wearing a Hawaiian shirt, which did little to hide his fat stomach. His chubby, flat face was damp from the heat. The sweat gave his yellow skin a slick sheen and as usual he was frowning.

"Where the othah half?" he asked in butchered English.

"Practicing with his picket."

Joe shook his head.

"You want beer?" he said putting a bottle on the bar.

Frank nodded and took a swig.

"Anything new?"

"SOS—same ol' shit."

"Nothing more on what we talked about the other night?"

The Chinaman looked carefully around to make sure no one was listening. His face was bloated and aged from years of serving—and drinking—cheap booze in a smoke-filled room. His black hair was dry and flaky.

"Cousin tell me, be careful. No baahk gwai, no truce."

"You tell your cousin they'll be plenty baahk gwai. Not all of us are on strike."

"Not you, Parker?"

"Not me."

Joe seemed to approve, although with him you were never sure. Like most bar and store owners in the city, he was worried. He had good reason to be. Joe Louie was one of the few persons in Chinatown who openly spoke out against the Son Lee Tong. When his nephew Ben was found dead, Joe put a sign in the window of the Kowloon accusing the tong of murdering him. His friends said he was crazy but Joe was his own man. Barney said it was because he'd been raised by the Paulists at Old St. Mary's and had a strong sense of right and wrong. (Schultz considered himself an expert on all Oriental behavior because he had been to Vietnam.) Frank thought it was because Joe was drunk more often than sober.

"We found a man floating in the bay this evening. He was wearing a rice sack for a hat."

"Son Lee?" the Chinaman asked sternly.

"We don't know. The man was a transient. A bum."

"No bum in Chinatown," Joe said, shaking his head. No one shook his head as much as Joe.

"That's the strange part. He was white."

Joe Louie looked sharply up at Frank. He was not the kind of man who was easily shocked.

"White man killed by tong. Make no sense," he said finally. But the expression on his face told Frank what he'd already feared.

When Joe excused himself to make drinks at the service bar, Frank tried to make sense of what made no sense: the tong execution of a white wino. If the Son Lee wanted a man dead they would usually get one of the gang shooters to take care of it. Shooters were fourteen- and fifteen-year-old illegal aliens brought in from Hong Kong, given a gun and pointed toward the victim. So why the rice sack? It had to be a warning of some kind. But why? The waterfront was all that made sense. Andropolus was supposed to be checking. He wondered if the truce was ending. Joe's information was usually good. But that didn't make sense either. The fei jai would break the peace, not the tong. Whatever the trouble, it couldn't have come at a worse time.

When Joe came back he brought another beer. Frank looked up when he heard the door open and saw two girls who worked the Kowloon. Joe had told him they were Korean. Anything but Chinese. Just as there was no such thing as a Chinese bum, there was also no such thing as a Chinese whore. Frank turned back to the bar.

"I think she work tonight," the owner answered without being asked.

"Monday night. Yeah, she works on Monday," Frank said.

"She not come in much lately."

"Yeah, I know."

"She come in last night."

Frank stopped the glass in front of his mouth.

"She did? Did she say anything?"

Joe shook his head.

"She with Patty Ho and some white girl from the restaurant. They make lot of noise. Then Sidney Yee come in with two friends and they all leave."

"She left with Sidney Yee?" Frank asked, feeling his pulse speed up at the name of the Kum Hon leader.

"She no good, Parker," Joe said solemnly. "She not know what she is. Half Chinese, half Hawaiian, maybe half crazy."

"You don't have to tell me about Rita Chan."

He recognized the high-pitched laugh before she was through the door. In the dim light of the bar her exotic features were more alluring than ever. She was with Patty Ho. When she saw him sitting at the end of the bar she whispered something to Patty and giggled. He moved uncomfortably on the stool as she walked toward him. She was wearing a flowered-silk shirt tied above the waist and a pair of white silk drawstring pants. He remembered the pants well.

"I didn't know you still came here," she said. Her voice

was loud and slightly affected, like many Orientals who learned English as a second language. The smile she gave him was neither friendly nor warm. It was a Rita Chan smile. Impossible to read.

"Yes, you did," he said calmly.

"Do you know my friend, Patty Ho?" she asked imperturbably. "She's Hong Kong girl like me."

He had met Patty many times. They nodded. Patty had the flat round face of a Cantonese. Frank thought she didn't approve of him.

Rita was wearing platform shoes which made her about five-feet eight. She looked as good as he'd ever seen her look, which was awfully good. He could feel her fantastic body teasing him through the silk.

"What have you been up to?" he asked.

She looked at Joe, then laughed.

"Just because I don't see you anymore doesn't mean I can't come here," she said. "Two wine spritzers, please, Joe."

The bartender shook his head and began making the drinks.

"You know what kind of a person Sidney Yee is," Frank said angrily.

She gave him the same enigmatic smile.

"Sidney Yee is a nice boy. We have fun."

"Sidney Yee is a murdering little punk and you damn well know it," he said, raising his voice enough that people at the other tables looked up.

"You don't tell me who I can see," she said just as loud. "You have lovely wife at home waiting. Some day have little Parkers. Rita Chan doesn't go out with married men."

Throwing back her head she picked up her drink and took it to an empty table. Patty joined her. The two girls laughed when they sat down.

Without saying a word he turned and walked toward the

door. He was almost running when he got to the end of the bar.

"Good-night, Frank Parker," she called after him.

There was a desperation in her voice that almost made him turn around but his cop's strong sense of survival kept him going.

He took a deep breath when he got to the alley, trying to regain his composure. He leaned against the back door of Hop Lee's Gifts and Novelties. The quiet of the alley was what he needed. The heat and the alcohol and the sight of Margarita Chan had almost gotten him into deep trouble. It wouldn't have been the first time. She had a strong effect on him, strong and dangerous. Her instinctual animal vitality attracted and frightened him. That was why he had stopped seeing her. She played by a different set of rules. Rules that a cop—a white, half Irish, married, San Francisco cop—would never be able to live with. Not for very long.

He walked out of the alley, letting the pungent smells of Chinese cooking work their magic on him. He felt an irresistible urge for moo shu pork on mandarin pancakes covered with plum sauce. It was his favorite dish and nobody made it any better than Rebecca Sing at the North China Restaurant. Rebecca once told him she was fifty but she didn't even look thirty-five. She was typical of the Chinese-American living in Chinatown, hardworking, thrifty, and deeply devoted to her family. He smiled when he thought of Barney's description of the people of Chinatown, "Out of one hundred thousand people only about one hundred are assholes. Pretty amazing when you think of it."

TUESDAY
AUGUST 3rd

8

THE mayor pushed his way past the newsmen in the corridor. For the first time in months he felt like working. The muscles were stiff and had lost their tone but they were still there. He and Topham had stayed at City Hall until after one A.M. the night before, making sure Chief Murphy and his supervising captain Bob Hartzell were able to keep the evening and night shifts covered. So far they'd been lucky. The strike had been far more effective than Murphy had anticipated, yet there had been no violence.

"How long do you think it's going to last, Mr. Mayor?" Harry Carl asked him before he could get into his office.

"When's your magazine go to bed, Harry?"

"Friday midday," Harry told him. Carl was one of the few reporters the mayor liked and respected. Unlike most reporters he seemed as interested in the truth as in his career.

"If it isn't over by then you might have to send your story by Pony Express."

Ken Topham and the mayor's press secretary, Eli Bergman, cleared the hall until only Miranda Stone of KSFT remained between Belardi and his office.

"Didn't I answer all your questions at the news conference, Miss Stone?" he asked, purposely emphasizing the title.

"Not the most important one, Mr. Mayor," the freckled brunette said. "You said under no circumstances would you let amateurs come into the city to do the work of professionals, but you didn't say what you would do if the governor called up the National Guard."

"I've been advised by the city parliamentarian that Governor Moffat can only take such an action if a state of emergency has been declared. I don't foresee that happening, Miss Stone. As I said earlier, this is not a police state. San Franciscans are civilized people. The protection being supplied by Chief Murphy and his police supervisory personnel is more than enough to ensure order."

"But what if order does break down, Mr. Mayor?"

"Let me worry about order, Miss Stone. You worry about getting your news clip to New York in time for the network news."

The mayor managed to disappear into his office before Miss Stone's epithetic remarks could reach him.

"My, my. Whatever happened to American femininity?" he remarked to Topham who was on the phone. "Who are you calling?"

"Fred Zimmerman. I told his AA you'd see him right after your press conference."

"Where's Eli? Tell him I don't want to see another reporter in this building."

Belardi began to pace across the Oriental carpet in his office. The give-and-take with the reporters had gotten the old juices flowing. He could feel the sweat dampening his collar. It was hot but he never used the air conditioner. There was something about the idea of a big-city mayor governing from an air-conditioned room that he rebelled against. Let the William Moffats and the Fred Zimmermans

66

govern from vacuums. They couldn't afford to sweat anyway, their makeup would run . . .

"He's on his way down," Topham announced. "Do you want me to stay?"

"No, I'll talk to him alone. Why don't you and Eli work up some kind of a 'keep cool' press campaign. Maybe I can walk through some of the neighborhoods. Go down to the Fillmore or into the Tenderloin. Show the folks there's nothing to worry about."

"You walk through those neighborhoods and you'll have plenty to worry about."

"I'll take Spivac with me and some community people. Why don't you give Jimmy Cleveland a call and ask him if he wants to take a walk down Fillmore Street with me later on?"

"You know Jimmy doesn't do anything for free. He'll want to know if he can get matching funds. Besides, Zimmerman won't like a councilman breaking ranks, especially Cleveland. He came down pretty hard on Wallace yesterday."

"Jimmy Cleveland does what he wants when he wants. He'll be there if he thinks there's going to be trouble."

"From what I've heard lately he's in a little trouble himself. More than a little trouble."

Before Topham could elaborate, the mayor's secretary announced Fred Zimmerman on the intercom. Topham left by the side door. Sam turned and waited to face his likely successor.

His reaction on seeing Zimmerman's boyishly attractive face was always the same. He despised the man. From the elfin hairstyle to the gold-chain loafers, Fred Zimmerman represented everything Belardi hated about modern politics. Like many post-Reagan California politicians his principal qualifications for office were a sincere smile and a cleft in his

67

chin. He had none of the ethnic or neighborhood character-
istics that the city politician usually had, he barely seemed
Jewish, but then he really couldn't be considered a city
politician. Cosmetic politicians, the mayor called them.

He'd often wondered if Ketty had done it to spite him. He
wondered if she found the man he disliked most in all of San
Francisco and then married him. The truth was he'd only
begun to hate Zimmerman after Ketty married him.

He'd been in love with Ketty Zimmerman—née
Stevens—since the first day he saw her swimming in the pool
of the Stevens's country house in Woodside. She was
seventeen then, two years younger than his own daughter,
Margaret, and he was the incorruptible city attorney Ketty's
father was molding into the next mayor. He watched her
grow up, got drunk with Bryce when she ran off with a ski
bum, stood in for Bryce when she wanted a church wedding
with the artist. When her marriages invariably ended he had
always been there.

He wasn't sure how it got to be more than that. For him it
had always been, although he would never let himself admit
it. Then one night she looked up. He was still there. Her
best friend's father, her father's best friend. They were
having dinner, just Ketty, Bryce and himself—Constance
hadn't been feeling well. It was a month or two after Ketty's
second divorce. Bryce was called away to the hotel and they
stayed at the restaurant, drinking wine, talking about the
men in her life. There had been a lot. She asked him if there
had ever been anyone else in his life. He said there had.

It ended before it began. He was too old, he was married,
he loved his wife. She was too beautiful. Too much.

Bryce never did know why he hadn't come to Ketty's last
wedding. For the last five years Sam had been waiting for
Zimmerman to break. He'd heard the rumors, everyone
had; Ketty was up to her old tricks, yet Zimmerman had
stayed. He went home every night as if she were any other

wife. Maybe that was what galled him so about the man. Or maybe it was his own guilt.

"I hear you gave quite a performance this morning," the younger man said, looking around the room as he entered. The mayor had noticed that each time Zimmerman came into his office he seemed to be mentally redecorating it.

"The important thing is that the people not panic. If they think they're safe they will be safe."

"Did Ken tell you I tried to get hold of you yesterday?"

The mayor didn't answer. He didn't like the familiarity of Zimmerman's manner. Zimmerman always was too friendly.

"You know, this whole mess could have been avoided if you'd given us another month."

"Is that why you've refused to meet with Pinch Murphy or Clint Wallace for the past six weeks?"

Zimmerman's careless laugh conceded the point. "If I thought it could have done any good . . ."

The mayor dismissed the remark with a wave of his hand. "Why don't you sit down? You make me nervous walking around here like a real estate salesman."

The councilman obligingly sat.

"I have a few things I want to discuss with you. A few things I want to get on the record while there's still time. Now, I don't know whose advice you've been taking lately . . ."

"I'm not following anyone's advice," the councilman broke in defensively, "It was a simple economic decision from the start. Dick Thornton came to see me last March and said there was no way the city could afford to give the policemen the full twelve percent raise the formula called for. I don't have to tell you what kind of financial shape the city is in. Our bond rating has been dropped to a *B* by Moody's because of Proposition Thirteen. The tax base is deteriorating faster than the city treasurer can subtract.

We've had to dip into the emergency fund the last two years to meet the payroll. It was time somebody around here said no, and that's what I've done."

The mayor studied Zimmerman's tan face for a sign of humor or facetiousness. There was none. There was only a sickening sincerity, the empty righteousness of an opportunist who must defend his every action.

"I didn't call you down here to lament the financial condition of the city. I called you down here to give you a little advice. I don't think you have any idea what you've started."

His voice and pulse began to rise.

9

THE phone was still ringing in Frank's ears after he picked it up. A painful turn of his head told him it was eleven thirty. At least it was still morning.

"You missed a lot of excitement last night, partner," Schultz said with a pronounced slur in his voice. "About one o'clock the newsmen started to complain about nothing happening so I shot out the street light. I was so loaded it took me three shots to hit the damn thing. In the paper this morning there was a big story on the strikers shooting out street lights in front of station houses to protect themselves against snipers."

Frank laughed, but it wasn't easy. His head felt like a blown gasket. His mouth like the inside of a broken radiator. He vaguely remembered driving home in his patrol car—with the lights flashing.

"If you were shooting out street lights last night, how can you be feeling so good this morning?"

"Haven't gone to bed yet. They wanted me to stay down until the day crew got here. I've been drinking so long I don't know whether I'm drunk or sober."

"So, is the strike still a big success?"

"I guess so. Almost everybody's staying out. Couple of older sergeants crossed the line, but that's all except for jerks like Sandy Gillespie. A few guys wanted to paint 'scab' on Gillespie's car last night but no stores were open."

"Did they say anything about me?"

"Yeah. Ted Thompson mumbled something about hoping you'd get smart. He said Clint was counting on guys like you and me to come through. When I laughed he walked away. . . . 'Look, why don't you come out for a drink? I'm down at the Worm's Eye. They have a new waitress, she's got tits like honeydews. I don't have to be back on the picket line until the eleven o'clock news. Come on."

"No way. I'm hurting this morning. Went over to the North China last night for some moo shu pork and plum sauce and ended up drinking two bottles of plum wine with Rebecca."

"That yellow hussy has been trying to get you drunk for years," Schultz laughed.

Frank heard the back door open and the rustling of groceries in the kitchen. It occurred to him that he and Kathy had something to do this morning but nothing was playing back.

"Sure you don't want to come out for a couple of shooters?" Barney persisted. "It's too hot to do anything but sit in a nice cool bar."

Frank again declined the invitation. He appreciated what Barney was doing. He understood that Schultz in his own way was worried about him.

Kathy came into the bathroom as he was searching for aspirin. In the bathroom mirror they were a good-looking couple. The dark-haired mustachioed cop and his cute chipmunk-cheeked wife.

He met her in his second year at City College. She was the prettiest girl in his geography class. Her gold hair was lighter then and somewhat longer. She looked like a cheerleader, wholesome and healthy, always fresh. She would cross her legs in the row next to him and he would miss the entire lecture. It was hard to think about scarps and alluvial plains when transfixed by the crease between her tan thighs. Luckily he managed to meet her before the final and copy her notes. She blushed when he told her why he needed help. He got a B in the course and she got an A.

Now she was back in school, getting her teaching credential at State. He'd encouraged her at first but lately they hadn't talked much about school. They hadn't talked about much of anything.

When she saw him staring at her in the mirror her expression grew tense. She left the bathroom without acknowledging his presence.

He had thought about telling her about Rita. Telling her the whole story, why it had happened, why he had broken it off—because he still loved her, because he didn't want their marriage to break up. He hadn't told her because he wasn't sure he entirely believed it, nor was he sure it would have made any difference.

"Didn't you say we had to move something out of the garage?" he asked her, walking into the kitchen. He was feeling a little rocky and balanced himself carefully against the drainboard.

She ignored his question, continuing to put away the groceries. He opened the refrigerator door and poured himself a large glass of orange juice.

"Can you eat anything?" she asked curtly.

"Maybe a couple of eggs."

She took three eggs out of the refrigerator, careful to stay as far away from him as possible. She was wearing a pair of white shorts and a halter top. She looked very good for a woman married six and a half years. She hadn't let herself turn to dough like a lot of her friends. Not that it was going to do him any good. They hadn't made love more than four or five times in the last five months. At first it had been her idea, then he had stopped trying.

The problem, as always, was children. He was a policeman because he wanted to protect human life, but as long as he remained a policeman she would never trust him with the life of their child, so as long as he was a cop there would be no little Parkers.

"Where were you this morning?" The orange juice seemed to have revived him.

"I went by to see Janis. She was upset because her neighbors won't talk to her."

"Why not?"

"Because Mike is out on strike."

Frank laughed scornfully. "I love it. People get mad at cops because we want a decent wage to protect them from themselves."

Kathy mechanically broke the eggs into a bowl.

"Janis was pretty upset. She was mad at you because you didn't go with Mike."

"You should have told her I didn't want to make the neighbors mad."

He waited for a response but she continued to beat the eggs without animation. They'd talked briefly before about the strike and he'd gotten the impression she didn't care what he did. That was generally her opinion about anything to do with police work.

"I'm going to be working long hours this week. Twelve-hour shifts—six to six. It's going to be pretty crazy if we don't get a settlement."

She beat the eggs harder. Her brown arm moved awkwardly. Women didn't have the same kind of coordination men had, he thought to himself. Especially their arms. They had no muscles. He'd wrestled with some pretty strong chicks in his career but their arms were usually weak.

"You're gonna kill those eggs, honey."

The bowl dropped to the kitchen floor, splattering the

74

eggs all over his feet. He looked up in surprise. She was glaring at him. Her cheeks were flushed with anger.

"Do you think I care!" she yelled at him. "Do you think I care about your eggs or your job or friends or drinking bouts or girl friends! It may surprise you, Frank, but you're not the center of the universe. People can actually live full normal lives without ever having had anything to do with you."

He watched her, dumbfounded.

"What are you talking about?"

"You! Your selfishness. Your image of yourself as being different, better than everyone. When Janis told me this morning how disappointed Mike and Fred were that you didn't walk out with them, it hit a familiar chord. You're that way with me, you're that way with our friends. You're that way with everyone. Frank Parker needs no one, so screw the world."

"Since when do you care whether or not I go on strike? I talked about it all last week and you never said anything."

"Why should I say anything? You'll do whatever you want, no matter what I say. You always do what you want. This morning we were supposed to go to your mother's and help clean up after her garage sale. But, no, you got drunk again last night so your father had to do it by himself."

"Jesus, that's what it was I had to do," he muttered.

Frank knew he had to get out of the kitchen quickly. There was no way she was going to stop and his head was throbbing. He tried to move but the eggs made his feet stick to the floor.

"Most cops never grow up. That's what Professor Wickstrom says. I believe it. He says they're victims of converging evolution. They take on the traits and manner-isms of the people they deal with and never develop mature character traits like love and trust and responsibility . . ."

"Don't give me that college crap, Kathy," he shot back,

"those pricks don't know anything about what it's like to be a cop. They don't know what it's like to be alive, period."

"Is that why you're afraid of education? Is that why you're afraid to find out about yourself? You might be a good cop, Frank, but as a human being you don't make it."

"Shut up, Kathy. I mean it. Shut up!" he yelled at her.

"Not this time, Frank. I'm not going to shut up. I can't stand it any more. I can't stand being married to a man I don't know. I didn't marry Frank Parker, supercop. I married Frank Parker, person. You don't need a badge and a gun to love someone."

The next thing he knew he had jumped up from the chair and was shaking her violently by the arms. "I told you to shut up!" he cried. He wanted to shake her until he couldn't hear her words anymore.

She screamed and he saw an unfamiliar terror in her familiar face. He realized what he'd done.

He let her loose against the drainboard. The sudden energy dissipated as quickly as it had appeared. For some inexplicable reason he was completely relaxed. It was the first time he ever remembered laying a hand on her in anger.

She was looking at him strangely. He hadn't felt her look at him that way in a long time.

His hands came back to her arms, gently this time, and he kissed her. He kissed her and closed his eyes, tasting her waxen lip gloss and feeling her warm, wet lips and tongue. Her body came alive with his as they pushed against the kitchen sink. He could feel both their tears on his cheeks.

The love that had been stored between them came easily to him. He was surprised that it had been so close to the surface, surprised and very happy. He held her tighter and she responded.

"Wow," she said when he finally stopped.

He couldn't say anything. He was afraid of ruining the

mood. Then, looking into her brown, teary eyes he knew it was impossible to break.

His hands slipped off her arms and over her buttocks.

"Let's go into the bedroom," he whispered.

"What's the matter with right here?"

He knew she meant it.

"Some breakfast," he said lifting her off the sticky floor.

10

POLICE ON STRIKE!

IT was a disturbing sight, even to Frank. He drove the patrol car slowly past Central Station. There were thirty men marching back and forth in front of the square concrete building, carrying picket signs. Many were wearing their sidearms in open view, looking not unlike a vigilante army. He recognized most of the men although he considered none close friends. They seemed to regard him with suspicion, as if he were a pimp or a pusher cruising the station in his hog before doing a number. He'd heard on the radio that strikers had vandalized squad cars at Taraval and Northern stations. He hoped there wouldn't be trouble at Central.

He was in too good a mood to be brought down by a hassle with drunken pickets. He and Kathy hadn't spent such a day together in a long, long time. From the kitchen they had moved into the bedroom. The way he felt he could have made love to her in every room of the house. How wrong he'd been to think those kinds of afternoons were history.

Afterwards they walked over to Golden Gate Park. They rented a boat and she rowed him around Stowe Lake. With his head in her lap he admired the miniature forests and trails of Strawberry Hill. They talked about things they hadn't been able to talk about before. There were promises to talk more, to make time to spend afternoons together. The next time they would take a picnic lunch to the top of the hill. It was going to work. The fact that it had come so naturally, so easily, made him sure it was going to be all right.

He parked across the street, near the Cellblock, Central Station's unofficial clubhouse. Before he crossed the street he looked up and down the block to see if anyone else was reporting. Seeing no one, he approached the pickets by himself.

As he reached the curb, Ted Thompson, the station strike coordinator, broke ranks and walked up to him. With Thompson was patrolman Ron Jones, the day watch picket captain. Both men were big, though not muscular, and had reputations for being hard-asses. Frank could smell beer and trouble.

"Your partner says we're supposed to leave you alone," Thompson said, showing a mouth of yellow teeth.

"He's right," Frank answered casually.

Both men stepped in his path.

"But your partner's not here and we don't like scabs," Jones said, poking the top of his picket lightly into Frank's stomach.

He stopped and looked at the two men. The rest of the pickets had stopped marching and were watching the show. No one made a move to help him. Not that he expected it. He wasn't afraid of the two men. Although they were big, he was younger and bigger and faster and tougher.

"Get that picket out of my gut, Jones, or I'll break it over your nose," he said calmly.

The patrolman tried to push the picket further into his stomach but hit muscle. Frank had two choices: step off the curb and walk around to the alley or splinter the picket on Jone's face as he said he would. He was leaning to the latter choice when the station house door opened in front of him.

Captain Woodruff Brady stood in the doorway. The sight of the lean, angular face was enough to make Jones quickly lower the sign.

"What's the problem, Parker?"

"No problem, captain, just waiting for someone to open the door."

"Now it's open," Brady said without changing his stony expression. "We've got a lineup at five thirty."

Frank walked past the two pickets, making sure to give Jones a slight nudge with his shoulder as he went past. "'Scuse me, fatso," he mumbled as he went by. Jones reached out to grab his arm but before his sausagelike fingers had closed, Frank pivoted off his right foot, taking Jones's arm with him in a one-move half-Nelson. The patrolman cried in pain as Frank bent his arm up to his head.

"God dammit, Parker!" Brady yelled, at the same time moving in front of Thompson to prevent him from assisting Jones. "Let him go!"

Frank slowly brought Jones's arm down to his waist. As he relaxed his grip it became obvious Jones wasn't going to try anything else. Frank doubted he would be doing much with his right arm for quite a while.

"If you or Thompson or anyone else out here try to stop another patrolman from reporting for duty you'll never wear a badge in this city again," the captain fumed at Jones. "You hear that?" he yelled at the others.

The strikers muttered compliance.

"I respect what you're doing and I expect you to show me and the men who stay on the job the same respect," he continued. "We're in this together, remember that. When the politicians are through with their games we'll be back on the streets with no one to count on but each other."

No one looked convinced but they weren't about to argue with Brady. Frank wasn't convinced either. He wouldn't want to ever have to count on the men who now watched him out of the corners of their eyes.

There were usually thirty cops in the briefing room for lineup before the evening shift. This night there were twelve. Five of the men were regulars from Central Division, the other seven were detectives. One of the detectives sitting by himself near the back of the room, smoking a cigarette, studying the proceedings with professional disinterest, was Phil Andropolus.

Frank had expected the detectives to show up. There was no great affection between them and the POA. The detectives considered themselves superior to the patrolmen and a few years earlier had voted to withdraw from the association. Most of them were caught up in what Barney called the "Mike Stone syndrome." They spent more time combing their hair and pulling their guns than they did catching criminals. Frank had considered taking the inspectors test that fall when he became eligible but the more time he spent on patrol covering for the flashy but usually slipshod work done by the detectives, the more he realized becoming a detective would take him away from the kind of street-level police work he enjoyed and considered important.

He knew the detectives were covering their asses by not striking. The way things worked down at the Hall of Justice the inspectors were probably closer to the politicians than they were to their fellow cops. Assignments and salaries were determined by the police bureaucracy, which was controlled by political appointees. By refusing to honor the picket lines they were only looking out for themselves, not the people of San Francisco.

"I don't think anyone else will be coming in," Brady said with a wry grin. The men looked around at each other. Usually they stood for inspection but tonight no one moved.

"I'm going to make this short and sweet. The sooner you get out on the street the better. The chief has sent all the district captains a copy of his strike contingency plan. There's no need to read it through, I'll paraphrase it.

"What we're going to be doing is essentially what we've been doing for the past twenty-four hours—provide basic police protection, which means that all calls will be thoroughly screened by Lieutenant Burns and me. Only emergencies—homicides, assaults, burglaries in progress—are to be answered. Because the inspectors have been good enough to volunteer for patrol duty, all criminal investigations are going to be delayed indefinitely. So make sure your reports are legible and informative. I don't want a novel, but chances are that it will be a long time before we can get back to the scene of any crime, so all we'll have to go on is what's in your reports.

"Property crimes, theft, stolen cars, vandalism, especially those committed hours earlier, are going to be handled over the phone, which means they won't be handled at all. I know people are going to be pissed but that's the way it is. If they don't like it, tell them to call their councilman.

"Any questions?"

If there were any his impatient look discouraged them.

"We're going to be breaking you into teams. An inspector will be riding with a uniformed officer when possible. Burns and I will be here to handle any bookings. Clint Wallace has been nice enough to exclude jailers from the strike so at least we'll be able to hold whoever you pick up. The communications people have also been exempted so we'll be able to talk to you out there even though we can't do much else.

"We're going to have five cars patrolling an area that is ordinarily patrolled by ten cars, four three-wheelers and five plainclothes teams. You're going to have little or no backup so be sure and keep your butts close to the ground. If you get into any trouble and we can't get to you, take care of yourself first. Shoot your way out if you have to. There's no reason for you to take any more risks than you already are.

What we're trying to do is prevent crime, not catch criminals."

"You don't want us to give pursuit then?" Frank asked.

"I want you to use your head, Parker. You see a guy shoot up a store full of people and run out with a sack full of money I want you to go after him. You see three Kum Hon walking down the street I don't want you stopping them on a four-seventeen. We don't need you to start a gang war tonight, Parker, because with the department at less than twenty percent efficiency I doubt if we could finish it.

"Any more questions?"

"How long are we going to be out?" one of the detectives asked.

"You're working twelve-hour shifts. Six to six. I know you fellows from downtown like to get your beauty sleep, but you're going to have to give your girl friends a break for the next few days or however long this damn thing lasts."

"Are we going to use the black and whites or our own cars?"

"Black and whites. Visibility is the key. We're more worried about the street punk than the professional criminal. The professional criminal is basically a cautious man, so we don't have to worry about the banks and the jewelry stores until he's had time to study our routine. But the minute the junkies and street toughs find out they can knock off the corner liquor store without even getting chased . . . it's all over."

"I heard on the news that the strikers weren't letting patrol cars out of the station," Sandy Gillespie said nervously. Sandy Gillespie was an asshole.

"That's not happening here," Brady said flatly.

"Some of those guys out there are pretty juiced up, captain," another detective said.

"You take care of the muggers, I'll take care of my men. I said there'd be no problem and I meant it."

"Lieutenant Burns has drawn up your teams. You want to read them off, lieutenant?"

"Ivy and Holms, car number one; Kendall and Gillespie, car number two; Andropolus and Parker, car number three . . ."

Frank laughed to himself. Schultz would love it. Just like Streets.

"You know the area better than I do, why don't you drive?" the detective said to him as they walked out to the garage. They'd politely acknowledged one another when introduced in the briefing room. Brady described Andropolus as the best homicide detective on the force. Frank said he'd heard.

Their area was from the Embarcadero to the Ferry Building and back up Broadway past the nightclub district to Columbus Avenue. He knew that Brady was purposely keeping him out of Chinatown. He and Brady had gone around before about the tactics he and Schultz occasionally used in dealing with the Chinese street gangs. Brady was playing it safe, but Frank knew if it came to the crunch the captain would go with him.

They drove down California Street, through the financial district. Foot traffic was heavy as bankers, stockbrokers and secretaries broke for their cars or the nearest bar. There were more hostile looks than usual, but the people, mostly commuters, seemed more concerned about getting out of the heat or having a drink than worrying about a police strike.

"I got an ID on that stiff you looked at last evening," Andropolus said as Frank turned up the Embarcadero a few piers below Pier 7.

"Oh yeah," Frank said, mimicking Andropolus's low-key professionalism.

"Guy named Leroy Krebs. His last known residence was Stockton. He worked there as a shipping clerk. That was four months ago. I talked to his former boss this morning, said he canned Krebs last May because he was a drunk."

"That's a lot of information for just one day."

"Not enough. His boss said he thought Krebs worked here a few years ago but he couldn't remember who for. I'm running an employment check on him through Sacramento, should get the answer tomorrow."

"You think he could have gone back to his old company?"

"His landlady said he was broke when he left Stockton. I'll find out tomorrow if he was collecting unemployment. If he wasn't, he didn't have a dime to his name. You don't put two dollars worth of lead in a man who doesn't have a dime. Not unless he knows something or has seen something he shouldn't have."

"Did the guy have a record?"

"D and D, vagrancy, nothing that clicks."

"You still think it was one of the Chinese gangs then?"

"I don't know who it was. Like most murder cases the more you know the more you don't know. Then you hit something that ties it all together."

Frank could feel Andropolus studying him.

"What makes you so defensive about those punks anyway? From what Brady tells me no one on the force has done more than you and your partner to fight them."

"I guess that's the reason. My partner and I have put a lot of hours in Chinatown the last two years. If the gangs are starting to kill whites I want to be sure. You see I have reason to believe it isn't the gangs. I don't know if Captain Brady has told you anything about R. Y. Ling and the Son Lee Tong . . ."

"I've heard rumors for years. When I worked out of Central fifteen years ago there were stories about the Son Lee. But no one's ever been able to prove anything."

"You're right, no one has. To most people, including the people who run this city, the Son Lee Tong is a highly respected community organization."

"But you know better?"

"I know the adults in the tong are far more dangerous and far more powerful than the fifteen-year-olds in the youth gangs. Narcotics, prostitution, loan sharking, extortion, smuggling jadeite . . . I'm convinced there's not an illegal activity in Chinatown that the tong doesn't control, either directly or indirectly. The way Krebs was killed, the rice sack, his hands and feet bound, that's the old tong-style execution. The only difference is that in the 1880s they'd also cut off the ears.

"If there's a link between the tong and the murder, which I think there is, I don't want to risk the confidence and connections we've built up by letting you or any other cop come in and start pointing fingers. Ling's the kind of man you don't get a second chance with."

"I like your thinking, Parker. You'd make a good detective."

"I've got enough work where I am," Frank answered.

11

THE mayor stood under the street sign at Taylor and Geary. He had just finished a mile walk down Market Street from City Hall, up Taylor, and through the sleazy Tenderloin district. Now he was waiting for a few straggling reporters to catch up before they went the final two blocks past the theater district to Union Square. The evening was warm and he was perspiring. He wiped his face gently with his handkerchief. The tour had been hard on him but he was glad he'd done it. It had enabled him to distinguish the reality of the strike from the politics of it. Being a political animal it was a distinction he had never found easy.

The ostensible reason for the evening stroll had been to show the reporters, and through them the people of the city, that the streets were safe. If he could walk through the highest crime area in the city, the Tenderloin, then anyone could. The pictures had been good and he thought the ploy had come off very well. There had been no violence, not even any intimation of trouble. The winos and bums of Market Street and the pimps and pushers of the Tenderloin had been on their best behavior. To them it was a grotesque party; to the mayor it was very serious business.

One pimp, "Eugene, the king of the Ellis Street scene" as he called himself, had taken Sam into a Tenderloin dive called Lucky's and introduced him to the patrons. The mayor had never seen such depraved humanity. They came in all shapes and colors. There were drag queens; men dressed as women, some who had silicone-injected breasts; whores, black and white, covered with cigarette burns and scabs; drug addicts whose cold, bloodshot eyes told him they would kill him for his shoes. Spivac couldn't believe it when the mayor patiently shook hands with everyone in the bar and even talked to one man who told the mayor he'd sent him to jail twenty years earlier. To the reporters Sam Belardi could have been a regular.

Yes, the pictures had been good. There were also shots of the mayor with his arm around Babe Tripuca, the owner of Babe's Billiards and a former Mission High football star; of the mayor shaking hands with Vera, the manager of the Golden Fleece Massage Parlor (a much more apropos name than Lucky's); of him buying a bottle of mineral water from Haziz, the Arab grocer on the corner of Taylor and Eddy. Haziz, whose store had been held up an incredible fifteen times in the last two years, had said he hadn't seen the streets so quiet in months. It had been like a campaign, and the mayor had always been able to press flesh with the best of them.

There was only one problem. It was a sham. The whole thing had been a lie. He'd known it in the first block, but it wasn't until he'd gone into Lucky's that he realized the depth of the city's charade. Everyone he'd talked to that evening had been afraid, even the derelicts, the dregs of the city, were frightened. They pretended to be happy that the police were gone, just as the law-abiding citizens pretended to be indignant, but the truth was they were scared. He'd seen it in their faces, heard it in their voices, and had felt it in his own heart. There was no escaping the disquieting knowledge that, for the first time in their lives, these San Franciscans were living in a city without a police force; they

88

were living in a society with no guarantee of order. The balance between order and anarchy was gone and no one understood the delicacy of that balance better than the pitiful denizens of the Tenderloin.

"Who's missing?" he asked Eli Bergman.

"Carl and Muldoon," the frazzled press secretary answered.

The mayor was fond of his press secretary, they'd been together forever it seemed, but Eli was not at his best under pressure.

"Better search the bars," someone suggested.

"You search 'em," Bergman told him, "I'm never going in a bar down here again."

Just then the two reporters came around the corner. Harry Carl was wearing his usual ironic smile. To the mayor he always looked like a man who was waiting for everyone else to get the joke.

"What's the matter, Harry, don't you like the tour I'm giving?"

"Is that what it is, Sam?"

The mayor ignored the question and led the reporters across the street. Now was not the time to get into a discussion with Harry Carl. The illusion of order was all-important. Until he was able to somehow get the police back to work the charade would have to continue.

"You know Geary Street was named after the first mayor of San Francisco, a Pennsylvania colonel, John C. Geary. When the City Council asked him to run for a second term he declined and moved back to Pittsburgh. There are a few members of the present City Council who I think might have gladly named a street after me if I had quit after one term."

The reporters seemed to be enjoying it. It surprised him how easily the banter came back. He'd gotten along with them better that night than he had in years. He wondered if they knew how important they were to him. How important it was that they played their roles as well as the pimps and hookers.

"Are you going to take us into the Redwood Room, Mr. Mayor, to show us how the other half is taking it?" somebody asked, referring to the stately dining room of the Clift Hotel.

"My guess is the people you'd find in there would want every striking policeman before a firing squad at dawn," he told the reporter as they passed in front of the hotel, "The only collective bargaining I've ever heard a rich man endorse was a cartel."

One of the remarkable features of that part of the city was that in one square block could be found a three-star restaurant, a massage parlor, a luxury hotel, and a pimp bar. For years the mayor had been under pressure from certain theater and restaurant owners to clean up the theater district but every time he'd make a move in that direction he had come under equal pressure from certain hotel owners, like Bryce Stevens, who although they would never admit it publicly, were not at all averse to the idea of so many varied "tourist attractions" being within walking distance.

The procession continued down the street. By now the group had grown to over forty and included the reporters, onlookers and the mayor's staff. Blocking their path was a large crowd waiting outside the doors of the Curran Theater. The mayor approached the theater crowd with some apprehension. He'd never been too popular with the cultural, intellectual set. William Moffat was more their kind of politician. He signed bills protecting endangered species and didn't accept contributions from oil companies. To these people Sam Belardi was an old ward heeler, an Italian who went to baseball games—not operas.

"Good evening," he said to a nicely dressed couple who smiled pleasantly as he approached them. "Good play tonight?"

"*The Cherry Orchard,*" the man answered. Sam guessed him to be in his late forties, possibly a lawyer.

"After Shakespeare and Pirandello, Chekov's my favorite," the mayor said.

"Have you seen the ACT production?"

"No . . . no, I haven't."

"You should. It's very good. It'll be here through the tenth."

"Maybe I will," the mayor said, "later in the week."

The couple nodded, again pleasantly, and got back in step with the ticket line. If they were in the least bit worried about the strike they didn't show it. None of them did.

"Amazing, isn't it?" he said to Bergman as they crossed Mason in front of the Commonwealth Club. "The people who can't afford it always have to pay."

"That's not amazing, Sam. That's the way it is. That's the way it's always been."

The mayor remained silent. Eli was right, it wasn't the least bit amazing. He, of all people, should know that. The day before, he had thought in some twisted, convoluted way that he could punish those San Franciscans who had turned their backs on him. He had wanted to show the city that it still needed him, that it couldn't continue without him. What a proud fool he'd been to think that he could teach men like Fred Zimmerman a lesson by abdicating his own responsibility. The ones who ended up suffering were the ones who always did. The poor, the destitute, the people who depended most on the government, on men like himself.

"What time is it, Eli?" he asked, stopping in front of Lefty O'Doul's.

"You were supposed to be at Bryce's reception for the Japanese Trade Commission twenty minutes ago."

"I don't want to see Bryce Stevens or anyone having anything to do with Bryce Stevens tonight. Come on, let's have a beer. I'm parched."

The mayor ducked into the saloon before Bergman could object.

"Draw one for the house, Kevin," he told the bartender, putting two twenty-dollar bills on the bar.

A raucous cheer went up from the patrons. The mayor knew many of the men sitting on stools around the bar and there was much handshaking and backslapping. Almost any night of the week you could field an entire pro team in Lefty's. Most of them never made it past the minors but to hear them talk you'd think they all played with Lefty himself. Nobody mentioned the strike, which told him they were worried. Unlike the theater crowd, these men worked on the street, not above it.

He took a satisfying gulp of the cold beer and watched the reporters come in behind him. Most of them were too young to have seen the Oakland Oaks or even the San Francisco Seals.

"Harry!" the mayor yelled to his favorite reporter. "What year did Lefty set the base-hit record?"

"Nineteen hundred and twenty-nine. Bill Terry tied it the next playing with the Giants."

"Not bad," one of the regulars said, then asked, "Who holds the PCL record for doubles in a season?"

Harry Carl smiled. "Give me a break, I'm from the East Coast. But if I had to guess I'd say you did."

"And you'd be right," the man said.

Harry came over to where the mayor was standing, loosening his tie, which was already loose. It occurred to the mayor that he had no idea how old Harry was. He had one of those faces that could be thirty-five or fifty.

"Is it true you're buying, Sam?"

"There it is," the mayor said, pointing to the money on the bar.

The reporter ordered a tall gin and tonic. When the drink arrived he asked the mayor to join him at a table in the corner. When they sat down, Harry proposed a toast.

"To a lame duck who won't stop flapping."

The mayor smiled and raised his glass.

"I'm going up to Sacramento tomorrow, Sam."

"Oh, yeah?"

"I don't know if you're aware of this or not but the governor sent a man down here yesterday from his office of emergency services. In fact, the guy was here before you even announced you weren't going to extend the contract."

"That's interesting."

"I called the Oakland Armory this afternoon. I asked for General Hinshaw but his aide said he was unavailable to the press because the Guard had been put on second-stage alert."

"That's also interesting," the mayor said, raising an eyebrow.

"I thought you might think so. Off the record, Sam, I think there's a lot more to the strike than we're getting in the press releases."

"What do you mean?"

"You know what I mean. I mean Bryce Stevens and the other Democratic power brokers of this state are setting it up as a campaign stunt for Moffat. We both know it's too big to be a Fred Zimmerman production. It's like we're following a fuckin' movie script. A remake of the Calvin Coolidge story using solar units in every home rather than two cars in every garage."

The mayor didn't comment. He hadn't known about the governor's man, nor the second-stage alert, but neither development was unexpected.

"They're playing a dangerous game, Sam. Hundreds of people could be harmed because a few powerful men think Bill Moffat would be a good president. And the farther it goes, the harder it will be to stop. New York's been on the telex all day. I must have had ten inquiries. Evidently it was the only comer at the story conference back there this morning. Most likely it will be next week's cover. And you saw the network news tonight. Cronkite gave it almost four minutes, so did Chancellor."

"I guess it won't surprise you to hear that I agree with everything you've said. The problem is we can't prove any of it. I can't use it, any more than you can write it. Motives don't count for much in politics—unless you have the proof, and we don't."

"But you *know* it, Sam, you know what they're going to do. In politics that does count. You're the only one who can stop them."

The mayor had never seen Carl so intense; the cynical reporter was a believer, just as the hard-bitten politician was a believer.

"I'm trying, Harry. I've been at this too long to make any promises, but I'm trying. I guess you already knew that?"

"I guess I did."

WEDNESDAY
AUGUST 4th

12

IT was one A.M. and Frank was glad he'd worn a short-sleeved shirt. The red, yellow and green neon lights blinked on and off, back and forth across the wide street. Working the Broadway beat was like working inside a pinball machine. He had always liked the night-club district. Kathy never understood how he could actually like working among such degenerates, but he enjoyed the far-out types who worked in the clubs. Listening to the barkers drag tourists off the street, each one promising that the live sex act in their club was the one you'd come to San Francisco to see. "Topless and bottomless. That's right, folks. Totally nude. Absolutely no cover. This isn't the Brown Hotel in Des Moines, friends . . ."

Frank could sense the changing mood of the street. There were a lot of people around—maybe not as many as usual for a hot summer night, but Broadway still seemed crowded. As usual, the tourists and visiting businessmen were getting louder and drunker as the night got later, but there was a certain caution in their celebration. They seemed to be forcing themselves to have a good time in spite of the strike.

An hour earlier he and Andropolus had responded to a fist fight in front of an outdoor cafe. By the time they'd arrived both men involved were bloody messes but also too

97

drunk to feel any pain. The woman cashier told him that the patrons just sat and watched the fight in silence, afraid to get involved because they weren't sure the police would come.

Even the locals were subdued. He had expected the barkers and the hookers to be dancing in the street, but they too seemed to be waiting. Only the Japanese businessmen were oblivious to what was happening, but then they were usually oblivious to everything but their maps and cameras.

"When I was a patrolman, we used to fight over this beat," Andropolus said as they walked past the Garden of Earthly Delights. A three-foot glossy poster of two giant breasts stared them in the face.

"It hasn't changed. The club owners pay the young guys in women and the old guys in cash," Frank said.

"All except you, huh, Parker?"

Frank was beginning to tolerate the Greek detective. He didn't trust him. He couldn't bring himself to trust any cop who carried an eight-hundred-dollar chrome-plated Browning automatic with a polyester pearl grip, but it was hard to dislike him.

"Not my style," Frank answered.

"Not mine either, but it didn't stop me," Andropolus laughed. "Let's go in the Oasis, I haven't seen those belly dancers in years."

They pushed through the beaded curtain into the darkness of the Oasis. Frank passed his hand over his magnum. The bar was half full. On stage was a young woman wearing a black veil across her nose and gold braids in her long dark hair. Her olive stomach quivered between two frenzied hips.

"I may be back in uniform before this week is out," Andropolus said admiringly.

Frank saw the club's owner making his way toward them. The man claimed to be a Turk but in fact was Mexican. His name was Mustaph and, like most club owners, he liked cops. Or at least pretended to. As in any well-run clip joint, cops were good for business.

Mustaph's wolflike face broke into a rare smile when he saw Andropolus.

"The only Greek I go fishing with," he said, shaking hands.

Both men laughed and started reminiscing about the old days on Broadway. Andropolus wanted to know where all the old dancers had gone and Mustaph said after he left the beat they all settled down and married hippies. Frank recognized a friend at the bar and walked over to talk to her.

"Slow tonight, huh, Tracy?" he asked the tall black lady leaning elegantly against the bar.

"No pigs, no johns," she said with a resigned smile. "Everyone's afraid they'll get ripped off."

"Maybe you better start giving discounts."

"I'm giving it away now, honey."

Frank laughed and Tracy flashed a toothy smile. She didn't like to smile because of her overbite, bad for business she used to tell him when they both worked in the Tenderloin. Now they'd come up in the world. He'd heard she was supporting a bad-ass pimp and a fifty-dollar-a-day habit. That was a lot of walking.

"How come you're not with the other pigs? Don't ya want no more money?"

"Somebody's got to keep you in business."

"Ain't that the truth."

"What's Mustaph think about you trickin' in his club?"

"He don't think nothin' of it long as I pay him with the brass off my ass."

She swung her regal rear end around defiantly. The sight was enough to divert the attention of a few customers away from the belly dancer.

"Frankie, honey, I think I see me a playboy over at one of

them tables. Why don't you go down and see Sophie at the Paradise? She's too ugly to be a whore anyway."

"I'd be glad to go and see Sophie if you'll do me one small favor."

She looked doubtful.

"Tell me what you hear about the hard business lately."

"How would I know about that? I've been clean for months," she said indignantly.

"Don't try me on like that, Tracy. You're a walking poppy bush and we both know I could prove it awful fast."

She looked away. "I've been hearin' Chinatown. My man says that's what he's been hearin'. It used to be paddies brought it in. Now it's the Chinks."

"Could he identify these Chinese?"

She shook her head.

"He don't see nothin' if he don't want to. 'Sides, he'd kill me if he ever knew I told you."

"Frank believed her.

"I guess we both better get back to work."

Frank joined Andropolus and Mustaph near the entrance.

"Who's your girl friend?" Andropolus asked.

"An old friend from Eddy Street."

The Mexican Turk shook his head.

"I tell her to stay away but what can I do? It's a free country. Her pimp say he kill me if I throw her out."

"It's not good business to throw out paying customers," Frank said.

Mustaph gave him a strange look and excused himself while Frank and Andropolus went back into the muggy street.

"Why are you looking so proud of yourself?" the detective asked.

"That hooker back there. She told me the Chinese are hand delivering into the ghetto."

"Hand delivering what?"

"Heroin. Before, the tong always sold it to the mob and *they* delivered it."

"What are you talking about? How do you know anything about heroin traffic? From a spade hooker?"

"You work on the street, you pick up a lot. She uses it. Her pimp buys it. He knows."

"Have you told Narcotics?"

"About the tong? At least ten times, but they're too busy busting coke pushers in Pacific Heights to waste their time in Chinatown."

"Can you prove it?"

"That's what the narcs say. Then they send some lame DEA man around to ask questions and nothing happens. They like to work from the inside and there's no way you can get inside the tong. You can't even get close from the outside. Chinese rarely use heroin. I've only known of two cases of heroin addiction since I've worked there, and both times the junkies were dead before I found out about their habit. The tong found out first."

"What do you think is happening now?"

"I'm not sure. I've had the feeling it's been awfully quiet lately. Something's been going on, but I didn't know what."

"Do you know now?"

"I think I might in the next few days."

"If you need any help I know one or two good men in Narcotics."

Before Frank could answer, a white-haired man came running up to them and began tugging on his sleeve. Frank had seen him many times along Broadway. They called him The Reverend because he was always giving biblical tirades outside the clubs. The club owners had tried to get rid of him as a public nuisance until they recognized his entertainment value.

"He screams for the Lord, but His ears are deaf to such sinners."

The old man had an unusual seriousness about him, even for a man who preached eternal damnation.

"What's he talking about?"

"Where is he, Reverend? Where's the screaming man?" Frank asked him.

"Near the Devil's corner," the Reverend said, pointing back toward Columbus, "the infidels are afraid to witness the Lord's judgment."

Frank started running before the old man finished. He knew the Devil's corner and when he got close he could see a small crowd had gathered in front of a cheap hotel next to the Condor. The screams sounded as though they were coming from the second or third story. He and Andropolus pushed their way through the crowd into the tiny lobby.

A lady with a splotchy face and a mustache pointed up the stairs.

"It's three hundred and eight. I bet it's three hundred and eight," she kept saying.

The two cops bolted up the stairs. The screams grew louder when they reached the third floor. They ran down the dingy hallway until they reached room three hundred and eight. A man's voice could be heard pleading with someone to keep quiet. Frank and Andropolus split the door, with their guns drawn.

"Police! Open up!" the detective yelled.

The screaming continued and before Frank could move Andropolus kicked open the door. When Frank got inside the door Andropolus had his automatic pointed at a nude, overweight middle-aged man who was standing, actually straddling the naked body of a much younger man. The older man held a broomstick in his hands. The boy on the floor had both hands over his anus. The end of the broomstick was bloody.

Andropolus pushed the man away from the boy, who then turned over on the floor still holding onto himself and moaning in shocked pain.

"I'll call an ambulance," Frank said in a helpless voice, looking at the boy but not wanting to get close to him.

"He gave it to me. It's his," the fat man said in a bewildered voice.

"Say another word, mister, and I'm going to blow your dick off," Andropolus said, pointing his gun at the fat man's genitals.

Frank couldn't bring himself to run down the stairs. He could taste the acid in his stomach. He wasn't a squeamish man but the depravity of the scene above had sickened him. The woman was still standing at the bottom of the stairs. Other residents and passersby crowded into the hallway.

"It was three hundred and eight, wasn't it? I told you it was. That goddamn pee-pee kisser, that'll be the last night he spends here."

He ignored her as he walked past. There were more people outside.

"Is he dead?" a woman asked.

"Sure took long enough to get here," another said.

He pushed his way through the crowd. Someone threw a coin at his feet. It was a penny.

"How much protection will that buy me?" a man in the crowd shouted.

"Not enough," Frank answered, taking a step toward a red-faced man.

The man and two of his friends backed off as Frank approached.

"They're drunk, please don't arrest them," said a lady with the group.

Disgustedly, Frank turned away. This was no time to get into a brawl with tourists.

He began running back to Broadway where they had left the patrol car.

It was after seven the next morning when he finished his paperwork. He was in no mood to joke with Andropolus about whether the offense in the hotel was rape, assault with a deadly weapon or sodomy. He was in no mood to do anything but sleep. He was amazed at how long Brady and Andropolus could keep going. The captain had set up a cot in his office but there was no sign of his using it. Frank asked Andropolus if he wanted a ride home but the detective told him to go ahead, he'd take a cab later. He had some homicide work to do.

On the way home Frank tried to analyze what Tracy had told him about the heroin traffic in the ghetto. He couldn't believe Ling would actually have tong members deliver the stuff. Something big was going on. He was going to have to drop by the Kowloon that afternoon. Maybe take Andropolus with him. It wasn't impossible that the body they'd found in the bay somehow tied in. If Ling was using a new delivery system, it meant trouble with the nickel-and-dime mobsters he'd been selling to. It also meant he was bringing the heroin directly into the city. That was what he'd been waiting for. A chance to tie the tong leader directly to the junk. If he could do that . . . if Andropolus could use his connections downtown to help him . . .

He wished Barney would sober up and get back to work. The strike couldn't have come at a worse time. He didn't know how many more nights he could take like the one he'd just been through. He had been awfully close to breaking three or four heads in front of that hotel. He was going to have to watch himself, not let his temper get the best of him. He'd always been inclined to hit a man rather than reason with him. It occurred to him that the few cops he did admire weren't like that. Men like Brady or Andropolus only used force when it was absolutely necessary. It was chumps like Wallace and his crowd who threw their weight around. You don't think with your right hook, Brady had told him more than once.

His small stucco house looked sleepy and comfortable. The morning still shaded it. He could see a few of his neighbors had started to stir. He hoped the plumber next door didn't pick this morning to talk football or register his complaints about the strike. He'd made the mistake of telling him that he and O. J. Simpson had played on the same high school football team. Ever since then the guy called him whenever O. J. was on TV, which seemed to be all the time.

The lawn needed watering and he promised himself he'd do it after the strike was settled. He didn't even have the energy to pick up the morning paper. Opening the front door quietly he carefully walked down the hall. He could feel the soft sheets of their bed before he got to the bedroom.

The room was growing light. He walked past the bed and put his off-duty two-inch .38 on the dresser. It was only when he looked down and saw Kathy's sleeping face with those cheeks he loved that he realized how much he wanted to talk to her. Only then did he realize how much he'd missed her and needed her and how glad he was to be home.

"Kathy, Kathy," he said softly.

Kneeling down on one knee he touched her bare shoulder. It was warm and inviting, like the bed. He gently kissed each cheek.

"I love you, too," he said and walked back around the bed to undress. He barely had the strength to get under the sheets. He lay on his back for a minute, letting her body heat soothe him. It struck him that he hadn't thought of Rita Chan once the whole night. He rolled over and found himself looking into her reassuring brown eyes.

"You better love me, Frank Parker, because no one else would have you," she said, and he knew it was true.

13

THE mayor held the dark-green ball cupped in his right hand as if it were made of heavy dough. Like the other bocce players his pants were rolled up two folds at the cuff. He knelt slowly, balancing himself with his left hand on the hard clay. With patient skill he rolled the ball down the sixty-foot court toward a cluster of red and green balls surrounding a smaller white ball. A midmorning quiet seemed to envelop the event. It was a needed respite.

"Corta, corta," a man yelled from the bench across the way.

The green ball continued to roll, hitting a small rise in the clay about four feet in front of the cluster, picking up the needed momentum to knock away a red ball and nestle near the white ball.

"Bravo, Sam, bravo!" a man yelled from the far end of the court.

The mayor smiled, shaking his right hand at the man who said his ball would be short. Reno Palimino, the other captain, used two short sticks, unmarked except for years of thumbnail scratches, to measure the distance. Sam and the other men crowded around while Reno held out the sticks. The mayor's ball was a winner. He held up his fist to his teammates. Palimino's team immediately demanded a rematch but he shook his head, pointing toward the ivy-covered gate where Spivac stood with Bryce Stevens.

Reno came up to the mayor, opened the string pouch that held the money and carefully paid out three dollars and fifty cents to Sam. They had grown up together in North Beach forty years before, in the days of Lusetti and DiMaggio. He and Reno used to play catch with Joe DiMaggio in the same North Beach playground where they now stood. Looking through the fence the mayor saw only Chinese boys playing on the diamond. The only Italians in the entire block were the old men on the bocce court.

"Why don't you come down to the restaurant later? I make you some pesto and we can split a bottle of Ruffino."

"Not tonight, Reno, this strike is no good for my stomach. When it's over then I'll come by and we'll split more than one bottle," the mayor answered, letting Spivac help him on with his coat.

Bryce was already in the limousine. They exchanged no greeting. They never did. Stevens had said it was important they talked . . . about the future, he had said. But it was the present that concerned the mayor.

The hotelman's face had a patrician gloss, like his daughter's. He was five years older than the mayor but didn't look it. They had fought many political battles together, but it was the mayor who wore the scars, not Stevens. Where Sam's face was craggy and his hair the color and texture of steel wool, Stevens's hair was still brown and his skin relatively smooth. Ketty once told him the reason her father looked so good was because he was too rich to have a conscience and too smart to regret it.

"I thought close only counted in horseshoes and hand grenades."

"What would you know about either?" the mayor retorted.

"Horseshoes is an old man's game and hand grenades a young one's."

"My father played bocce all his life just as his father played before him in Lucca. It's a game of skill, not of age."

In all their years of friendship an underlying competitiveness had persisted. As they had gotten older the competition had become even keener, at least on Stevens's side. This morning the mayor was in no mood for Stevens's jibes.

"Sheriff, drive us down to Pier thirty-five, I want to show the mayor something."

Spivac looked in the rearview mirror for confirmation from the mayor. On getting it the black limousine pulled away from the clay courts and headed down Mason Street toward the wharf.

The mayor sat back and let his mind make the transition from an enjoyable game with friends to this far more dangerous game with Bryce.

The city's luck had continued to hold the night before. The crime rate had actually been lower than normal for a Tuesday, but as he and Chief Murphy agreed, statistics were a poor indicator in this situation. With less than ten percent of the city's fifteen hundred patrolmen on duty even one incident would be enough to transform the generalized fear he'd seen in the Tenderloin into panic.

The City Council and the POA leadership had a closed meeting tentatively scheduled for later that afternoon, but he knew the meeting was for appearances, not negotiation. It was, as Harry said, another scene in the script.

"You should have come to the reception I gave last night for the Japanese Trade Commission," Stevens said.

"If you haven't noticed, the city's in the midst of a police strike."

"You don't have to tell me about the police strike, Sam. The Bankers Convention representative told me about it this morning when he cancelled their reservations for next week.

I hear Western Retailers will be next. That's nearly four-hundred thousand dollars worth of business."

"You should have thought of that before you put your son-in-law up to it."

"You know as well as I do that's patently ridiculous," Bryce snapped. "But I didn't come all the way down here to argue about Fred. I came down to talk about your future . . . our future. That's why I wish you had been there last night. Those are the kinds of people you're going to have to start spending time with if you want to put together the consulting firm we talked about."

"I've been stroking Jap businessmen for years and the only thing I ever got for it was a ticket for a massage my wife wouldn't let me use."

Stevens made a gesture of exasperation. "How many times do you have to hear it—business isn't politics. It isn't playing bocce ball with your high-school friends or riding horses in Mexican parades or pumping hands at Candlestick Park. Once you're out of office, the rules change. You start paying for your suits. The day your term ends you're going to have fewer friends and a lot more enemies than you ever thought."

The mayor laughed to himself. There was something absurd about Bryce Stevens warning anyone, least of all Sam Belardi, about the perils of the cruel world.

"Stop here, sheriff. Just pull in through the main gate."

Spivac crossed the Embarcadero and pulled the limousine up to the large triangular-shaped marshalling yard. There was a barbed-wire-topped fence running across the railroad spur that entered the outside loading area. Two security guards stood at attention behind the fence. The sign over the entrance read PACIFIC SHIPPING COMPANY.

Stevens and the mayor got out. The guards immediately opened the gates and the two men walked through, leaving Spivac and the car outside. Pier 35 was bustling, forklifts loading and unloading the freight containers on truck beds and flat cars.

"Remember when I took over this company a little more than a year ago? I wanted to be on the north end of the Embarcadero, and East-West Lines was the only company up at this end with enough adjacent space for containerization. What I paid for was space. East-West ran four break-bulk Panamanian freighters between here and the Philippines and two of the four ships were making the run from memory. They were losing more in towing fees than they were making in cargo. The first thing we did was scrap the two junks and charter two container ships. Last month PSC had nine container vessels under charter with a tonnage of over a million, and we were running at over ninety percent capacity. Close to a one hundred percent on some of the Japan–U.S. runs."

The mayor nodded. He knew more about Stevens's company than he wanted to admit. He'd heard from Mark Marcucci of the International Longshoreman and Warehouseman's Union that Pacific Shipping was a mover.

"As you can see, we have completely modernized the facility. Look at those gantry cranes," Bryce said, pointing to two huge container cranes, one on each side of the pie-shaped pier. "Those two forty-ton monsters cost three and a half million dollars apiece—that's more money than anyone has spent in the Port of San Francisco since the war. But they're worth it. You better believe they're worth it. It costs four dollars a ton to load break bulk cargo with ship's tackle, it costs thirty cents a ton to do it with a container crane. If your friends on the Port Commission had their way those hoists would be made out of old telephone poles, not steel."

The reference was to Stevens's current battle with the Port Commission, but the mayor refused to respond. Quinn Bucklin, the chairman of the Commission, was convinced

Stevens was using PSC as a front to buy up the entire northern waterfront for a huge real estate development similar to The Cannery or Ghiradelli Square. The mayor had declined to intercede, figuring Stevens, as usual, was drawing to both ends of a straight. Once Fred Zimmerman was elected in November Stevens could appoint the Port Commission himself. Bryce Stevens, even at age sixty-eight, was a man who could afford to wait.

Again the mayor wondered why he was there.

"Come into the shed, I want to show you what a modern container operation looks like."

They walked over to the north shed. It had been completely renovated. It didn't even smell like a pier. Rows of stainless steel containers were stacked alongside one another. Further down were hundreds of Japanese cars. The mayor was impressed.

"Tartan floor. Feel it," Stevens told him.

He stooped over to touch the hard-rubber surface.

"It's supposed to last for forty years with almost no upkeep."

"You must have a forty-year lease."

Stevens laughed. "When we get finished this will be the best container facility on the West Coast."

Again Belardi said nothing. They walked back out into the open air, Stevens leading him to a deserted part of the yard. The two men sat on a table-size wooden cable spool.

"In ten years, we'll be the biggest and fastest shipper in America. We've already put orders in for five new container ships. And when those are delivered, we'll order five more. This is where it's happening, Sam. The Japanese now, but soon the Chinese. That's going to be the market that makes us. The whole Pacific Basin is our oyster."

"So I gathered from your company name."

"*Our* company name, Mr. Mayor. I want you to run it."

The mayor scrutinized Stevens. Sam had to admit he had balls.

"I want you to start January first. Two hundred thousand dollars a year and I'll finance your purchase of ten percent of the company."

"I don't get it. Why me?" the mayor asked, getting it all too clearly.

"You're an excellent administrator and a damn good salesman. I think you'd work well within the company as well as with the foreign trade people—also the unions. You know the leadership of the ILWU and the Teamsters. They respect you. To operate successfully on the waterfront you need respect. You don't have it and they'll bleed you dry. . . . And there's another reason. My partner wants you for the job as much as I do."

"Your partner?"

"Silent partner. And he prefers to keep it that way for a while. We've both wanted to do this for a long time and we needed each other for reasons you'll understand later. We also need you."

"Two hundred thousand dollars. That's a lot of money for a man whose only business experience consists of running the family bakery for six months. When we talked about this before, it was on a consulting basis . . ."

"I've always found that a consultant is a euphemism for a business dilettante. They can tell you what to do with your money without taking the risks themselves. As far as your business experience goes, well, running San Francisco for sixteen years is pretty good experience."

"How long can I think about it?"

"Today's the fourth of August. How about September first? We're going to need a heavyweight in there soon, Sam. We're growing too fast for the management people we have now. I go to a board meeting and all they do is smile. They think because our revenue has grown four times in one year that they're geniuses. They don't understand the kind of capital outlay we've made. We're going to have to be doing three times again that much by next spring."

"This silent partner of yours, do I report to him as well as you?"

"Of course, my investment is larger but his is still considerable. Essentially, it will be the three of us who run the company. You'd be the chief executive officer. I don't think I have to tell you, Sam, but it's an opportunity very few men ever get. You've spent your entire life working for people. Now I think it's time you put that talent of yours to work for yourself. Money is a very enjoyable commodity. Some men even prefer it to power."

"Others equate the two."

"Only in political years," Stevens smiled.

The mayor opened his coat. He was beginning to feel the heat of the midmorning sun. He could feel his shirt sticking to his back. Meanwhile Stevens's starched white collar remained crisp and cool against his thin brown neck.

"I suppose Fred reported our conversation yesterday," the mayor said, seeing no reason to continue the preliminaries.

Stevens nodded calmly, not surprised by the sudden change of subject.

"I don't know how much this conversation has to do with what I told him, but if your offer is contingent on my letting him and the governor play heroes by breaking the strike, forget it. . . . I mean that, Bryce."

"The offer has nothing to do with the strike. I made it because I have confidence in your judgment. Politically and otherwise. Naturally I've been talking with the governor over the past two days. He's very concerned, so is Fred. I don't blame them.

"A police strike is the kind of gut issue that can make or

114

break a political career. Obviously, Bill has much more to lose than Freddy. I know you don't like him, he isn't like his father, but Bill Moffat has a damn good chance of being the next president of this country. There are some very influential people in his corner. National figures you know and respect. I know of three former cabinet members who are with us, and I have commitments from more than ten national committeemen."

The mayor laughed scornfully.

"I pity this country if Bill Moffat ever gets into the Oval Office. He's a spoiled, arrogant brat who was handed his political career on a platter. He is the kind of ambitious, demogogic politician whose lack of compassion is interpreted as principle. And I'm telling you right now, Bryce, I'll do anything in my power to fight him."

"There are things even you can't control, Sam," Stevens said softly.

"In San Francisco there's nothing I can't control," the mayor shot back.

"I don't want you to get hurt, Sam. You love this city. We all do. If you get in the way you might not be able to recognize it afterwards."

The mayor stood up. He took a deep breath and tasted the sea.

"You can threaten your business associates, Bryce, and you might be able to buy politicians like Bill Moffat but don't ever try to threaten me, don't ever try to buy me. You do and I'll take you to the bottom of that bay if I have to drown doing it."

The two men stared at one another. The mayor thought he detected a bead of perspiration glistening on Stevens's forehead.

"Fred was right. You have changed."

"We all change, Bryce. I can remember when you and I celebrated your election to the County Central Committee."

From the way Stevens looked at him he could have been talking to a total stranger. The hotel man stood up and walked toward the shipping office leaving him alone.

The mayor stared up at the big crane above the north shed. He thought of the school-book incident. It was much simpler then. All you did was bang a few heads together and your mind was at ease. Now, everything was done automatically. Seldom did you see a boom crane or even a grappling hook on the waterfront.

He made a mental note to check with Quinn Bucklin about Stevens's silent partner.

14

"I wanted a chance to talk to you before the meeting," Fred Zimmerman said with a quick smile, offering Jimmy Cleveland a chair.

Jimmy knew the council president well enough to know he had some kind of a proposition for him. Something about the way Fred's eyes shifted back and forth between the door and him, as if he were afraid someone might overhear them.

"How do you think it's going?" he asked as soon as Jimmy was seated.

"How do I think what's going? Your campaign for mayor?"

Zimmerman frowned. Jimmy enjoyed teasing him. He did business with Zimmerman but he didn't like the man. There was too much form and not enough style. Sam Belardi had style, Fred Zimmerman never would. That was one thing Bryce Stevens's money couldn't buy him.

"I'm talking about the strike," Zimmerman said.

"Right now the cops look bad and you're lookin' good. If I were you I'd get it in the barn, man. People start getting crazy and we're all in trouble."

"I can't back down now."

Jimmy did a mild double take.

"What are you talkin' about, back down. You're a

politician. Compromise. Give 'em a couple more bucks and take your bows. Isn't that what this big meeting with Wallace is all about?"

"Just because we're having a meeting doesn't mean we have to come to an agreement."

"Slow down a minute, Freddy. Are you saying you want this thing to go on?"

Zimmerman smiled. His sincerity was so transparent Jimmy sometimes thought it was real.

"I'm saying I'm not going to let some fat-ass cop push me around. We voted the police a fair raise. If they don't want it we can find someone else to do the job."

Jimmy howled.

"I don't believe this. Aren't you forgetting something, man? The only reason we got Thornton to come up with that phony five percent recommendation in the first place was to give your campaign a lift. You didn't even know the formula could be broken until three months ago."

The beady green eyes were impassive. He looked at Jimmy as though he had never heard of anything he was talking about.

"I'm going to press it, Jim, and I want you to help me. This thing is too big not to see through to the end. I've talked with the governor and he's with us all the way. America is not a police state."

"Time out, man. Time out," Jimmy said waving his arms. "Don't you lay that 'police state' bullshit on me. America's been a police state as long as I can remember. If your father had been given twenty years for trying to hold up a bank with an empty gun you'd know it. Don't go laying that white man's law-and-order trip on me. You and I are in the same business but we don't buy the same records."

Zimmerman frowned. He was distressed again. Jimmy smoothed his new Sulka tie over his stomach. He was going to have to lose some weight. Kim didn't like her man being fat. The way it was going these days what Kim didn't want Kim didn't get. He was even going to speak to her summer-school government class tomorrow. Maybe he'd tell them about Fred Zimmerman's police state . . .

"I talked to the governor this afternoon. He thinks this is a once-in-a-lifetime issue. There are some very large political benefits to be reaped. I mean national benefits. Enough for every politician who has the courage to stand up to the police. They couldn't in New York, they couldn't in Detroit or Baltimore. But I think we can. And so does the governor. It's a chance to be out in front on an issue that's going to be with us for the next generation. It confronts the question of collective bargaining for public employees head on. We break this strike and every beleaguered, downtrodden taxpayer in the country is with us. You said yourself the strike was tantamount to blackmail."

"What I say in public and what I believe are only coincidentally the same," Jimmy commented.

"The California National Guard has been put on alert. General Hinshaw has assured the governor that he can have ten thousand troops ready to march from the Oakland Armory six hours after a state of emergency has been declared. Neither the governor nor Hinshaw believe fifteen hundred cops with handguns would actually try and stop ten thousand guardsmen."

"You're talking about declaring a state of emergency and bringing in the Guard like it's a game. Sam Belardi's not going to invoke the emergency powers provision unless a major riot breaks out. And let me tell you, man, if this city does break loose you're gonna need a lot more firepower than ten thousand farm boys and school teachers commanded by a few retired generals."

"Who said anything about a riot, or Belardi for that

matter? The council can declare a state of emergency and request state aid if they feel the situation warrants it. It's in the charter."

"And Belardi can veto it."

"And the council can override with eight votes."

Jimmy nodded. He should have guessed sooner.

"That's where I come in."

"You can deal with Chacon and Mayberry better than I can. All you have to do is convince them it's in the best interests of the minority community to bring in the Guard."

"Even when I know if those trigger-happy punks got near the ghetto or the barrio you'd have to wash the blood off the streets with a fire hose."

"It doesn't have to be that way. Not if we can get the right community people with us. There's enough for everyone."

Jimmy laughed appreciatively.

"You boys are really serious, aren't you?"

"This is the big time, Jimmy. The presidential primaries are a year away. Bill Moffat has a shot. A good shot. I don't have to tell you what that would mean to us."

Jimmy pulled on his soft chin. Zimmerman's talk was intoxicating. Very intoxicating. Ambassador James Cleveland. It would solve a lot of problems.

"You can put the crayons back in the box, Fred, I get the picture."

"I thought you might," Zimmerman said.

"It's mighty tempting," he said, pausing to give the temptation a final chance, "but I can't do it. The risk is too great. It's dry down there, man. One spark and . . . boom. The only thing that's changed in the ghetto since the sixties are the prices—they've gone up. Everything else is down. Real low. I couldn't be part of a scam that put two thousand shitless paddies in the Fillmore with rifles in their hands. No way."

"The governor will be sorry to hear that, Jimmy. So will Bryce."

There was a coldness in his manner that Jimmy didn't recognize. If he didn't know him better Jimmy would have thought his fellow councilman was threatening him.

"We made a deal, Fred. I deliver the votes against the cops and you make me council president after you're elected mayor. The way it is now you're going to win big. Let's quit while we're ahead."

The white man shook his head.

"I can't quit, Jimmy. You can't quit either."

He looked at Zimmerman.

"It's not my decision, Jimmy. It's Bryce's. Either you play ball or the city attorney's office opens an investigation of the Redevelopment Agency. The builders of the King Center have a lot to say about the unorthodox way you awarded the construction contracts. You'll be indicted before Christmas if the Muslims don't get you first."

"Why you slimy, sheeny son of a bitch."

Jimmy breathed out slowly.

Zimmerman continued in the same monotone. "After the meeting with Wallace I'm going to ask Judge Ewing for a restraining order on the police. It should be granted by tonight. If Wallace doesn't comply, which I'm sure he won't, I'm going to ask for a vote tomorrow on the emergency powers provision. If everything goes as expected we can have the Guard in the city by tomorrow night."

Jimmy tried to laugh. It had to be funny. He thought of the years he'd spent playing the edges with liberals against conservatives, blacks against whites, law against justice. And now the edge had slipped. He could feel its sharpness against the skin on his neck.

"You're going to thank me when this is over," Zimmerman told him.

121

"And I always thought you Jews were too guilty to put it to us black folk."

"You should know better than to generalize in politics," Zimmerman told him. Jimmy considered it possibly the most profound thing he'd ever heard Zimmerman say.

"How did Stevens find out about the Redevelopment Agency kickbacks?"

"You're not the only wolf in the woods," Zimmerman laughed.

"Muhammed?" Jimmy asked, feeling his anger rise as he stood up to leave. "It was Muhammed, wasn't it?" The other man didn't answer and Jimmy knew it made little difference.

"You know the three most common lies?" he asked Zimmerman abruptly.

The other man looked at him quizzically.

"Black is beautiful, the check's in the mail, and I promise not to come in your mouth."

The white councilman tried to smile. Jimmy tried to laugh as he walked out the door.

15

FRANK found two messages waiting for him when he got to the station. The first was to call Joe Louie, the second to call Rita Chan. He dialed Rita's number first but there was no answer. She had never called him at the station before, and he was debating whether or not to go to her apartment when Andropolus came into the squad room.

"You were right. My friend Lipscombe in narcotics made Tony Redlick as a buyer. He's been around for three or four years. Never deals in more than a couple of pounds. Steps on it with boxing gloves then moves it along."

Already it had been a long day. Andropolus had awakened him at noon with the news of Redlick. They'd found him down at Pier 24, right under the bridge. Number twenty-four was the last pier before the Embarcadero swung south. Andropolus guessed the bodies were being dropped from somewhere north of the Ferry Building, probably up around the wharf but, like the Pier 7 watchman said, it was only a guess when it came to the tide in San Francisco Bay.

"Lipscombe says most of his dealers work in LA. But your theory about the tong moving in new wholesalers sounds good. This is the kind of guy they'd be burning. Lipscombe's going to run a check on other buyers who might be out a source."

"If we could only find out who they're using now. I have a hunch it's somebody I know."

"The street gangs?"

"That's my guess. I'm going over to the Kowloon right now. Wanna come?"

"I've got to finish up that check on Krebs. Sacramento says he worked for East-West Lines from February of '74 up until March of last year. The only problem is there's no such company listed in the phone book."

"What time does Brady want us for patrol?"

"Five thirty" Frank answered.

The detective swore softly. Frank noticed he hadn't changed his gabardine suit from the previous day. The bags under his black eyes were fleshier than usual.

"If you keep it up I might have to change my opinion of detectives."

"Don't do me any favors. Did you talk to your partner about the stakeout on the tong headquarters?"

"He said he'd put in an appearance on the picket line then sneak up to Chinatown."

"Is there a chance of getting anyone else off the line?"

Frank laughed.

He tried Rita's number again. This time it was busy. He left by the side door. Since it was only four-thirty he could stop by her place before he went to the Kowloon.

Rita lived in one of the many faceless old apartment buildings on the south side of Nob Hill. Thirty years before the buildings were fashionable, but now they were only a block or two from the Tenderloin. She had always liked it when he walked her home in his uniform. He felt strange being back on Pine Street. He remembered the anticipation he used to feel. It wasn't completely gone.

He parked in front of a fire hydrant. With no meter maids working, parking was a predictable free-for-all. As he was getting out of the car two figures halfway down the block caught his eye. Their shapes and dark baggy clothes set off a silent alarm. Young Chinese males carried themselves in a certain way that was unmistakable. Their manner was both self-conscious and hostile as they walked with their rigid heads and bodies bent forward, their styled black hair bobbing with quick steps. Both were wearing jackets, their hands in the pockets. Frank automatically felt under his arm, then tensed. He'd left his jacket and his off-duty .38 in his locker.

He stopped and waited for them to come to him. He knew who they were before they looked up at him. The smaller one was Sidney Yee. His apelike face was easily recognizable. Frank noticed that he was starting to grow a mustache in a so far vain attempt to cover the pink birthmark that ran from his nose to his upper lip. The punk with him was Danny "Banana Boy" Pong. Called Banana Boy because of his preference for white girls, "Yellow on the outside, white on the inside" was what they said about him, though never to his face. Banana Boy, like his Kum Hon boss, was a killer.

"Haven't seen you two boys around lately," Frank said as the two came closer.

They ignored his greeting and not surprisingly neither seemed too happy to see him.

"Nice watch you're wearing, Danny," Frank said, admiring the gold Rolex on Pong's wrist. Jade luck pieces and expensive wristwatches were important status symbols to gang members.

"I bought it from a nigger on Market Street," the Chinese tough said arrogantly. "You like it, Parker, I sell it to you cheap."

"No thanks, I don't like wearing stolen watches. Never know when you might run into the owner."

Banana Boy gave a laugh. Yee looked past Frank down the street. He seemed tense, very tense.

"Going somewhere, Mr. Yee?"

"This is a public sidewalk, man. You want to say something, you say it."

Frank moved a step closer to the Kum Hon leader. He studied Yee's prehistoric face. He wondered what Rita saw in the little Chinese punk.

He wanted to pull them both in right there and then but with no gun and no backup it would be suicide. He also remembered Brady's words about starting a gang war.

"I don't suppose either of you would know anything about the bodies we've been fishing out of the bay lately—the ones wearing rice sacks?"

Neither of them flinched. Maybe they half expected the question. Yee again glanced down the street. It wasn't like him to be so agitated.

"All right, boys, you're excused," he said lightly, not wanting to show his concern. "Try not to get lost in any jewelry stores on the way home."

For a second neither boy moved. Banana Boy looked over at Yee. Frank could feel his hands tingle. He was considering diving at them both when Yee began walking off down the street. Pong followed, his hand still in his pocket, laughing at Frank's helplessness.

Frank turned after them, looked, and saw an elderly couple coming his way. They were pushing a metal grocery cart up from the store. He knew then what had happened. Pong had been asking his boss for a hit sign. The old couple had kept Frank from being a dead man.

There was only one reason the Chinese would risk killing a cop.

Frank ran all the way to Rita's apartment building. He didn't bother looking back for the two hoods. He knew they were gone. He jabbed at her buzzer. No answer. He rang every other apartment he could reach. Finally the door buzzed open. He took one look at the ancient elevator and grabbed the stairwell door. Seven flights later he staggered into her musty hallway. Two heads popped out but he ignored them.

He knocked once, twice, at her door. The only sound he could hear was the gasping of his lungs.

"Rita! Rita!" he shouted. Still there was no answer.

He put his hand around the doorknob and hesitated. Once before, in the Tenderloin, he had opened an unlocked door.

His entire body ached with tension and dread as he stepped into the apartment. The living room smelled of jasmine. He checked it out with one professional pass. Nothing seemed out of place.

He was halfway across the room when he noticed that the turntable of the record player was on. An album, one of her favorites, "All in All" by Earth, Wind and Fire, lay out of its jacket next to the spinning turntable. She had told him fifty times to put the albums back in their jackets. Her records were one possession she seemed to care about.

He had to force himself to go into the bedroom. Once inside, his eyes registered the scene without blinking. He accepted the expected without shock. His experience had prepared him for the reality.

She lay naked on her stomach, her arms and legs splayed out on the bed. Her white buttocks arched above the plane of the mattress, revealing a tuft of pubic hair. Her face was covered by the pillow, except for her mouth, which was slightly open. Even in death she was the most sensual woman he had ever seen.

He reached over and picked up the pillow someone had used to suffocate her. Her saliva was still wet. He pulled the bedspread over her body and combed her hair out of her face with his fingers. He wasn't supposed to touch her but he didn't care. He was doing it to protect himself. There were times when police reactions were not enough.

16

HARRY Carl looked distractedly at the miles of steamy rice fields on either side of the causeway. The eighty-five-mile stretch between San Francisco and Sacramento was one of the most boring routes he'd ever driven. He had known Bay Area politicians who commuted daily to the state capitol but that was back in the days of the sixty-five mile-an-hour speed limit and the urinalysis test for alcohol.

He had been in a miserable mood when he left the city and the hot ride up in his Ford hadn't done much to improve his humor. New York woke him up that morning with the news that they were sending the LA bureau chief, Matt Fleming, to assist him with the strike story, ostensibly because his usual three-man bureau was down to just two—him and the photographer. But Harry suspected another reason. Brit Jefferson had recently been appointed managing editor of the magazine. He and Jefferson had been contemporaries from the days of Joe McCarthy and Duke Snider. Harry once said that Brit Jefferson could report the apocalypse without using an adjective. The line had been a standing joke around New York for years but now the joke was on Harry.

For the last eight months, ever since Jefferson had taken over, Harry hadn't recognized his own copy when it

128

appeared in the magazine. Now came the final blow, they were bringing in someone else to write the biggest story of the year.

Miranda had put it all in perspective the night she had told him she was leaving.

"You've had your career, now let me have mine."

Had. He'd laughed to himself.

"You know what I mean," she had said, oblivious to the pejorative connotation of her words.

"Sure I do."

Four years earlier they'd been introduced at an advertising agency party. She'd asked him how he could work for the same magazine for twenty years. If anyone else had asked the question he would have taken a swing at them, verbal or otherwise, for the obvious reason that it was a question he had asked himself too often. But with Miranda the question was neither patronizing nor condescending. She simply wanted to know. Miranda Stone wanted to know everything. It was a quality that made her one of the best reporters in the business—that and the fact that she looked like a *Vogue* model.

If he had any sense he'd keep on driving over the Sierras and into the Nevada desert. He'd stop off at the Mustang Ranch to wash the "Coriandre" out of his mouth, then at the *Lovelock Gazette* to drop off his press card. Maybe he'd give the *Gazette* editor a final interview before he disappeared into the Nevada brush. An epitaph for the millions who had read his words and never knew who he was. A Saigon correspondent who once ate dinner with Henry Luce and Joseph Alsop and never worked for the CIA. A husband who never missed an alimony check. A father who remembered every birthday, if not every age. . . .

He was approaching the end of the causeway. The gold capitol dome was just beyond the Sacramento River. San

Francisco was a city, Sacramento was a town. A town made important, some (not Harry) would say exciting, some (including Harry) would say dangerous, by its one industry: politics. The difference between the lazy, sun-baked streets of the old downtown area and the carpeted, fluorescent, air-cooled halls of the Capitol Building was essential. Walk two blocks from the capitol and you could be in Stockton, Tracy, Modesto or any one of the other hot, dusty farm towns of California's great Central Valley. It was a town into which God knows how many squeaky-clean legislators had come, ready to change the world, only to leave twenty years later with nothing more to show for their government service than a closet full of expensive ties, half of them stained with bernaise from years of dining with lobbyists at Sacramento's one San Francisco restaurant.

He remembered a big fund-raiser a few years ago for the Democratic State Committee at Bryce Stevens's San Francisco hotel. A bright, young black assemblyman from Los Angeles had that day been appointed chairman of the Ways and Means Committee, the most powerful committee in the lower house. The only way the young assemblyman could get to the dinner on time was to fly down from Sacramento. Stevens volunteered to pick him up at the airport in his Rolls-Royce. When the two men came back to the open bar in one of the suites, Stevens was wearing a chauffeur's cap. The black legislator had been more impressed than insulted and the rest of the Democratic bigwigs had thought it hilarious. Harry had been standing next to Sam Belardi when Stevens walked past and whispered loud enough for both to hear, "Buy 'em early, buy 'em cheap."

Belardi had laughed, but not convincingly. Before that moment Harry had wondered where the mayor drew the line with Stevens. Like everyone in the city he'd heard rumors of collusion between the two men, of this real estate deal, of that labor deal, but no one had ever been able to prove their political alliance was anything more than just that.

"With him it's a game, isn't it?" he had asked the mayor when Stevens left them.

Belardi hadn't answered but Harry knew he had hit it. To Stevens, politics was amusement, it could just as well have been polo; to Belardi it was his life. That's where the line was drawn between the two men. That's why he knew he could trust Belardi.

He waited under a redwood—the sign said *Sequoia semper virens*—adjacent to the east nave of the capitol. The governor's executive secretary said Moffat preferred Capitol Park to his office at this time of evening. Harry said he didn't know why it was still hotter than hell. The executive secretary, a prematurely gray, Ivy League type who had gone to law school with the governor, laughed at the non-joke.

It was nearly six when Moffat descended the east stairs and walked toward him. He was tall enough not to be short, and thin, in keeping with his much-publicized austerity. The face was photogenic but not personally attractive. His mouth was too small and his skin had a sickly pallor. He looked like a young eastern lawyer who had gotten lost on the New Haven shuttle, which was part of the reason he was elected. "An anemic Kennedy," Harry once termed him, in a description that didn't survive the telex.

Moffat smiled as he approached but the smile wasn't friendly, only calculating. He was the brightest star in the American political sky. "Realistic humanism" was his solution to the failures of the liberals who had come before him. Who could argue with that?

"Hope I haven't kept you waiting too long, Mr. Carl. The speaker pro tem is mad at me again. He says I don't understand the hallowed tradition of the state senate."

"Does that mean you're going to take away their limousines?"

"It could," Moffat smiled, sitting down on the grass where Harry joined him. The ground was cool and felt good to a posterior that Harry sometimes felt was half vinyl.

"So what is it that brings America's leading news weekly up to this den of inequity?"

"I think you can guess."

"I told the capitol reporters this noon that I'm staying out of San Francisco's problems. At least until I've been formally requested to do otherwise."

"And if you were requested to intercede?"

Moffat hesitated.

"*If* the mayor or the City Council declared a state of emergency and state intervention proves necessary—I'm saying *if*—then according to the State Constitution I have to send in the Highway Patrol or call up the National Guard."

Harry nodded as he scribbled on his notepad.

"And have you given any consideration to which of those alternatives you might pursue, governor?"

"Only the most cursory consideration, Mr. Carl. You're aware the mayor has said he wants no interference."

"Could you describe more fully the extent of your consideration?"

Moffat didn't like the question, but he answered it.

"From my information, the Highway Patrol is not anxious to be dispatched into a major city. They have to maintain a working relationship with local police. There could be some real damage done if they went into San Francisco in what was regarded as a strike-breaker role."

"So you would go with the Guard then?"

"I didn't say that. There are problems with the National Guard also. Bringing a military organization like the Guard into a city presents certain psychological problems."

"With the minority communities?"

"With the minority communities, and with the strikers themselves."

"Do you think Clint Wallace is going to back up his threat to prevent any outside law enforcement agency from coming into the city?"

"I have no idea what Mr. Wallace will do. Right now it's not my problem and I hope it stays that way."

Harry waited a moment, reading notes he had made previously while pretending to study the governor's responses.

"Are you familiar, governor, with what Calvin Coolidge did in 1920? As governor of Massachusetts he brought in the state police and broke a strike, which propelled him into the presidency four years later on a campaign of law and order."

"So that's the game." The governor grinned. His was a shameless guilt.

"Actually, governor, it began very innocently. Monday afternoon I was standing in the city council chamber waiting for the vote on the police pay package when I ran into a man from your office of emergency service. It struck me as odd that he would be in City Hall before the council had even voted to reject the police offer, not to mention a good two hours before the police themselves voted to strike."

Moffat continued to smile. This was the kind of exchange he enjoyed. It was what made him so effective with the news media, his ability to make newsmen overcommit with their questions, then turn the question around on them. Harry knew the ploy but continued talking.

"I asked him a few questions and his answers were quite interesting. He said you'd sent him down personally in the event you had to intercede."

"That's a lot of talking for a second-rank civil servant."

"He seemed excited about the possibilities of the situation."

"Surely you can't blame me for being cautious. As I recall, didn't Mr. Wallace start talking about the possibility of a strike as early as last Thursday?"

Harry ignored the question.

"That's when I thought I'd better check with General Hinshaw of the California National Guard. Unlike you, I waited until the strike was official, then I called the Oakland Armory. I talked to a very polite major who told me the general couldn't talk to any newsmen at the present time. When I asked him what the trouble was, he told me no trouble, it was just that the Guard had been put on a stage two alert and the general was very busy."

Moffat's smile disappeared and his tone became formal.

"A perfectly ordinary procedure. The Guard was used over seventy times last year, for everything from fighting fires to picking peaches during the farm-labor dispute. They must have been put on alert over a hundred times. That's General Hinshaw's job. He'd do the same thing for a big storm."

"When the general didn't return my call I thought I might do a little investigating on my own. So this morning I went over to the armory and asked a few of the men what was going on. To my surprise, the first three men I talked to weren't even from the Bay Area. Two were from Oroville and one was from Merced. All three were reserve officers but none seemed to know anything."

The governor's thin black eyebrows came together.

"That's when I decided to wander down to the motor pool. I've covered enough combat to know you can find out more from a motor pool sergeant than you can from a battalion of brass. I showed him my press card and asked him how many men were being called up. He said he wasn't sure but thought it was in the neighborhood of seven thousand, at least that's what they were told to grease up for.

"Those numbers were impressive enough, but my biggest shock came when I called a friend at the Presidio and asked him how many reserves there were on the California National Guard roster. Do you know what he told me, governor? Nineteen thousand. That's right, nineteen thousand. That means you must have every guardsman in northern California mobilized."

"Congratulations, Mr. Carl. You've done a lot of legwork today. Now that you have this untimely but hardly spectacular information what do you plan to do with it?"

"Ask you another question."

"Be my guest."

"Have you considered how many hundreds, maybe thousands, of lives could be lost by sending an army of white farmers and salesmen into ghettos like the Bayview of Hunters Point?"

The young governor's cheeks flushed in anger. Harry had never seen him angry before.

"Mr. Carl, lest this discussion continue to deteriorate I want to make something exceedingly clear to you. I, and I alone, am ultimately responsible for the safety of the people in this state. At this moment in San Francisco the lives and property of hundreds of thousands of law-abiding citizens are being jeopardized by a small group of militant police. Every minute that the strike continues those lives and that property are increasingly threatened. This morning I received reports of a great number of lootings and muggings in the city, most of them unreported by the police. It is obvious to everyone but Mayor Belardi that the emergency personnel currently deployed by Chief Murphy are unable to guarantee public safety. Within the next twenty-four hours state intervention will be necessary, and when that intervention is requested the State of California will be ready."

"What happens if it isn't requested?"

"It will be."

"You're determined to send in the Guard . . ."

"If the only reason you drove all the way up here this evening was to impugn the motivation of executive actions I have yet to take, Mr. Carl, I suggest you're wasting your time. I'm getting very tired of reporters who insist on imposing their own morality on me or any other politician. As a professional reporter I find it hard to believe you can't separate fact from innuendo. I'm sure your editors in New York will find it equally hard."

Harry leaned back against the redwood. For a wistful moment he felt like the martyr he promised himself he'd never be.

"I was there, governor." he said slowly, forcefully. He didn't even sound like himself. "I was with Belardi last night when he walked through the Tenderloin. Those people are afraid, they're afraid and they're dangerous. It's amazing how much the pimps and the whores and the junkies depend upon the police to protect them from each other. You send in those gas station attendants with M-1's on their hips and all hell is going to break loose."

"That's an interesting sociological point, Mr. Carl. But you must remember it is not the whores and junkies who vote."

17

THE mayor took note of the only playground in Chinatown as Spivac brought the limousine down Clay Street. A solitary backboard with a netless hoop for ten thousand children. And people wondered why there were street gangs. If there was anything left of Chinatown after the strike ended he would go out and buy a net for that basket and the city would buy a decent piece of land for the children to play on.

For a man who'd grown up next door in North Beach, lived in the city most of his life, and been its mayor for almost sixteen years, Chinatown was still a mystery to him. He couldn't deny he'd ever wanted it any other way. Like most San Franciscans he'd heard horror stories for years about the "gilded ghetto"; the overcrowding (seven to ten people in a room); the exorbitant rents (two hundred dollars for a one-room apartment with a shared bath); the underemployment (a typical working day in Chinatown was fourteen hours, six days a week); just as he was aware of the historical prejudice (as recently as the 1920s Chinese youths weren't allowed in public schools). But although he was the mayor, he was also white, and the rule in Chinatown had always been that a white man can look, he might even be able to touch, but he'll never know.

In the tradition of so many San Francisco politicians

before him, his contact with the Chinese community had always been through intermediaries, and there had been very few personal appearances. That was the way the Chinese liked to operate. They were never pushy, always very polite but firm and businesslike. He knew the old families were generally conservative and Republican while the new leaders were more liberal and mostly Democratic. He had always carried Chinatown by a wide margin, thanks mainly to the work done by R. Y. Ling. "Mancat" he was called because of his pale-blue Siamese eyes. Ling was the leader of the Son Lee Tong, the most powerful family and business organization in Chinatown. More influential than even the fabled Chinese Six Companies, the hundred-year-old organization set up originally to return Chinese corpses to their native land, but which for decades had been the dominant political and economic organization of Chinatown. That distinction was now however the Son Lee Tong's, whose Council of Elders was said to comprise the leaders of every major Chinatown business. All Ling and the other Chinese leaders had ever asked for in return for their support was more low-income housing and bilingual schools, facilities the mayor would have provided even without their support. Other than that they preferred to be left alone.

Mayor Belardi had always honored their wishes until the gang wars of the previous summer. Sixteen murders in less than four months. He formed a special police task force to investigate. It was after he'd authorized the task force that he'd had a conversation with R. Y. Ling that he'd never forget. The tong president had come to his office. It was the first time Sam had ever seen him upset. Ling said he'd read that a task force had been set up. He wanted to know why he hadn't been consulted. The mayor had apologized, saying that he was under a great deal of public and community pressure to do something. "We can take care of our problems, Mr. Mayor. We don't ask for, or expect, help from anyone," the Chinatown leader said coldly. The next day one of the Wah Chung gang was found dead. There were five bullets in his head and he was wrapped in a rice sack floating in the bay. The day after, a known friend and supporter of the rival Kum Hon was found waterlogged. He also had five or six bullets, and the rice sack . . . The murders continued all week . . . one day a Wah Chung, one day a Kum Hon . . . then they stopped. Not surprisingly, so did the gang wars. Until an hour ago.

Grant Avenue had been blocked off from St. Mary's Cathedral to Sacramento Street. It seemed like every police unit in operation was crammed into the block in front of the Imperial Garden restaurant. On the sidewalk outside the restaurant three Chinese youths lay dead. The mayor wasn't looking forward to facing the cluster of newsmen gathered on the corner. The mood of the city was tense enough without the added spectacle of the late news beaming pictures into every home of dead bodies lying on San Francisco's streets.

Pinch Murphy looked like he'd aged another five years in the two days that had passed since their meeting in his office. His eyes were sunk deep in their sockets, the old sparkle missing.

"I can't say much for their timing," Murphy said as the mayor stepped onto the curb. The area had been cordoned off by a motley-looking collection of supervisors and detectives.

The two men walked over to where the bodies lay. Blood was splattered all over the sidewalk and street. The lab crews were just getting started. Standing over the victims was the Central District commander, Woody Brady. Pinch had told him more than once that Brady was the best district commander in the city, and the mayor had never quite understood why. The lean captain made him nervous. He was too intense, too by-the-book. Sam preferred cops like Pinch, who understood the good in people as well as the bad.

Brady pulled the sheet off one of the bodies before the mayor could stop him. All he needed before dinner was to see the lifeless face of a teenage Chinese boy. His pale yellow skin was already turning a hideous purple. He looked to have been shot three or four times, once under the ear. There was something about death in Chinatown that was different from death anywhere else in the city. It was so anonymous. There was more violence in the ghetto and in the barrio, and there you heard about it. There were bereaved families, lawsuits, and if the police were involved, charges of brutality. In Chinatown a boy could die, be taken to the morgue, then buried without anyone knowing who he was.

"What do you have, Pinch?"

"We think the three dead boys are members of the Wah Chung gang, Mr. Mayor," Brady answered. "We're pretty sure it was the Kum Hon who gunned them down."

"That's right, Mr. Mayor. Sidney Yee and Danny Pong are the principal suspects. They're the same two who patrolman Parker saw leaving Rita Chan's apartment this afternoon, shortly before he discovered her body."

"I still don't understand what a policeman is doing going over to a beautiful Oriental girl's apartment during the height of a police strike."

"He was off duty at the time," Murphy clarified.

"He was following up a lead, Mr. Mayor. Parker probably knows more about Chinatown crime than any cop in Central. And that includes the Asian cops."

"What was this lead?"

"We don't know. She left a message for him to call her.

He knew she was dating Yee. When her line was busy he thought he'd go by and check.

"And you think her death ties in to these?"

"It could," Brady answered. "Or else it might just have been business as usual. You know the history of the two gangs."

"But there hasn't been any trouble recently?"

"No. Not for six or seven months. But in the last week there have been signs it might start up again. I don't know if the chief has told you about the man we found in the bay Monday."

"He mentioned it."

"Well, we found another today. Also a white man. Also in a rice sack. But this one wasn't a bum, he was a known drug buyer."

"What you're telling me is that five people have been murdered today in San Francisco. And all of them have some connection with Chinatown."

"Five that we know of," Brady said caustically.

"It's bad, Sam. Woody thinks the Kum Hon are trying some kind of power play, possibly involving narcotics. Judging from the only witness we've been able to find, the Wah Chung boys had just come out of the dry goods store next door when a light sedan came up and four young Chinese males with handguns jumped out. They were wearing ski masks but two of them fit Yee's and Pong's physical descriptions. The Wah Chung boys didn't get off a shot."

"We think the store they were coming out of was one of their pickups," Brady said. "The owner won't say anything but we know the Wah Chung got everything south of Grant after the truce last fall. We think the Kum Hon knew when and where the Wah Chung boys were going to be tonight. We think it was a setup all the way."

"But what about the truce? After what happened last year, you'd think the gangs would be more careful. The Chinese businessmen aren't going to like this."

"You mean Mancat Ling isn't going to like it," Brady said in a hostile tone.

"For one," the mayor agreed.

"I wouldn't be surprised if Mancat Ling wasn't the one who set it up."

"Wait a minute, captain." the mayor protested. "I've known R. Y. Ling for a number of years. He's a very powerful man down here, granted, but that doesn't make him a master criminal. He's done a tremendous amount of good for the people of Chinatown."

Brady looked at him with tolerant disrespect.

"Woody and I have had our arguments about Mr. Ling before," Pinch cut in.

"It's all right for him to smuggle millions of dollars worth of heroin yearly into the country as long as he delivers money and votes to the right people."

"That's enough, captain," Murphy said sharply.

"No, Pinch. Let him talk. Who are these right people, captain? Me?"

"Anyone who's in a position to threaten his power. I didn't give the orders to disband that special task force on Chinatown crime."

"As I remember, the task force was broken up because the violence had stopped and the crime rate had sharply decreased. There was no mention of any heroin."

"As I remember the task force was discontinued because Mancat Ling thought it was getting too close for comfort."

"Do you have proof Ling is involved in heroin traffic, captain?"

"Sam, this is no time to get into an argument about Chinatown drug traffic. If Captain Brady has come up with any hard evidence against the Son Lee Tong or against Ling

142

we'll discuss it after the strike. Right now let's concentrate on catching those crazy China boys before anyone else is killed."

"Are you amenable to that, captain?"

Before the captain could answer, Miranda Stone walked out of the Imperial Garden into their conversation.

"Do you always take him with you when you go out to dinner?" the mayor said, nodding toward the bearded cameraman.

"Only when I can expense it," she said, fumbling with her tape recorder.

"I'm sorry, all reporters are to wait behind the barricade," Brady told her.

"You can let her stay, captain. We better bring the others over, too. I'd hate to let KSFT get an exclusive."

Brady reluctantly signalled his men to let the reporters through. Then he and Murphy walked over to the lab truck.

"Doesn't the chief want to talk to us, Mr. Mayor?" Miranda asked in a little girl's voice. Every time the mayor thought he might be beginning to like the brassy reporter she would blow it.

"Chief Murphy has a lot of work to do. I'm afraid you're going to have to settle for me."

The other reporters pushed their way onto the sidewalk. They looked almost as tired as the police. Electronic vultures he heard someone call them. The name fit. He smiled cordially, clicking his tongue against the back of his teeth.

"Do you have an opening statement, Mr. Mayor?"

"We have a preliminary identification on two of the three boys murdered. Both were believed to be members of the Wah Chung gang. Judging from descriptions provided by witnesses we believe the assailants to be members of the rival Kum Hon gang. As you know, the two gangs have been fighting for control of Chinatown crime for the past few years. We have no evidence that the murders have any connection with the police strike."

"Is it true, Mr. Mayor, that Governor Moffat is sending General Hinshaw of the California National Guard into the city to make his own assessment of public safety?"

"I wouldn't send Pinch Murphy to Sacramento, I don't see why the governor would send General Hinshaw to San Francisco. He said in his news conference this morning that he wouldn't interfere. I see no reason why he should change his mind."

"How about five murders in the last ten hours?" Buddy Mullahy asked.

"We can all count, Mr. Mullahy, including the police. I assure you everything possible is being done to apprehend those responsible. In fact, we have reason to believe that two of the Kum Hon members involved in the shooting here were also involved in the murder of the cocktail waitress on Pine Street."

"How about the rice sack murders? Is there any connection there, Mr. Mayor?" It was Al Landi, a veteran police reporter.

"Not that we can determine, Al. But we are following every possible lead. The important thing is for people to remain calm. The violence here tonight is an isolated instance. It has nothing to do with the general public safety. Pinch Murphy told me just a few minutes ago that the crime rate is lower than usual tonight."

"Do you care to comment on the restraining order Judge Mendel Ewing issued this evening to Clint Wallace calling for an immediate cessation of the strike?"

"I hope Sergeant Wallace and the POA membership will abide by the judge's decision."

"Would you ask Ewing for a contempt finding if they don't?" Miranda asked.

"Let's give the POA a chance to respond before we find them in contempt, Miss Stone."

"What about the meeting this afternoon between the council and the POA leadership?"

"I wasn't there so I have no idea what happened. All I know is that nothing was resolved."

"How many more days do you think the city can hold out, Mr. Mayor?"

It was Mullahy again. The mayor ignored the question.

"What do you think might happen if the National Guard *does* come into the city? Do you think they can be an effective deterrent?"

Belardi hesitated.

"I've said from the beginning I can forsee no probable circumstance where the National Guard will be asked to come into San Francisco. This city is completely under control and will remain so until the strike is settled. As for the National Guard's deterrent capability, it's been my experience that calling up the Guard is like going to the Giant's bullpen before the sixth inning. They both have an uncanny ability to turn a close game into a rout."

18

FRANK had never known Chinatown to be so quiet. Maybe it was because he couldn't hear anything over the din of his own thoughts. It seemed that his mind had been roaring for days . . . like being in a car wash with the windows down. There was so much to understand. So much to analyze and examine. He knew it fit: the rice sack murders, the new delivery boys, Rita's death, the Wah Chung massacre. He knew what made it fit—R. Y. Ling. What he didn't know was how. Only Sidney Yee could tell him that, and he had a strange feeling that he would never see Yee's ape face again, or if he did, Yee wouldn't be alive to answer his questions.

"It has to be Ling. He's the only one heavy enough to make Yee come out in the open like that," he thought aloud as he and Andropolus walked down Waverly Place on their way to the Kowloon.

The detective lit another cigarette and watched Frank out of the corner of his eye. He had helped Frank a great deal the past few hours. Frank had been amazed at the methodical and disciplined way that Andropolus's mind functioned. It was Andropolus, who, after Rita's death, had kept him from unsnapping his magnum and putting it to the head of every Kum Hon associate he could find. It was Andropolus who convinced him to move carefully, to step back and try to get it all. Brady had put them both on full time on the Chinatown killings. Two men in a community of over a hundred thousand. Those were the odds the tong counted on.

"I'm beginning to think you're right about everything," the detective said, taking a deep drag. "The narcotics people aren't looking too good. That's what happens when you mix politics with police work. Lipscombe told me earlier tonight that they've suspected most of the heroin on the West Coast was brought in by the Chinese underworld. But, like you said, the problem has always been that so few Chinese are users. The narc squad gets ninety-five percent of their information from junkies. So you figure by the time it gets to the street it's passed through maybe four or five connections, including the mob. All they've ever gotten were rumors. Third-hand rumors at that, because Chinatown is so isolated.

"Lipscombe told me they've been waiting for some hard evidence before moving on Ling and the tong, but I can't buy that. The stuff you and Schultz gave them, along with other pieces that they had and you didn't, should have been enough. They should have started their own investigation, or at least helped keep your task force in business."

"Did Lipscombe have anything else on Redlick?"

"Not yet. They have him working patrol out in the Sunset now, so he won't be able to have any free time until tomorrow morning. I have to admit this fucking strike is starting to piss me off. At first I kind of thought it was amusing. Cops pretending they're hired guns and politicians pretending they can take care of themselves, but now the bad guys are beginning to take advantage. A lot of important police work isn't being done.

"Speaking of that, I forgot to tell you. I checked out the East-West Lines. They were bought out last year by Pacific Shipping Company. If we have time, which I doubt, I thought we might drive down to Pier thirty-five and see what we can see."

"You think that first body's important, don't you?"

"Coincidence only exists for television cops. Life is based on a personality continuity, so is crime. The dots may not always connect but you're not doing your job if you don't try to draw the line between them. That's what Lipscombe and the other narcotics people should have done. I'm only sorry we can't move faster now, and with more manpower. Patterns appear and then disappear. I have a strong feeling it's there for us, all we need is the right perspective . . ."

Frank had already made up his mind that, when and if the strike ever ended, he was going to talk to Andropolus about taking the inspectors test. For the first time he was beginning to see another side of police work. A patrol cop relied on observation and reaction. A detective relied on perserverance, thoroughness and instinct. He'd been wrong about Andropolus, he'd been wrong about a lot, but he could learn.

They crossed Washington Street to Ross Alley, past the office of the *Chinese Times*. Although it wasn't yet midnight, tomorrow's edition was in the window and a crowd of old Chinese men was gathered in front of it. Some wore hats, others wore their hair straight back. All were dressed in shapeless main-floor department-store clothes, with pants either too long or too short. Barney often remarked that the only tailor-made suits sold in Chinatown were sold to tourists.

The old men were talking excitedly, rarely gesticulating, usually keeping their arms folded or at their sides. Frank couldn't speak Cantonese but he didn't have to, to know what the worried-looking men were talking about. Still, he wished he could join in their conversation. There was so much these old men had seen that he would never get a chance to see.

148

"I've never liked these alleys," Andropolus said as they moved further down the narrow passageway.

The only colors in the steamy, foul-smelling alley were the painted fire escapes. Faded graffitti covered the bricks. "China Rules" was the favorite. They passed a slightly opened door and Frank took the detective by the arm to make him look in. There were twenty women sitting at twenty sewing tables, each one numbered. The room was so small it seemed impossible to walk between them. The women looked up for a second at the two cops then resumed their sewing and talking. They talked fast but they sewed even faster.

Andropolus shook his head.

"There's a story about this alley. They say this is where the street gangs all began," Frank said. "In the late sixties, when immigration laws were relaxed, the Chinese began to come into the city from Hong Kong and Taiwan by the thousands. Many of the boys were used by the tongs, particularly the Son Lee Tong, as looksies for the gambling establishments and whorehouses. They were paid a few dollars a week by the tongs for being lookouts and janitors.

"It didn't take the immigrant boys long to figure out they were getting screwed. That's when the Wah Chung gang was founded: the foreign-born or outside gang. Their first scam was supposed to be on Ross Alley. Two Wah Chung would stand at each end of this alley every morning at seven o'clock and hit up the old Chinese women coming and going from the sweatshops. I think they started out at a dime a trip."

"And I thought Greeks were born criminals. These people would extort their dead mothers."

"A few years later, the Son Lee Tong began recruiting their own youth gang, the Kum Hon or inside gang. The tong was then content to let the gangs fight each other, rewarding the stronger gang, usually the Kum Hon, with the best jobs in the high-rolling gambling halls and cathouses. It worked perfectly because the police and public were distracted by the gang violence and never could get close to the real underworld activities of the tong.

"And, of course, it's still going on. The papers tomorrow will talk about a new flare-up between the youth gangs over territory for the extortion and protection rackets. Or maybe over the sale of firecrackers, that's one they use a lot. One thing for sure, there won't be any mention of the millions of dollars worth of heroin that Ling brings into the country or the stranglehold he has over everyone in Chinatown."

Andropolus had been watching him. The Greek was smiling, his rough olive face showed an affection Frank had never seen before.

"You really love it down here, don't you? I mean you take it all so personally, not just the girl, but everyone down here."

"I care, if that's what you mean. They're good people. I don't understand them but I've always felt they needed . . . they deserved all the protection I could give them." He hesitated. "Maybe it's because I'm so different. Not better. I don't think I'm better than they are. Maybe I used to."

"But the girl, she was more than different."

Frank thought of her perfect body lying on the bed. She had been more than different, yes. She had taught him how much he was like those cops he detested.

"She would still be alive if I had left her alone."

"You aren't the first cop who's been caught in that trap. It's so easy when you work in a world that isn't yours. It's easy to step over the line once, then twice, and before you know it the line is gone. Only when you try to step back do you discover that the line is really a wall. And someone always gets hurt."

"But never the cop."

"Always the cop. One way or another."

They turned down Jackson toward St. Louis Alley. Barney

was waiting for them in front of the Kowloon.

"You two look like you could use a couple of Joe's mai tais."

"Have you been inside yet?"

"Just got here ten seconds ago. Had to go down to the Cellblock and check in. Thompson is telling everyone the city's about to roll over."

Barney was wearing his picket uniform, as he called it. A forty-niner T-shirt and Levis with his .357 magnum on his hip.

"Don't bet on it," Andropolus said, "We saw Belardi down on Grant Street earlier and he was looking very cool. That man doesn't rattle easy."

"That's what I told those jerkoffs. They're out of their fuckin' heads if they think a few dead gooks are going to shake up the snakes that run this city."

Barney saw Frank stiffen. He put his huge arm around him.

"Sorry, partner. I didn't mean Rita."

"Hey, it's me," Frank told him.

"Did you see anything interesting up on Powell Street?" Andropolus interjected.

Barney looked up and down the alley, then up at the dark windows above.

"Old Chinese saying, 'never talk where you can't see who listen!'"

The men moved across the alley and walked down while Schultz pulled out his notebook.

"I parked across the street from the service entrance on Trenton Alley at six-thirty P.M. A little after seven two old Chinese dudes, tong elders by the way they were dressed, real expensive three-piece suits, silk ties and handkerchiefs, came down and got into a limo that had pulled up."

"Recognize 'em?"

"One might have been Fong Wong of the Superior

Trading Company but I'm not sure. Anyway, they had to be members of the council because about five minutes later Mancat himself came down with three bodyguards. His whiskers were up and he was acting real nervous. He kept looking up and down the street while one of his men ran into the garage to get his Continental. . . . I tell you, there aren't many men who scare me, but I'm afraid to look him in the eye. There's nothing there."

"You said that was a little after seven. Almost the same time that Yee and Pong were blowing away the three Wah Chung. Was there any other activity after that, Barn?"

"A few coolies came in and out of the garage. And there were two deliveries. One around seven-thirty, a Golden Gate Fish Market truck; and another about ten-thirty, a Nob Hill Laundry truck."

"That's pretty late for laundry service."

"Did seem sort of suspicious, but there was no way I could see into the trucks. Both of them were panels, and the garage doors were shut right after."

"What do you think, inspector?" Frank asked.

"Both of you guys, my name is Phil. Okay? As to what I think . . . my large Greek nose tells me that meeting was more significant to Sidney Yee and the Kum Hon leadership than it is to us. Ling knew they were going to waste the outside gang leader. What was his name?"

"Richard Soo."

"Yeah, that's it. Ling knew they were going to waste him. What that meeting was about was what they were going to do with Yee and Pong. You have to figure they're either setting them up for a fall or taking them out of the country. After Frank ID'd them in front of Rita's apartment, they're too hot to keep around. Even with ninety-five percent of the force out."

"So where does that leave us?"

"We have to find 'em before the gong does."

"And the heroin. What about Ling using the Kum Hon as delivery boys?"

"There are plenty more Kum Hons and Wah Chungs where those two came from. You know that. There must be a thousand punks in Chinatown who could be recruited into those gangs. Not to mention Honolulu and Hong Kong. When you're as big as Ling, you don't worry about losing a few lieutenants.

"Hey, what do you say we go inside? I have to be back on the picket lines in an hour. Remember, I'm on strike."

Harry Jew was in his usual place in the middle of the bar but all the tables were empty except one. A Chinese girl sat in the corner. Frank thought she might be there.

Joe Louie shook his head as the policeman walked to the end of the bar. He was wearing his most gloomy expression. Frank guessed a night of hard drinking might have helped his melancholy. When a Chinaman's face begins to color even in the dull light of the Kowloon, he's had too much scotch.

Barney introduced Andropolus to Joe while Frank went over to the girl at the table. Her eyes were wet. He could see where the tears had run off her flat nostrils down along the sides of her mouth.

"I hope you might come tonight," she said haltingly.

"I hoped you would too, Patty."

"Rita like you very much. Even though she say horrible things."

"I know," he said feeling his throat close. "There was no one like her."

Patty Ho began crying again. He put his hand on her frail yellow wrist.

"I'm sorry. I can't help . . ."

Frank held her wrist tighter, struggling with the unresolved sorrow and guilt he felt about Rita.

"Last night she told me Sidney didn't like her anymore.

153

She said she told him about you. He got very mad. Said she was a whore for *lo fan*. She was very afraid."

"She tried to call me this afternoon . . . it was too late when I got there."

Patty began sobbing again. Frank wondered if she had any other friends. He'd only seen her with Rita. An ugly Chinese girl in a strange town.

"Do you know where I can find him, Patty?"

"Once we go to an apartment with him and Banana Boy. Near Broadway Tunnel."

"Which side?"

"Other side. By playground."

"Near the Helen Wills playground?"

The name didn't register.

"Tennis courts?"

She nodded faintly. Her eyes were almost swollen shut.

"Can you remember the building?"

She shook her head. "Tennis courts in back," she said then.

Frank kissed her softly on the forehead.

19

BARNEY parked the squad car above the tunnel at Hyde and Broadway and from there the three men walked down the west side of Russian Hill toward the Helen Wills playground. All three were in street clothes but their profession was obvious. Andropolus carried the Remington pump shotgun from the car and both Frank and Barney had their Smith and Wesson magnums drawn. They'd called the Northern District dispatcher asking for assistance but they weren't counting on getting any, nor could they afford to wait.

There was only one apartment building that backed on the tennis courts. It fronted on Pacific Avenue in the middle of the block between Polk and Larkin. Because of the high cyclone fence around the courts the only entrance was from the front. The Polk Gulch neighborhood, as it was called, was composed mostly of gays and Chinese. They expected no trouble from the gays . . .

The three of them approached the building from the north side of the street, using the other apartment buildings on the block for cover. The strike was beginning its third day and the streets were almost completely empty. All communication was by hand signals or whispers. They knew the procedure—locate the apartment, two men go in the front and one works his way to the back.

Frank shone his light on the mailboxes in the alcove. It was a matter of deduction. There were six units: three in front, one, three and five; three in back, two, four and six. Apartment two was a Mr. Pristine Condition.

"No Kum Hon has a sense of humor like that," Barney whispered.

Apartment four was interesting because there was no name. Apartment six was interesting because the name was Chinese.

Andropolus held up four fingers, then six. The other two nodded.

Schultz went around the side of the building to cover the rear fire escape. Andropolus jimmied the lock with a police "credit card." The apartment building, like most in that neighborhood, was probably forty years old, had a small lobby and high narrow hallways. The entrance to apartment one was directly off the lobby and the door marked two was at the end of the hall off the stairwell.

The hallway was quiet and smelled like cooked vegetables. The man in two was watching television, judging from the light under his door. Frank followed Andropolus up the stairs.

At the first landing the detective stopped. He pointed the barrel of the Remington toward the door of apartment four. Frank listened but could hear nothing. His hand was wet against the walnut grip of the revolver. Andropolus continued up the stairs, his expression implacable.

Frank held onto the bannister as the detective leaned into the wall one step below the second-floor landing. To their right was apartment four, to their left apartment three. The distance between the two apartments was the width of the staircase . . . less than ten feet.

Voices could now be heard coming from four. The abrupt

cadence and high tone of pidgin English was unmistakable. Andropolus motioned Frank to move further back down the stairs. Frank took one step backward. There was very little room to maneuver, but with all the police firepower Frank thought this would be to their advantage in a shoot-out.

A girl laughed, and a voice could plainly be heard telling her to shut up. Frank recognized that voice immediately. It was Danny "Banana Boy" Pong.

He gave Andropolus the sign to move. The detective nodded, banging on the door with the barrel of his shotgun, then crouching behind the wall.

"Police! Open up!"

There was commotion inside. Then the light went out.

"We've got the building surrounded. Throw your guns out and come through the door with your hands up."

The girl shrieked. There was shouting in Cantonese. A window slid up, followed quickly by two bursts of Barney's magnum. Andropolus wheeled in front of the apartment, leveled the Remington and blew the door open.

There was another high scream, but this one was from a boy. Andropolus was again behind the wall. Frank still held his revolver pointed in the direction of the broken door.

In the back Schultz was trading shots with a small caliber handgun.

"Let's move!" shouted Andropolus.

Frank tried to take three steps at once and slipped. He fell to the carpeted hallway and saw the figure of Danny Pong ducking into a room less than eight feet away. There was a flash from Pong's hand and Frank blinked. Andropolus put two quick rounds in Pong's direction, shredding the door-jamb and giving Frank a chance to bounce back up and take the left side of the door. Andropolus held his position on the right. Frank felt the trickle of blood running down his arm just below the elbow. He let the blood drip to the floor, not wanting to release his grip on the magnum.

157

The two men entered the apartment. The light from the stairwell skylight shone dimly on a small buckshot-riddled body lying in the hall. Frank didn't have time to study the young Chinese face. On the floor next to the body was a cheap handgun. There was something about fighting fourteen-year-old boys that he would never get used to.

From the back of the building came more shooting, but Schultz seemed to have things under control. Frank thought there was only one other gunman, but he didn't think it was Yee. A girl could be heard whimpering in the kitchen. Andropolus nodded toward the bedroom door to their right, where Danny Pong had disappeared.

Andropolus blasted another load of size-two shot into the blackness as Frank jumped across the doorway. This time there was no return fire. Pong wasn't going to give away his location unless he had a sure shot.

The two men stood across from each other in the quarter light. Frank could see that Andropolus was in control, his expression both intense and confident. He motioned Frank to stay low. Frank knelt on one knee while the detective quickly shoved four more cartridges into the magazine of the Remington.

Because he was concentrating on the dark room before them, Frank didn't notice the shadowy movement in the stairwell behind Andropolus until it was too late. He looked up just in time to hear three sharp pops and see Andropolus grimace—more, Frank reflected later, from the knowledge of what had happened than the actual impact of the shots.

Frank rolled away from the falling body. He shot three times at the small dark form in the hallway. The boy was knocked through the bannister by the force of the shells.

Frank, in partial shock, lay for a moment between the bodies in the narrow hall. Andropolus moaned. The back of his light suit was dark with patches of blood. He didn't know how many times Andropolus had been hit but he knew the detective needed medical attention fast.

Frank crawled over the detective and back to the doorway. He waited for a few seconds, reloading and giving his eyes a chance to adjust to the dark.

The room opened to the right. Pong was either in the right-hand corner or in the closet along the left wall. Frank made the choice instinctively.

Raising himself to the stance of a down lineman he dove forward, putting three shots in the deep corner before he hit the floor. The flash of the magnum illuminated the room. Pong's gun fired spasmodically into the ceiling as he slumped into the corner. Frank squeezed off two more shots at the limp figure.

THURSDAY
AUGUST 5th

20

AFTER washing the dried blood off Frank's forearm with a wet cloth, the medic wrapped the arm in gauze and adhesive tape. It was only a superficial wound and Frank had refused to go in the ambulance with Andropolus to the hospital.

The detective had been unconscious when he was carried out. It was hard to walk in the hallway because of the bodies and the blood. The medics said they thought Andropolus would live, but with two .32 slugs in his back there was some question as to what kind of shape he'd make it in. There was no question about three of the four fei jai. The only place they were going to make it was the morgue.

Frank had never killed a man before. He was surprised at how easy it was. Barney had once told him that shooting a man was harder than catching a football but easier than skiing down a mountain. Frank held the Galileo High School single-season reception record and had been skiing once. From his experience Schultz was right.

A backup unit from Northern had gotten there a few minutes after the shooting just as the remaining Kum Hon had thrown his gun into the hallway. The girl, who was white, went into hysterics when she saw what had happened to Pong. She didn't look like one of Pong's girl friends; Frank noticed that immediately. She was wearing a sweat shirt and old jeans, her blond hair was straggly and unwashed, her face pale and used. Banana Boy's girls were pretty and very stylish. They had to be because they were lo fan, and all whites were considered inferior by the Chinese.

It was Schultz who put it together. They were looking around the apartment. (It was the plushest gang hideout he'd ever seen.) The furnishings were new and expensive. There was a color TV and enough stereo equipment to start a small store. The walls were decorated with posters of Bruce Lee and Mao Tse Tung. The floor was littered with car and kung fu magazines along with soul and R and B records. He and Schultz were admiring the expensive stereo components when Schultz abruptly walked over to the girl who was sitting handcuffed on the couch.

"I bet I know why she's so broken up about Banana Boy," he said, grabbing her arm above the elbow.

"Get your fuckin' hands off me, pig," she screamed, trying to loosen Schultz's ham-hock grip.

"Shut your mouth, junkie," he said, pulling the girl's sweat shirt above her elbow, revealing a line of bruises and scabs along the inside of her arm.

"I thought there was something familiar about her," Schultz said. "Can't believe it took me this long to figure it out. I can usually smell junkies. She's probably an old girl friend of Banana Boy's who he strung out."

"Danny loves me!" she screamed again and then began to cry.

"Sure, blondie, he loves you. He loves this little gook over here, too. That's why he made you into a scag queen and him into a ten-dollar-a-day killer."

Schultz turned his attention to the young Chinese huddled in the corner of the room. His eye was swollen where Schultz had punched him.

The boy watched Schultz; like most fei jai, he kept his expression motionless. Frank didn't think he was more than fifteen. He didn't shave, yet he carried a gun. And killed on command. And because he was American born he'd serve a year or two in juvenile hall and then be back on the streets of Chinatown. His parents would be broken hearted and he'd be a hero.

"I doubt if this little duck soup could even get his rocks off at one of Madame Wu's cathouses." Schultz spat.

"He's old enough to kill a cop," Frank said, and this time it was he who hit the prisoner. He hit him with an open right hand. The boy's head snapped back from the force of the unexpected blow. Blood began to trickle out of his mouth, but still his expression didn't change.

"Hey, that's your pitchin' arm, partner," Schultz said, pulling him away from the boy.

"Both of you take it easy," the lieutenant from Northern said. "Just because we're the only cops left doesn't mean we can break the rules. Your captain is on his way over. I'm sure you don't want him coming down on you."

"When's the lab crew coming, lieutenant?" Schultz asked.

"I phoned 'em when I got here. Last I heard there was only one photo-and-lab crew working the whole city."

"Maybe we should develop some of our own evidence then," Schultz said, grabbing the girl again.

"Fuck off, fatso," she yelled.

Schultz was ready to pull the string when Brady walked into the apartment. Seeing Frank, three dead bodies, two prisoners, and Schultz with his fist cocked, all the captain could do was shake his head.

"Schultz, I'm not sure if the city's better off with you on or off the picket line."

"Captain, I'll bet Frank's overtime pay there's some horse hidden in this apartment. She wouldn't be here with these gooks if there wasn't."

Brady looked at the girl, then at the Chinese boy.

"Okay, let's take it apart."

It didn't take Schultz long. He went directly to the stereo speakers. Two bags of what looked like finely granulated sugar were hidden inside two of the speakers.

"The last time I saw this much shit was in Saigon," he said, weighing the bags in his hand. "Look at that rich white color. This ain't that dirty Mexican junk, no way. You're looking at China white—two one-pound bags. I bet you could get two hundred thousand dollars apiece for this on the street right now."

Frank had never seen that much of any drug before. Brady came over and took the two bags away from Schultz.

"Aren't you going to let me taste it, captain?"

"That's what we have a lab for, Schultz," Brady told him.

"How did you know where to look?" Frank asked his partner.

"When I got back from Nam some friends of mine were doing a little smuggling. Mostly small shit. A pound of grass, couple ounces of hash. One was always talking about using stereo speakers to ship it in. When I saw those extra speakers it hit me."

"You think then that they were going to ship this someplace else?"

"Maybe. Or maybe this is how it got to them. One-pound bags, though. These punks must have some connection."

Schultz didn't have to tell Frank who that connection was.

21

JIMMY Cleveland woke up with a hard-on. It was going to be one of those days. He slowly slid his hands onto Kim's caramel-colored shoulder.

"Just a little lovin' early in the mornin'," he whispered.

She rolled over. His hand went to her small soft breast.

"Are you going to come to my class this morning?"

"Baby, I told you last night that's goin' to have to wait until this damn police strike is over."

He kept massaging her breast. The nipple was getting firm. He moved his leg between hers, gently rubbing back and forth.

"Jimmy, you promised it was going to be this Thursday. I've been telling them for two weeks. Summer classes will be over next week."

"Baby, that was before. A cop got shot last night. The Chinks are going crazy down in Chinatown. I can't be off lecturing ninth graders about civics."

"But it seems to me this is the perfect time for the kids to be made to realize how important the government and the laws are."

"That's exactly why I have to be going downtown," he sighed, losing more than his concentration. "I've got to be in front of those cameras telling all the brothers and sisters in the ghetto to be cool, not just the twenty-five kids in your class. There's already been looting out in Bayview along Third Street and on Fillmore down near Mint Hill. If it happens again today I don't have to tell you what's going to happen. Come Friday and you won't have a school to teach in, much less kids to teach."

She wrapped her long arms around him.

"Honey, I'm scared. I don't like the way some of the boys are talking in class. They say they're going 'shopping' after school. You know what that means, Jimmy. Those boys are going looting with the older boys. Fourteen years old and they think because there's no police they can steal anything they want."

"Like I told you before, baby, today's niggers think all they have to do is get in line. Everything is free. But that ain't how it works. That's just the white man's hook gettin' deeper in. Just because you're poor and dumb doesn't mean you have to act it."

"You have to tell them, Jimmy."

"I've *been* tellin' 'em, baby. But they don't listen to me. They listen to the bad-ass and the Muslim who tells them how much Whitey owes them. That's why they go looting and burning. They don't understand that you got to play the game. White folks have insurance, black people just got each other."

"You have to go tell them, Jimmy," she said again, closing her legs around his.

He shut his eyes and rolled her on top of him, squeezing her with his thick brown arms. She was the only one he cared about. He was going to tell her that after it was over. He'd done enough playing; it was time Ruth Cleveland's boy got out of ghetto politics and into something where a man of his talents could do himself justice.

She rubbed his temples with strong fingers.

168

"What are you thinking, honey?" she asked him in a low tone.

He didn't answer. His mind had taken him back to another time. He could see the gutted ghetto streets as if it were yesterday. He could smell the twice-burned wood and cherry wine. He could hear the sirens wailing in the distance and the glass breaking at his feet. He could feel the heat and excitement and fear in the roving bands that came down the street. It had been ten years since that night and nothing had changed.

Yes, it was going to be one of those days.

22

"WHERE do we start?" the mayor asked Ken Topham.

The aide glanced up at him from behind his bifocals.

"Does it make any difference?"

"Pinch?" the mayor asked the other man sitting in his office.

"You both have copies of the crime report," came the police chief's somber answer. "Our estimation is that these figures reflect approximately a third of the crimes committed last night."

The mayor's forehead creased above his thick gray eyebrows. The partial figures were more than double a normal night's total for most crimes. What little control they had was slipping away.

"We were very close to losing her last night," Murphy continued. "We had twenty-five cars and three wagons for the whole city. They were cuffing kids to the streetlights in the Bayview. If the same thing happens again tonight, we're going to be running up the white flag in front of at least four stationhouses before midnight. Northern, Park, Mission and Southeast all reported looting in the black and brown neighborhoods. There's no reason to think it won't be the same or worse tonight. It's still hot, the looters are finding out they can get away with it and, of course, there's still Chinatown."

"What's happening with the POA?"

"You already know Wallace refused to receive Judge Ewing's restraining order. A court deputy went to the Cook and Stewards Hall to serve him and Wallace's bodyguards chased him away. From what Al Neilsen tells me, Wallace is getting crazier by the minute. Al tells me Wallace sees himself as some kind of police savior. You remember I told you a while back about that group he started up within the POA—Officers for Equal Justice?"

"The Fascists who wanted to start locking up every black teenager who spit on the sidewalk?"

"The same gentlemen," Murphy said. "From what I hear, Wallace had a cadre of about twenty hard-core supporters from that OEJ group. Most of them are his station-and-watch leaders for the strike. When the strike is over they're talking about instituting new police procedures based on OEJ guidelines. 'Victim-oriented crime prevention' is their name for it."

"What about Neilsen and the old guard, Pinch? I can't believe Al and people like Linc Noll are sitting on their hands watching Wallace radicalize the assocation."

"There's not much they can do as long as the strike goes on. And it will, as long as the council keeps telling the press there's not a police department and the public keeps trying to run down our guys on the picket line."

"What?"

"I forgot to tell you," Murphy said with a faint smile. "Some idiot got his nerve up in Kelley's Tavern out in the Portals last night and drove his car up on the sidewalk in front of the Taraval Station. Fortunately he was too drunk to hit anyone."

"I always said the people in the city could drink better

than they could drive," the mayor said, but the chief's smile was gone.

"Let me tell you, Sam, three-fourths of the men would go back on the job right now if they thought they could do it without losing face. They can see what's happening. It's eating them up that a guy like Phil Andropolus was dropped last night. This is their city. They feel a responsibility for it. I mean that. At first, I think they considered it a dare. You know how bull-headed cops are. But now they're looking for a way out. The trouble is, Wallace and the council aren't about to give them one."

"What are the chances of getting a strike solidarity vote?"

"Three votes out of five from the POA executive committee are needed for a vote of confidence."

"You've got Neilsen."

"And that's all. The other three committee members were appointed by Wallace after he won the election."

"Got any ideas, Kenny?"

"If you're planning on getting the cops to go back to work, you better do it fast. Zimmerman's called a special meeting of the council for two o'clock this afternoon. He's going to ask them to declare a formal state of emergency, which will grant him full emergency powers. And my sources down at the hall tell me he has the votes to do it."

"But he doesn't have the votes to *override*. He can't so much as declare the Pope a Catholic if I don't want him to."

"You're wrong, Sam. He does have the votes to override. Both Cleveland and Chacon are voting with him. That makes eight out of nine. My bet is that the National Guard will be crossing the Bay Bridge by six o'clock tonight."

"Who told you Jimmy was voting with Zimmerman?"

"His AA, Virgil Parks. I told you a long time ago, you can rent Jimmy Cleveland but you can't buy him. Zimmerman is playing hardball on this thing. I hear the governor has been calling people, too."

"Hardball my ass. Jimmy knows better than anyone else what will happen if the Guard is turned loose. I don't believe it. See if you can get Cleveland in here."

Topham left the office. Pinch Murphy rubbed his chin. The mayor recognized the gesture and waited.

"I was thinking, Sam," he began hesitantly. "I'm not so sure bringing in the National Guard would be that bad an idea. Why wait for the city to blow before reacting? There's a chance that if we bring the Guard in now, we can stop the trouble before it starts."

The mayor's glance locked with Murphy's blue eyes. He needed his friend with him on this.

"Two reasons," the mayor said forcefully. "One: Clint Wallace has said repeatedly he won't allow any other law-enforcement agencies into the city. You told me yourself the man is playing without face cards. He's not about to let Moffat and Zimmerman break this strike. Even if he only has the support of those twenty fanatics from the OEJ, you know damn well that twenty professionals—well-armed professionals—could take out maybe two hundred Guardsmen before they went down. Can you imagine what that would do to this city, or to the whole country for that matter?"

"Just worrying about the city is enough for me," Murphy said.

"We've got to get them back on the street, Pinch. The only reason we've been able to hold on this long is because no one knows yet how undermanned we are. I've told the press more lies in the last two days than I have in my entire political career."

Murphy overlooked the mayor's exaggeration. "I want you to get in touch with Neilsen and the other POA members you can trust. Tell them to spread the word that there's going to be a solidarity vote tonight at the Cooks and Stewards Hall at eight o'clock."

"But I told you, Wallace . . ."

"I know what you told me. You told me the cops would come back if they had a chance. So we're going to give them that chance."

Murphy looked unconvinced. The mayor wasn't completely convinced himself but he had said what had to be done.

"Let me worry about Wallace and the City Council. You just get your men to the Cooks and Stewards Hall at eight o'clock."

The buzzer rang and mayor flipped on the intercom.

"Captain Brady and Inspector Lipscombe are on their way in, Mr. Mayor."

A moment later two very tired-looking men walked into the high-ceilinged office. Brady appeared stiff and ill at ease. Lipscombe, whom the mayor vaguely recognized, seemed much more relaxed. Murphy had told him once that a good narcotics officer had to have the metabolism of a smuggler.

He told the policemen to sit down. Brady was holding a manila folder. The mayor had been bothered by his conversation with the captain the night before, and by Schultz's discovery of four hundred thousand dollars worth of heroin in a Kum Hon hideaway early that morning. There were things he didn't know about his city, things he had never wanted to find out.

Lipscombe made a perfunctory motion toward Brady to begin.

"I've brought some notes that I've been making on Chinatown since I took over command of Central Station eight years ago—"

"I'm sure your notes will make very interesting reading, captain, but considering the circumstances, we don't have the time to cover any deep background," Belardi said hastily. "What the chief and I need from you is an assessment of the situation in Chinatown now and, more importantly, your thoughts on how we can prevent another outbreak of violence like the one last night. I don't think I have to tell either one of you this city is very close to the edge. Another gang killing might be all that's needed to kick off a full-scale riot."

Brady listened to the mayor without blinking. His intensity made the mayor nervous. The captain began speaking again without hesitation.

"I told you last night I considered the Imperial Gardens massacre a continuation of the rivalry between the Kum Hon and Wah Chung gangs. Since then we have positively identified the Imperial Gardens victims as Wah Chung members. Ballistic reports indicate that three of the guns found in the Kum Hon hideout this morning were used in the restaurant killings."

"What about this fellow Yee?"

"We assume the fourth gun used in the restaurant executions belonged to Sidney Yee. Four of the five slugs found in Richard Soo were from a .38. It's been a gang custom that the leader of one group must personally kill the rival leader. But unlike previous gang violence, this battle isn't over territory, or control of firecracker sales, or plum jobs in the Chinatown gambling dens and cathouses. What's going on now is a heroin war."

"Tens of millions of dollars worth of heroin," Lipscombe put in. "What we found in the Pacific Avenue apartment is only the tip of the heroin iceberg."

"You found two pounds of heroin in an apartment. What makes you think you've discovered a multimillion-dollar smuggling ring?" Murphy asked.

"Because this heroin is China white," Lipscombe said with professional enthusiasm. "There are three major heroin connections in the world. The French connection— you saw the movie—opium grown in Turkey, processed in Marseilles and smuggled into the U.S. through either New

York, Montreal or Miami. French heroin is usually ninety-five percent pure when it's brought into the U.S., and it's pure white. Second is the Mexican connection—opium grown in the northern Sierra Madres and processed into heroin in Durango or Culiacan, then brought into the United States through the border towns. The trade is controlled by a few powerful families in Mexico. Mexican heroin is dirty, a clay-colored brown, never more than fifty percent pure. It's processed quickly and doesn't have to be as pure because it's easier to bring into the country. Number three is the Chinese connection—opium grown in the plateau region of southeast Asia, where the Burmese, Thai and Laotian borders intersect: the Golden Triangle. The morphine base is processed into heroin in Rangoon and Hong Kong. China white is processed using the same seventeen steps as the French heroin labs in Marseille. The difference is that the Turkish opium has a higher morphine content than Southeast Asian opium, so the Chinese stuff isn't quite as pure. Anyway, the lab boys verified this morning that the heroin found in the Kum Hon hideaway was China white. It was a little less than eighty percent pure. They also said it hadn't been stepped on—diluted—yet, which means it was probably just brought into the country."

"So what makes the Chinese connection so important?" the mayor asked.

"Over the last five years the federal government has choked off the French and Mexican connections with aggressive policing by the Drug Enforcement Administration and Customs officials, and by putting intense pressure on the governments of Turkey and Mexico. The DEA estimates that over two-thirds of the heroin now brought into the U.S. comes through the Chinese connection. The problem is, and always has been, that there have been so few seizures that it's impossible to trace trafficking patterns, much less find the actual importer. You hear Vancouver one week, San Pedro another week, sometimes it even comes via Amsterdam and the East Coast."

He looked at the mayor, then at Murphy.

"This time it's different. This time we're one man away and it doesn't take a whole lot of imagination to know who he is."

"R.Y. Ling," Murphy said, caught up in Lipscombe's narrative.

"R.Y. Ling," Lipscombe concurred. "I wouldn't be surprised if the Son Lee Tong controlled the entire operation, from the harvest to distribution by Chinese youth gangs."

"If Ling really is responsible for bringing millions of dollars worth of heroin into the country—which I'm not ready to believe, but if for conjecture's sake he is—why would he involve the youth gangs?" Belardi asked. "From what Captain Brady has been telling me, the secret to the tongs' underworld success has been their anonymity and secrecy."

Brady answered his question.

"Using the gangs is a recent move by the tong. It's our guess that the white wholesalers the tong had been selling to wanted a bigger cut."

"The word our department has been getting is that the local heroin wholesalers have been frozen out," Lipscombe added. "I hear from the DEA that it's the same up and down the coast. Tony Redlick didn't like it, for one, and he wound up with the fishes."

"You mean the tong can just cut these people off without fear of retribution?"

"This isn't New York or New Jersey. The heroin wholesalers operating out here today are mostly independent. They're no match for an organization like the tong. When you think about it, it makes sense for Ling to use the two gangs. They both have branches in every major city where there's a Chinatown: Honolulu, Los Angeles, Seattle, Vancouver, New York. It's like having a built-in distribution network. What he's done is eliminate a step and double his profits. Those kids last night were probably going to ship those speakers to New York. A pound of eighty percent pure heroin can be cut and sold there for nearly three hundred thousand dollars."

"If there's so much money to be made, and the operation is nationwide, why are the gangs fighting each other? Wouldn't it be easier to combine forces?" the mayor asked.

"The tong won't let that happen," Brady answered. "Traditionally both the Kum Hon and the Wah Chung have competed for the tong's favors, and that's the way Ling likes it. Neither gang gets too strong."

"Wait a minute, captain. I always have trouble with all these Chinese names," the mayor said.

"Wah and Chung are common surnames in China," Brady said, "so the Wah Chung gang was named after two foreign-borns who started the gang in the early seventies. They're both dead now. The Kum Hon gang was named after the Chinatown restaurant where the American-born Chinese hoods used to hang out. Originally the Wah Chungs were exclusively foreign-born and the Kum Hon exclusively American-born, although now both gangs have begun recruiting FOBs."

"FOBs?" Murphy asked.

"Fresh-off-the-boat," Brady explained.

Murphy and the mayor exchanged looks.

"And the Son Lee Tong?"

"Tong is just a Chinese word meaning 'hall.' In China people used to hold meetings in regional halls to discuss their grievances; that's where the tong concept began. Tongs are different from family associations. Anyone with the same surname can join a family association, but tong members are almost exclusively adult males. A family

178

association is basically a benevolent organization that takes care of the old and the sick. A tong is more secretive, more interested in making money and providing protection for its members. Before the 1906 earthquake and fire, the tongs ruled the streets of San Francisco by reign of terror. Before the earthquake there were over thirty tongs. After the earthquake, when Chinatown was rebuilt, there were only six. For the past seventy years they've been kept more or less under control by the Six Companies, the de facto Chinese chamber of commerce, with the help of people like Jack Manion."

The mayor had heard of Sergeant Jack Manion. Almost single-handedly he had put the remaining criminal tongs out of business during the late 1920s. There was a lot of Jack Manion in Captain Woodruff Brady.

"Today there are thirty-five family associations in China-town, which is why less than one percent of the population is on welfare, even though their poverty is as great as or greater than any other minority's. But there are only five tongs, and by far the most powerful is the Son Lee. The Son Lee is said to be descended from the Chee Kong Tong, the first Chinatown tong. The Chee Kong were famous for their blood-brother rituals and anti-Manchu fanaticism. They flew a black flag over their headquarters instead of the Imperial yellow and white flag. The Chee Kong faded out when the Emperor was overthrown. But it reappeared under a new name, Son Lee, in the late forties when the Communists threw out the Kuomintang. At first the Son Lee was just thought to be some kind of anticommunist business society. It's only been in the last few years we've found out how far-reaching their influence is."

"Sounds like the Mafia."

"Like the Mafia, except no one knows about it. To most outsiders the Son Lee Tong is a respected community organization made up of the most prosperous and influential men in the Chinese community. The mayor can attest to that."

"I'm hearing theory this morning, captain. Interesting theory, granted, but nothing tangible, nothing that would make me want to arrest a prominent citizen of Chinatown."

"You'll have that tangible evidence, Mr. Mayor," Lipscombe said. "We know there's a huge amount of heroin somewhere in San Francisco. If it weren't for this damn strike I'd guarantee we'd locate it before the weekend was over."

"How many men do you need?" the mayor asked.

"Twenty would be a good start," Brady suggested.

"That's impossible," Murphy said. "Keep Parker and Schultz on special detail and get three men from Narcotics, but that's all we can afford."

"What about the DEA, can't they help?" the mayor suggested.

"The Feds won't go near Chinatown," Lipscombe scoffed. "It's bad for their batting average."

"I can't blame them; I've been mayor of this city for sixteen years and every time I go down there it's like I've never been there before. I'll always be fan kwei. Isn't that the name they have for us?"

"Foreign devils," Brady translated. "I don't think any white man can ever really understand Chinatown. You have to flow with it, you can't force it. It's the Chinese philosophy, yin and yang, the path of least resistance."

"Captain Brady, you don't seem like the kind of man who would follow the path of least resistance," the mayor observed.

"I'm a policeman, Mr. Mayor. I do what I have to do. I follow whatever path is necessary to get the job done."

"So how do you propose to find this heroin?" Murphy broke in before the mayor could reply.

"Wait and watch," the police captain answered. "Frank

Parker has developed some good contacts in Chinatown over the past few years. He can be impetuous at times, and his partner, Barney Schultz, is a maniac, but people trust them."

"Aren't there any Asian officers on the police force?"

"We have only three Chinese officers in the whole department, and they're out on strike," Murphy said.

"They don't work in Chinatown anyway," Brady added. "Two of them wanted to, but their families were threatened so they went to the Avenues."

"Jesus, it's a wonder we know anything at all."

"That's our one advantage. R.Y. Ling thinks he's invisible to the white world. When he finds out about the confiscated heroin, maybe he'll make a mistake."

23

THE antiseptic perfume failed to mask the real odor lining the corridors of County General Hospital. Frank had no love for hospitals. "People factories" his father used to call them when Frank took him in for periodic transfusions due to a chronic blood disorder. Frank would take him down to County General after school because his father usually felt too weak to drive. Finally the strain of loading and unloading over a hundred kegs of beer a day defeated both the man and the treatments. Now his father was lucky to make it up a flight of stairs.

For years Frank's mother and the doctors had told Tim Parker to get a less strenuous job. But his father wouldn't hear of it. Like his son he didn't know how to take advice. Tim Parker said it was the Irish in them. Kathy said it was a sexist syndrome. But Frank liked his mother's explanation best: "Stupid men are stubborn, stubborn men aren't always stupid." Frank loved his father, but he understood what his mother was talking about. . . .

He wasn't sure Andropolus would be conscious yet. He'd been in surgery until five that morning and a nurse had told him over the phone that the surgery had been successful. Neither bullet had hit the spinal cord and the doctors thought that no permanent damage had been done. They couldn't be sure, of course, but Frank's experience with doctors had taught him that they rarely made a positive statement unless one hundred percent convinced.

Two men were standing outside Andropolus's door. Both were about Phil's age, in their late forties, and Frank assumed that both were homicide detectives.

"You must be Parker," one of them said.

Frank shook hands with both of them, feeling only a slight twinge in his arm. There was implicit approval in their greeting.

"He's just come out of the anesthetic. Lila is in with him now."

"Lila?"

"His wife," the detective told him.

"Oh," Frank said and took a chair in the hallway. The detectives resumed talking. He felt foolish for not knowing Andropolus was married. He remembered their conversations about Kathy and Rita, but the detective had never said anything about a wife. Frank had just assumed that he wasn't married.

He felt the note in his shirt pocket. He could still see Kathy in the kitchen that morning. She had known Andropolus was married.

"I don't understand you, Frank, I really don't."

Her voice had cracked with frustration. Her eyes were bloodshot from crying. She'd gotten up to fix his breakfast but he couldn't eat. He was too tired. He hadn't had a total of eight hours sleep in the past three days.

"Yesterday you tell me you're disgusted with being a cop. You tell me you're sick of being spit on by the people you're supposed to protect. You tell me that your fellow cops want to beat you up because you cross their picket line. Now, after killing two people, after seeing your friend get shot in the back, after getting shot yourself, you want me to move over to Janis and Mike's where I'll be safe. What about you, Frank? Who's going to make you safe?"

"I just don't want you here alone at night. There's a man I'm after. He knows my name. He may know where I live. It will only be for a few days."

"I'll go on one condition. You tell me why. Tell my why you're doing this to us."

It was a typical Kathy question, which he couldn't answer.

"It's my job," he said lamely, after a helpless pause.

"That's not good enough," she shouted. "I love you, Frank. You're the only man I've ever loved. You're my life. I have to be worth more to you than your goddamn job."

"I wish you could see inside of me," he said slowly. "I wish you could see that what I do and who I am are the same. They're the same person who loves you. The same one who thinks about you out in the street, the same one who cares about you all the time. I'm a whole man, Kathy, not two halves. If you'd seen Phil Andropolus's face when he turned to me . . . I'm alive because he took two bullets that just as easily could have hit me."

She watched him without seeing.

"And that makes you do it? Because you think he saved your life? So now you feel you owe him yours. How about me? Don't you feel any responsibility for the woman you married? Do you want me to be like his wife someday, sitting home in an unpaid-for house, with three children, waiting for the hospital to call and tell me whether my husband will ever walk again?"

He remembered shutting his eyes. He wanted to block out what she was doing to him. Always she made it a choice. They had been so close a few days before and then . . . children. She would never let him forget why there was no family.

184

"I'm going to bed, Kath. Can we finish this later when I take you over to Mike and Janis's?"

"You think it will be any different?"

"No," he said, without wanting to.

She started crying again. He didn't blame her. If he hadn't been so tired, if his arm hadn't ached so much, he would have cried too.

When he woke up she was gone. The note was on the kitchen table.

My darling Frank,

You've always said I think too much. You say I should experience life not worry about it. This morning I finally realized what you have been talking about. You risk your life for what you believe in, all I do is cry and wait. It's time I stopped crying and started living.

Much love,
Kath

He had checked the bathroom and their closet. He thought a suitcase was missing, and maybe some of her clothes, but he wasn't sure. Her toothbrush and comb were gone, but a lot of her other bathroom junk was still there.

He had called the De Angelos's and both sets of parents. No one had seen or heard from her. His mother was upset and thought he should call all Kathy's friends. Her mother was unperturbed, probably thinking she had left him—a move she had none-too-quietly favored for years, ever since Kathy's father became a mild success in the meat business and they had moved to the suburbs. Having a cop for a son-in-law was okay for a butcher but not good enough for a meat-packing mogul.

"You can go in now, Parker," one of the detectives told

him, coming out of the room. "But don't stay too long. He's pretty groggy."

Frank entered the room cautiously, not sure of what he was going to say. It was a semiprivate room; Andropolus was in the window bed. His face was wan and loose, like a faded first-base glove. The usual professional confidence was gone. The detective's black eyes followed him around the bed. His wife was sitting on his left, holding his hand with both of hers. Intertwined in their hands was a rosary. She was a small sturdy woman with handsome Mediterranean features and the same dark coloring as her husband's. When she saw Frank she smiled. It was a smile of warmth and reassurance.

"Did you get the bastard?" the detective asked in a hoarse voice.

Frank nodded and Andropolus closed his eyes.

"We found two pounds of heroin in the apartment. Lipscombe says he's certain Ling was the importer," Frank announced.

"Be careful, Frank. Make all the connections," the detective said, his eyes still closed. "Don't guess when you can be sure."

"Brady and Lipscombe met with the mayor this morning. Every on-duty cop in the city has a picture of Yee. Schultz and I are working a special with Narcotics."

The detective opened his eyes. His voice was thick. "Now that they've shot one cop they won't hesitate to shoot another. Ling is deadly. If he thinks you're close he won't think twice."

His wife stood up to adjust the intravenous tube sticking in her husband's right arm. Andropolus smiled with tender resignation at his wife's solicitude. Frank was surprised and impressed by their apparent closeness and the dependency they shared. He was beginning to understand that there was more to Andropolus's confidence and character than he realized.

"When this is over I think I'm going to take the detectives' test," he said impulsively.

Andropolus watched him. "There are some things about police work you can't teach. You had the right feeling on this thing all the way."

"And now I have to finish it. Yeah."

The detective again shut his eyes. He was too tired to keep talking, but Frank knew he'd said the right thing. Andropolus's approval was very important to him. It wasn't like Kathy said. It wasn't that he felt responsible to the detective for saving his life. It was just that he respected Andropolus more than any cop he'd ever met. He respected his toughness and his tenderness, his courage and his intellect. Andropolus was the kind of cop Frank hoped he could become. He had shown it was possible to be a cop, a husband and a human being.

Mrs. Andropolus followed him to the door.

"He likes you very much. He usually doesn't take to the new ones, but he liked you from the start," she said.

"He talks to you about each day?"

Frank asked the question naturally and the woman immediately understood.

"There was a time at first when I didn't like to hear," she said. "Then later he was the one who would never talk. But it is very hard to be a good policeman by yourself."

"Yes, I know," Frank said squeezing the woman's small, hard hand.

He was supposed to meet Schultz at the Kowloon but instead he drove from the hospital to the coroner's office. He wanted to see the autopsy report on Rita. There were aspects of her murder that bothered him. He hadn't had the time to analyze his doubts but there had been entirely too many coincidences surrounding her death. He remembered Andropolus's advice about coincidence and police work.

Patty Ho had told him that Yee killed Rita when she told him about the cop she was in love with. Somehow that didn't sound like Margarita Chan. It was true that Chinese men hated their women to go out with whites, especially a baahk gwai. But Frank's romance with Rita hadn't exactly been a secret in Chinatown. In fact, he had a vague recollection of seeing Yee once or twice when he'd been sitting with Rita in the Kowloon.

There was also the problem of timing. It was hard to believe Yee would go into a jealous rage only hours before a well-planned hit like the Imperial Gardens massacre. Nor was suffocation a retribution fitting the spectacular style of an enraged Kum Hon. Although he could never pretend to know how Rita's mind worked, he had gained some insight into the fei jai over the past few years. Like all punks they were predictable in their rituals. Their killings were dramatic, done for effect as much as anything else.

The coroner's office was in the Hall of Justice, a large eight-story building between Harrison and Bryant, stretching the full block from Seventh to Eighth. Southern Station was on the ground floor of the Bryant side of the building and Frank could see a line of pickets in front of the building. He parked his car on Eighth and ducked into the medical examiner's office on Harrison.

A few minutes after identifying himself to the secretary, he saw the assistant coroner come out. His black-plastic ID said his name was Dr. Joseph Fay. He looked just like Frank imagined a coroner would: cadaverous face, with a pointed nose, thin lips and small eyes parodied by the magnification of his glasses. Dr. Fay told him that only supervisory personnel were allowed to see preliminary autopsy reports. Frank would have to have the detective in charge of the case come down, or get his lieutenant. Frank patiently explained that there was a police strike going on and all detectives were being used on patrol duty.

"I can't help that, officer. If you people don't think more of your responsibilities than to go out on strike . . ."

Frank resisted a strong urge to pull the man over the desk.

"Listen, asshole, I'm the officer who discovered her body. I've been put on special duty by my captain to look into this case . . ."

"Are you Officer Parker?" the doctor asked almost reverently.

"That's the name I gave your secretary."

"She didn't give me your name, only that . . . here, let me see if I can find my notes on the preliminary examination. The pathologist is in with the corpse now. We've finished with the others though."

"I know how they died," he said, as if it were all in a day's work.

Fay was busily thumbing through a sheaf of papers he'd picked up from his secretary's desk.

"Here it is. I hope you can read my writing."

Frank took the paper. He had no trouble with the writing, but he could not make much of the medical language. He saw that the approximate time of death was four P.M., the opinion as to cause of death was anoxia due to suffocation. After that he was lost in a maze of words he couldn't pronounce, much less understand. There was one phrase that stuck out in the body identification: "mouth and teeth, not remarkable." It was obvious Fay had never known Rita Chan when she was alive.

"Can I help you with anything?" the coroner offered.

Frank handed back his notes.

"Please. I'd like to know if there were any signs of a struggle. Anything that might help identify the killer."

"I'm not an investigator, of course, but I'm sure when the inquest is held the epidermal tissue found under the fingernails of the deceased will be mentioned."

Frank looked puzzled.

"There was some skin found under her fingernails. I ran a test on it this morning and the blood type was A. Miss Chan's blood type was O."

"So you think she scratched her killer and that his blood type would be A?"

"That's how they do it in homicide," the coroner said.

"Did you get a blood type on Danny Pong?"

"Let me look."

Again the long fingers delved into the sheaf of papers.

"Danny Pong is type O."

"Is there any way I could find the blood type of someone who is living?"

The coroner adjusted his glasses.

"I'm not sure he's been in the hospital lately and I don't think he's ever done time," Frank added.

"How old is he?"

"I'd say nineteen or twenty."

"Did he go to school in San Francisco?"

"He grew up in Chinatown, so he probably went to Galileo."

"They might have a record there, if they'd let you see it."

"I don't think that will be a problem. I went to Gal myself and the school nurse and I are old friends."

"There's one other thing I think you should know. There was a mark on her body, on the right thigh. A very strange mark . . . like this."

The coroner drew what looked like an inverted trine. Frank was familiar with the scar but said nothing.

"At first I thought it was a scar or a tattoo but when I examined it more closely I discovered it was a brand."

"A brand?" Frank asked abruptly.

"Yes, a brand. Like they put on cattle. It must have been very painful."

24

THE large brown eyes of Jimmy Cleveland watched him from across the table. There was always a hint of mischief in those eyes, like a bull following a parade of heifers across the road. Belardi never knew whether Jimmy was getting ready to break down the fences or lie down in the grass.

The mayor liked the councilman; he trusted him, against the better judgment of almost everyone in his office, particularly Ken Topham. Over the years he and Cleveland had developed a relationship that only their own kind of politician could appreciate. As a second-generation Italian lawyer and a black chief petty officer they had struggled to attain power and learned how to use it. When Belardi had first been elected, before John Kennedy's death, Cleveland had run his Fillmore Campaign headquarters and had impressed him with his knowledge of both the black and white worlds.

They had been part of the Great Society together, just as they had stood together during the Hunters Point riots and the Zebra killings. His relationship with Cleveland had never been stilted or strained like his dealing with the new crop of minority leaders. There was no posturing, no stroking, no righteous bullshit. With Cleveland it had always been straight.

"What did they promise you? A cabinet post?" the mayor said with sardonic pleasure. "You know as well as I do Willie Moffat doesn't have the guts or stamina to be the White House groundskeeper. If it weren't for his father and Bryce, he'd still be trying to get into law school."

"They got you going this morning, Sam," Jimmy said with an easy grin.

"You're the one who's got *me* going. I expected the others to belly up, but I thought you'd at least make it interesting."

Cleveland stopped smiling. The mayor found himself wondering how old Jimmy Cleveland was. He guessed mid forties—the age where a politician either moves up or moves out.

"Eight—One," Cleveland calmly told him. "Chacon will be with me. Your friend Barbara Mayberry will be all by herself."

"I don't have to tell you what will happen after this emergency resolution passes and the Guard comes in. You and I were both in Hunters Point in '68. The more bodies brought in, the more people killed."

"It's too late, Sam. Breathe that air. The people are gonna go no matter what you do. It's too hot. The city's too ripe for any self-respecting nigger to let it slide another day."

"Bullshit!" the mayor yelled suddenly, slamming a cuff-linked hand down on the desk. "You're giving them no other choice. I've never gone to the wall with you, Jimmy, but I'm going to this time. You vote with Zimmerman this afternoon and you're signing a death warrant for God knows how many people. Black people, Jimmy, they're the ones the Guard will be shooting at."

Cleveland's business-like cool remained. Like many good politicians he only got dramatic in public.

"A few years ago I would have bought that story, Sam, but no more. I was out there last night. It's been ten years

192

since the riots, and you know what my people have learned? Nothing. They're still out there on the street jivin' and snortin', getting fucked up waiting for the fun to start."

"Well, I've been talking to people this morning. Community people like Clay Prestone from Social Services and Reverend Wright, they think we can hold on another day. They plan to walk the neighborhoods, make the parents keep their kids in the house. There's a chance, Jimmy. All we need is another ten hours and I think I can have the cops back."

"This isn't 1962, Sam. You can't make a few phone calls and expect to get results in the ghetto. Those bloods you talked to, they can't stop it. They may get paid for telling you they can but they're part of the problem, not the solution. It's a little late to start talking about keeping your kids off the street and walking the neighborhoods when you don't know where your kids are and you haven't been on the streets yourself for five years. The dudes who set the tone down there are the destroyers, the hate mongers, the Muslims, the dealers, the enforcers. They're the ones who call the signals.

"Community people? Listen, you take away their government money and those turkeys would run to Tiburon. I should know, I'd probably be leading them."

The mayor stood up. He couldn't argue; most of what Cleveland said was true. When was the last time Sam Belardi had been to the ghetto? Not since the last election, and then only long enough to shake hands with a few black ministers and city workers.

"I'm sorry, man. If I had thought it would make a difference I'd be with you," Cleveland said.

But Sam had already resolved his doubts. His mind traveled back over the quarter century of memories. He couldn't walk away like Jimmy. There was something Jimmy wasn't getting. Something that had nothing to do with their own political vulnerability. He had seen the same tendency over the past few days in people like Pinch, Ken, Reverend Wright, Harry Carl, Mark Marcucci—old friends and community leaders who he'd thought were too safe and too fat to lay it on the line again—but they had all volunteered, they all had asked to be counted in, not out of any allegiance to him but out of their love for the city.

"There's a distinction between can't and won't. There's a larger distinction between caring and not caring. I don't think you give a damn."

Now Cleveland stood. He and the mayor were both broad men.

"Maybe it's time you went and found yourself another nigger," Cleveland said, challenging him to accept the language as much as the proposition.

The mayor studied the man across from him. He knew Jimmy better than that.

"What do they have on you?" he asked softly.

The councilman's anger passed as quickly as it had appeared. He exhaled slowly, regarding the mayor with a bemused affection.

"About ten years worth."

The mayor looked toward the heavens but had to settle for the office ceiling. It needed patching.

"I've been sloppy, Sam, real sloppy. They got me by the *cojones* and they're squeezin' with both hands."

"Is there anything I can do?"

"Yeah. Promise me they won't get to you."

"You got it." the mayor said, coming around his desk and putting his arm around the councilman. "When this is over, we're going to have a talk. You might have been sloppy but you have more savvy than anyone in this city. I'm old enough to retire, but not you. You can still make a difference in the sixth district and you know it. A big difference."

Cleveland smiled wearily.

"There's a saying in the ghetto, 'with one knee on the canvas you don't knock anybody out'. I can feel my knee in the resin, Sam, sometimes both knees."

"A little of that wouldn't hurt either," Belardi told him.

The councilman didn't argue.

"Topham," the mayor bellowed into the intercom after Cleveland left. The bald-headed man hurried into the office. "Call Pinch and tell him to meet me in the old Lobbyists Lounge at three P.M. Tell Eli to set up a press room across the hall from the lounge. Tell him to get phone banks put in on both sides of the room . . . No, you do that. We'll need two large maps of the city with outlines of the nine police districts and enough tables and chairs for twenty people."

Topham watched him with his mouth open. "Do you mind if I ask what you're doing?"

"What do you think I'm doing? Setting up a command center. We're going to war."

"Do you mind if I ask who we're going to war against?"

"Anyone who thinks this city can't take care of itself."

"Does that include the governor and Zimmerman?"

"Particularly the governor and Zimmerman. What time is that meeting?"

"Two o'clock. That's in fifteen minutes."

"I want to be in the Council Chamber when they pass the resolution. See if you can get me an appointment with Clint Wallace sometime this afternoon before five. It won't do me any good to see him later than that."

"What about the Mexican-American leaders and the Samoans? You've got them at three-thirty and four o'clock.

"Then try to get me in with Wallace by three. You and Pinch can start putting the command center together. Tell Pinch to use the riot procedure in the police manual, not that stone age civil defense plan. We're probably going to need three or four field command posts—one in the Bayview, one in the Fillmore, one in the Mission and one in Chinatown. Each one will need a special radio channel so make sure Pinch alerts communications. I want us to be patched in directly to the police operations center, but we'll coordinate it from here."

"Who do you propose to man these command posts with? Or have you forgotten we don't have a police force."

"You and Murphy are just alike. No faith. What's the name of that guy coming from La Raza?"

"Jaime Gutierrez. He's not one of our people. An independent. Wouldn't support Chacon in the last election."

"I don't blame him. I hope he doesn't mind talking to an old machine politician who wears monogrammed cuff links."

"I talked with Alex Jimenez. He'll be with the Raza leaders. He told me the parish summer schools are telling the kids to go straight home."

"Nothing like nuns to scare a kid to death. How about the high schools?"

"You're going to have to call the Board of Education personally. They say they can't announce public safety instructions unless a state of emergency has been declared."

"So get Dr. Kiner on the phone. I want an announcement made to every class in the city. If Kiner won't take the responsibility, I will. I also want you to call the Recreation and Parks Department. Tell Phil Stewart if he wants to keep his job he better start pumping up the balls and organizing a few tournaments. A boy who's played three full court games of basketball isn't as likely to spend the night looting as a kid who's been hanging out waiting for the sun to go down."

"You better give Mark Marcucci and Mo Howard a call. From what I hear, the Labor Council is seriously thinking about sanctioning the strike. That could hurt us with the firemen."

"You can get a sanction from the Labor Council for not drinking Japanese beer. Come on, they aren't going to touch

196

this thing. What do you hear from the Chamber of Commerce?"

"Bryce is telling the other big hotels to write the weekend off and wait for the Guard to come in and make the city safe. But the small restaurant and hotel people can't afford it. They want to stay open and pretend nothing has happened."

"Jesus Christ. Those people would bid for the concessions at an earthquake. Let Stevens worry about the business community, they're no good to us in this anyway."

"Last, but not least, Tab Hudson of the Gay Activist League has been calling all morning. He wants to know what the gay community can do to protect themselves and their stores from barrio looters. They're scared to death that thousands of macho chicanos are going to invade the Castro Street retail district."

"Who's Tab kidding? From the size of those Castro Street fairies, it's the chicanos who should be scared."

25

MRS. Douglas was on vacation but she made a special trip
down to the high school to meet Frank. She asked him all
sorts of questions to which his answers were barely ade-
quate. Did he finish college? No. Was he married? Yes. Did
he have any children? No. Was his mother still active in the
Society of St. Vincent De Paul? He wasn't sure but he didn't
think so. Did he still like to play gin rummy? Yes, but he
didn't play much. Most cops he knew didn't like cards—it
took too much concentration. What happened to his arm?
He got shot, but it was nothing. She wanted to check the
dressing but he told her he was in a hurry to get back to
work. "I knew you wouldn't be one of the ones on strike,"
she said.

When he finally did get her into the school's files he
explained that only for athletes was a physical examination
mandatory . . . Speaking of athletes, she got a Christmas
card from the Simpsons last year . . . She bemoaned the fact
that because Galileo was almost sixty percent Chinese the
football teams were getting worse and worse. . . . Maybe
Yee played lightweight basketball, Frank suggested, at-
tempting to get her back on the track. As it turned out his
guess was right. Sidney Yee had played 112-exponent
basketball and furthermore his physical record showed

blood type O—the same as Rita Chan's and Danny Pong's but not the same as that found under Rita's fingernails.

Frank grappled with this new information as he drove back to the Kowloon to meet Barney. Both the crime and photo labs were swamped with extra duties and it would be hours, maybe even another day before the fingerprints lifted from Rita's apartment could be processed along with the other evidence. He wished Andropolus were with him to guide him through the maze of evidence and conjecture. *"The more you know, the more you don't know"*—he knew exactly what the homicide detective had been talking about.

But if Yee and Pong didn't kill Rita, who did? Her neighbors had heard nothing. The only real sign of a struggle was the skin under her nails. The door hadn't been forced, and she always locked it. Did that mean she knew the killer? He tried to visualize the room as he'd seen it the afternoon before. The only thing that stuck in his mind was the record album. She had obviously been listening to it. Did that mean she had been with a friend? The murderer couldn't have been gone ten minutes before Yee and Pong got there, and those two wouldn't have had to be there long to know they shouldn't be there at all. So the question returned—who would want her dead, if not Yee? He wished he knew more about the girl whose death, like her life, became more intriguing, more frightening the closer he got to it.

There were so many things he'd been afraid to ask, as if by asking he was making more of a commitment than he could keep. It was one thing for a disillusioned cop to find solace with a beautiful girl on his beat. It was another to take responsibility for that solace. He could tell her his problems between cool drinks and hot lovemaking, but when she needed him he had walked away. She had been asking for help that night in the Kowloon, asking in the only way she knew—in the bar girl manner she so often hid behind. Like the singsong girls of pre-earthquake Chinatown, slaves brought over with their feet still bound, she was afraid to act anything but the coquette. But what had she been afraid of?

He could see the tiny black mark on her right thigh. He had asked her about it once. She laughed and said it was a vaccination mark. "They used different needles on Hong Kong girls," she said. If what Dr. Fay had told him was true they used different needles indeed.

He wasn't even sure she had been in the country legally. The little he did know about her he'd found out one night in the Kowloon, after four of Joe's mai tais. She was born in Hong Kong. Her father was from Shantung Province and her mother from Hawaii via the Cook Islands. Her parents had met when her father went to Honolulu in 1947. He was part of a Nationalist Chinese commando unit the U.S. Government trained in demolition techniques so they could fight the Communists. When the Chiang Kai Shek government fell in 1949 her father fled to Hong Kong. There he sent for her mother, and the two were married soon after. Rita was the third and youngest child in the family and the only girl. Her father blew himself up two years after she was born trying to detonate a bank safe. Rita lived with her mother and two brothers in a Hong Kong tent house until she was sixteen. When she was finally unable to stand the squalor any longer, she ran away. What happened after that she wouldn't say. "Who cares how I come here, you happy to see me," she laughed, knowing he wouldn't push it. Was she a Ming Dynasty princess or a Hong Kong call girl? She was right, he didn't want to know. . . .

Frank didn't see one camera, one pair of white shoes, one broad midwestern smile as he turned up Columbus to Stockton. The morning headlines FEAR GRIPS CITY and front page pictures showing the bodies of three Wah Chung lying on a Grant Avenue sidewalk was doing wonders to kill off the tourist business. There were benefits from a police strike after all, Frank thought to himself. Reports of the Pacific Avenue shoot-out hadn't made the morning papers but he expected to be back in the news by the afternoon edition. He'd told his mother about the shooting but not Kathy's parents. Mrs. Purcell didn't need any ammunition from him.

He parked his Camaro on the sidewalk next to St. Louis Alley. There was the ubiquitous odor of fish and poultry. Two Chinese boys, no older than ten, were flipping baseball cards against the shaded brick wall. They were wearing Levis which covered their shoes and their hair had been sheared under a bowl. Their English was perfect.

"Fuck you, mine is touching," one of the boys yelled.

"Yours ain't touchin', man," the other boy said, looking plaintively at Frank.

The argument was over George Foster and Steve Garvey. From Frank's viewpoint it looked like Garvey was touching, but he never had liked the Dodgers so stayed out of the argument.

Sociologists blamed the increasing juvenile crime rate in Chinatown on Americanization. Frank didn't doubt it. When both mother and father had to work fourteen to sixteen hours a day to pay inflated Chinatown rents and prices, Chinese parents didn't have time to maintain family and cultural traditions. Not that such economic rationalizations made it any easier for the families of the fei jai. In the Chinese culture, Frank knew, any crime of the "dutiful son" was shared by the entire family. Maybe that was why he still felt no remorse about killing Danny Pong.

The Kowloon—and the Kowloon's owner—looked horrible. Half-empty glasses and dirty ashtrays were still on the tables and the bar. There was even a glass in Joe's tip tray. The place smelled like stale beer and cherry juice and its owner seemed in no great hurry to clean it up.

Barney was standing on the other side of the bar watching

the television screen. He looked peeved. Miranda Stone was giving a live report from City Hall and Schultz seemed distracted.

"What's Miranda talking about?"

"The council overrode the mayor's veto and declared the city in a state of emergency. Evidently Zimmerman's on the phone now to the governor. Miranda says the National Guard will be coming over the Bay Bridge by six o'clock tonight."

"That's all we need."

"No, this is," Barney said handing Frank a red piece of paper. The writing on the paper was in Chinese and Frank was about to hand it back when he recognized a marking on the bottom of the page. It was an inverted trine with a line through the top like a crossed T.

"What's this?"

"That *chun hung*," Joe answered. "I find it on my door this morning. All over town. Chun hung is tong reward for head of enemy. Very old tradition in Chinatown."

"What's this chun hung supposed to say?"

"It say Sidney Yee wanted for murder of Rita Chan. It say $10,000 reward for Sidney Yee."

"What's this character down here mean?"

"That sign of Triad Society," Joe said respectfully. "Very old society in China. Three points mean heaven, earth and man."

"What is this Triad Society?" Frank asked casually.

"Triad Society secret organization two hundred years ago. Fight Manchu Emperor. Very dangerous. Kill many Manchus. Triad Society set up first tong in Chinatown. Chee Kong Tong. Chee Kong Tong now called Son Lee Tong."

Frank remembered something Captain Brady had told him about the origins of the Son Lee Tong. It seemed to fit what Joe Louie was saying. The reward for Yee seemed to fit, too. Not that he knew what it all meant, but a pattern was beginning to emerge. What he saw made him shudder.

"Can you believe it?" Schultz said, "They actually put their name on a death warrant. This whole thing is starting to piss me off. I don't mind a few slants shooting at one another—no offense, Joe—but if these bastards are going to start advertising. . . . What do they think we are, their fuckin' stretcher bearers?"

"Have you heard anything about what the Son Lee are up to?"

"Old Chinese proverb: 'Better to be dog in peaceful time than man in time of unrest.' Many dog in Chinatown all time."

"You don't know where I can find Patty Ho, do you? Didn't she work up on Powell Street somewhere?"

"What do you want her for?" Schultz asked.

The bartender made a derogatory sound which Frank understood to mean he didn't know, or didn't care.

Frank ignored his partner's question. He didn't want to tell Barney, or anyone else in the department, about the blood type findings. Under the best of circumstances police procedure had a way of depersonalizing crime just as the justice system had a way of depersonalizing a victim. He felt responsible for what had happened to Rita. He didn't want to lessen that responsibility by throwing the case open. The coroner's inquest would do that soon enough. He wanted a little time to see what he could develop on his own.

It was three P.M. when they got back to the station for their meeting with Brady. The pickets were three abreast. It was obvious that the strike was coming to a head—the pickets' mood was somber and tense. Their sidearms were still strapped to their belts but the liquor and bravado of previous days were gone. They weren't happy with the way things were turning out but now they had to see it through.

None of the men, including Thompson and Jones, made any attempt to intimidate Barney and him when they pulled up, and a few even yelled encouragement.

He stopped for a minute to talk with Mike De Angelo. There was still no word from Kathy. Frank told him to get in touch if either he or Janis heard anything. He suspected Mike knew more than he was saying—Janis and Kathy were pretty tight—but he didn't have the time or the right frame of mind to deal with Kathy Parker now.

Lieutenant Burns was laying out the riot equipment when they walked into the lineup room. Bullet proof vests, extra long 36-inch batons, helmets and masks, tear gas guns, Remington pumps and automatics, even a few AR-15 rifles were being put out.

"Expecting company, lieutenant?" Schultz asked.

"Yeah, about two thousand of your friends from China-town."

"The Chinese would never riot, lieutenant," Frank said, "They would never loot their own stores or attack this station."

"Don't tell me, tell Captain Brady. He's the one who told me to get out the riot gear."

Gene Lipscombe was in Brady's office along with two other bearded narcs. Frank and Barney reported their conversation with Joe Louie and the posting of the chun hung death warrant. Nobody seemed surprised.

"We knew the minute Ling learned about Danny Pong and the heroin bust that he couldn't afford to let Yee live," Brady said. "If what we think is true—and nothing so far contradicts it—Yee can implicate Ling or his tong representatives directly."

"But why would he put up a public notice? He's just drawing more attention to his own involvement," Lipscombe asked. "Does he think we're so stupid that we don't know why he's doing it?"

"The Chinese are gamblers," Frank said. "He knows the police strike can only last a few days longer. He's gambling he can get to Yee before we can. It's a good gamble because once Yee's dead there's not much we can do. There's no way to trace a chun hung. You think any printer in Chinatown would ever admit to setting a notice for the tong?"

Frank got no argument.

"We don't have a hell of a lot of options," Brady said. "With our manpower and the time limit of the chun hung, I'd say all we can do is stake out the Son Lee building and hope we get lucky."

"Does anyone know where Ling lives?" Lipscombe asked.

"In one of those Russian Hill apartments on Green, isn't it?" Brady said, looking at Frank.

"Nine hundred and sixty-five Green. Ling has the top two floors. It's the old Crocker family penthouse. He's supposed to have one of the most valuable art collections in America."

"I wonder what else he has?" one of the narcs said.

"It might be worth a try, Gene," Brady said. "We could put your two men at the Son Lee building; no one knows them. Then Schultz and Parker at Ling's penthouse. I doubt if Ling will ever get close to Yee *or* the heroin, but someone in his organization is going to have to get dirty."

"I talked to the regional head of the DEA this morning," Lipscombe said. "He says once we get anything that looks solid, he'll give us all the men he can spare."

"What does 'solid' mean?" Schultz asked.

"Anything over a half a pound, where the U.S. attorney has a good enough case to prosecute," Lipscombe answered.

"In other words, anything they can get headlines with," one of the other narcs said.

"They aren't too careful are they?" Schultz said.

"You oughta try to make a buy with them. They get receipts for coffee."

"Captain, what's Burns doing putting out the riot gear?" Frank asked.

"The chief wants us to be ready for anything. Evidently the black and brown neighborhoods are about to blow."

"But you know the Chinese would never riot."

"Parker, you worry about finding Sidney Yee before the tong does and I'll worry about running Central Station."

26

WHEN Kim had phoned Jimmy Cleveland she had been close to hysteria. Two of her students were being held at gunpoint by an Arab grocer. A third boy, Malcolm Dexter, was already dead, killed by the grocer when he and his McKinley Junior High classmates had foolishly tried to loot the Arab's store half an hour before. An angry crowd of blacks had gathered in front of the store at Fillmore and Ellis, threatening to burn it to the ground unless the boys were released. The police were on the scene but were hopelessly outmanned.

Jimmy swung his Mercedes left off Van Ness and up Geary Street to the top of Cathedral Hill. The three and a half day old police strike had cleared much of the traffic off the streets. The late afternoon sun blinded him momentarily as he reached the top of the hill at Gough Street. Below the glare he could see the familiar outline of the Fillmore Basin—known to those in the urban planning business as the Western Addition, to those in politics as the sixth district, but to most other people as the ghetto.

He could see two columns of smoke rising listlessly; and the ominous blinking of red lights. He felt a tightening in his stomach. It was a different fear from the kind he had known in the Navy. Then he had been too proud to acknowledge the dangers of the white man's world. This present fear, this dread, went back to the lining of his gut, to the essence of his blackness. It stemmed, he knew, in part from his ghetto childhood, when he had been continually afraid, surviving by his savagery. It was the memory of that savagery, as seen in the faces of others, that taunted and terrified him now more than it ever had before. When you're young and black, you can only lose what you know. Now he knew too much of life to lose it like this.

Geary Street took him into the shell of the Western Addition. When he had taken office nearly twelve years ago, the Fillmore had been one of the worst ghettos in America. Now it was a crazy quilt work of redevelopment projects, vacant lots and broken down buildings waiting to be condemned. Most of the blacks in the district had been forced to move south to Mint Hill or out to the Bay View-Hunters Point area because they were unable to afford even the low income housing in the Martin Luther King Center and the Marcus Garvey Plaza. He knew that if the ghetto—or what was left of it—burned tonight, it would be out of plain frustration, not rage.

"Slum clearance projects" they were called in final days of the Great Society. The urban riots had started a flow of federal money that hadn't stopped until John Erlichman told Richard Nixon he was the biggest honky stooge of them all. But by that time Jimmy Cleveland and his friends were up to their elbows in the Redevelopment Agency trough. Looking back, he could have lost an arm and still hung on to the power base he'd spent ten years building. But losing the arm meant losing the French cuff, tailored suits and gold rings that dressed it, and the Mercedes steering wheel that it held.

Two uniformed police stood at the Fillmore Street off ramp. They were white and looked uncomfortable. Probably refugees from the mounted patrol in Golden Gate Park,

Jimmy thought. They must have recognized either his face or the C–6 license plate because they let him pass.

He drove slowly south on Fillmore, through the ghetto shopping district, trying to avoid broken glass and debris. Young kids no older than eleven or twelve were running from store to store. Most of the businesses were being protected by their proprietors, but one abandoned little grocery was being picked clean. Older brothers stood in small groups on the sidewalk, drinking and smoking, making no attempt to hide either the booze or the grass. They knew who the dude in the white Mercedes was, and their bloodshot eyes made no attempt to disguise their hatred. They were watchful and waiting. Jimmy Cleveland could feel his threads, his gold rings, his car being picked clean like the mama and papa store he had just driven past. Ten years ago, when he and Styles had done the job in Hunters Point, Jimmy Cleveland had been part of the ghetto. He had shared their outrage, their injustices, their hunger. Now he was afraid of it.

He parked his car in an alley in back of Hawk's House of Ribs. If his car was going to be safe anywhere in the Fillmore it would be with the Hawk, an old friend from St. Dominic's schoolyard.

"Shee-it, I don't believe it," the tall man with the beak nose said when Jimmy walked through the back door.

"How you flyin' today, Hawk?"

"Close to the top, JC, seein' your face come through the door," the tall man said, coming from behind the counter.

Jimmy took a deep breath of the aroma from the Hawk's special sauce. He could almost taste the ribs. "You still going to Europe this fall, man?"

"Sweden ain't Europe, JC, it's black paradise. All you gotta do is step off the plane and start handin' out numbers."

Jimmy laughed at their old joke, then said, "Listen, man,

I want you to keep an eye on my machine for a while. Some crazy Arab down on Ellis Street just killed one of Kim's students and he's threatening to kill two more. I gotta get down there fast and the way these niggers is actin' I'm afraid to leave it on the street."

"You sure you want to go showin' that pretty face of yours down there, man?" the Hawk said with sudden seriousness. "They been a lotta jive goin' down 'bout you, man, bad jive."

"Since when you start worryin' about me, Hawk?"

"Since Ray Robinson say he wants you dead, that's when."

Jimmy waved disdainfully and opened the door. "You know that nigger never could take me to the hoop," he laughed.

"Let me come with you, man. There ain't no business today anyways."

"If you come with me, then who's gonna watch the car?"

The Hawk sighed and sat down at the counter as Jimmy waved goodbye and turned down the street. There the Hawk's special sauce gave way to another familiar smell.

The market was on the southeast corner. The crowd, which he estimated at over five hundred, was backed up half a block toward him on Fillmore. About twenty uniformed police were keeping the intersection clear. He could see a police command post had been set up in a van near the intersection on Fillmore. Everyone—the police, the crowd and the Arab—seemed to be waiting for something.

He pushed his way into the crowd, knowing Kim would be at the front. The bodies were warm and smelled of sweat, malt-liquor and super market perfume.

"He weren't nothin' but a boy," one woman said, "no robber neither."

"He didn't have no gun, that's what," said another.

"They take our money, but that ain't enough. Let me tell

you, that mother fuck A-rab is gonna regret he ever show his ugly face down here."

The deeper he got in the crowd the more hostile it became. Each rumor, each threat, fed another. He'd seen this kind of ghetto courage build itself up before.

"How many are left?"

"I heard three . . ."

"No, only two. The teacher said there were two. Ain't that right, JC?"

"I don't know, brother, I'm just gettin' here myself. I heard there were two but I don't know."

"You gotta do it to him, JC. You hear?" an elderly lady in a faded print dress yelled at him. He recognized her as a friend of his mother's. He hoped Ruth Cleveland wasn't in the crowd. That was all he needed.

"Don't you worry, Mrs. Rose. We'll take care of him."

Other people yelled out to him. He tried to reassure them. Most were older, his constituency. He knew they saw him as a possible way out without any bloodshed. It made him feel good to think there were still people in the ghetto who believed in him.

Of course, the others were there too—so-called radicals who knew all about Marcus and Huey but nothing about power or politics. He pushed past them. They saved their best shots for the TV cameras, and like the song said, "the revolution won't be televised."

The people who did scare him were the street people, the dudes on the corner—and the Muslims. They were easy to pick out in the crowd. The hair cropped short, the uniform suit and tie, the polite smiling mask over a fanatical hatred.

Kim turned when she heard his voice.

"Jimmy, hurry, this man's crazy," she said, pulling him forward in the crowd.

She was excited but her movement was controlled. There was none of the hysteria of their phone conversation. He couldn't help but notice how great she looked. Her hair was pulled straight back in a school teacher's bun, and her high cheekbones held her skin taut. He was lucky to have her, and he would do anything to keep her.

She dragged him toward the command post, composed of a police van and two patrol cars parked in a triangle about two hundred feet from the store. He was quickly introduced to a Captain Gray who had been alerted by the police operations center that he was coming down. Jimmy Cleveland was hardly the police department's favorite councilman, but Gray, who worked out of Taraval station, seemed happy to see him. With Gray was a Sergeant McAdams, head of the Tactical Assault Team. He talked like a farmer, and had skin as smooth as a peach, but the bloodlessness of his eyes betrayed the metabolism that found killing natural.

The police were waiting for the hostage negotiator to arrive, and Gray briefly outlined the situation to Jimmy. His version was essentially the same as Kim's, with a little more background. The market owner's name was Faisal Abdafi. His Ellis Grocery and Liquor Store had been held up ten times in the last three years. Jimmy had heard of the market and its owner—Abdafi's brother, Abdul, had been paralyzed from the waist down in a previous robbery attempt.

"He knows what will happen to him and his store once he lets the boys go. He knows we can't control this crowd," Gray said. Cleveland noticed that Sergeant McAdams and Henry Styles stood apart, each studying the two-story building in the corner.

"Don't be so sure you can control it much longer even if he doesn't let the boys go, captain," Kim said.

Gray didn't argue. Standing on the corner of Fillmore and Ellis surrounded by angry blacks and dealing with a crazy Arab looked to be the last place in the world he wanted to be. He kept looking to McAdams for instructions. The assault team leader ignored the captain. He was waiting for

212

something or someone, and Jimmy didn't think it was the hostage negotiator.

"What do you make of it, Henry?" Jimmy asked his friend.

"Nothin' fancy. Put the negotiator out on the street as a diversion, let one of the pigs blow the Arab away."

"And risk killing another innocent boy," Kim objected. "What happens if he misses?"

"I don't miss, lady," McAdams said softly, signalling the rest of the team to approach the command area.

Four flak-jacketed policemen came into the cordoned off area. Gray explained that there were usually eight men on the advance team but because of the strike there were only four. The captain seemed anxious to absolve himself of any responsibility.

"What do you mean there are only four men?" Kim demanded.

Jimmy closed his hand firmly around her arm and stepped forward protectively.

"Two boys' lives are at stake here, captain. We don't want one of your usual half-assed police operations. I think I should talk to Abdafi. If I could guarantee him safe passage . . ."

A brick crashed against the store's wire-meshed window, starring the glass at the point of impact and triggering a new chorus of threats and epithets from the crowd. Gray said no shots had been fired yet but it seemed only a matter of time until someone in the crowd opened up.

For the first time Jimmy could see the Arab sticking his face in front of the window. He didn't look much older than twenty-five, but, of course, Arabs were like Chinese—you could never tell. His eyes, even from sixty yards away, were darting and wary. He held one of the boys in front of him as a shield, enraging the crowd even more.

McAdams had been talking in a low drawl during the

213

commotion. He carried a high-powered .30–30 rifle himself and the other men had either shotguns or AR-15s. Jimmy knew enough about Tactical Assault teams to know that there were shooters, those with the semi-automatics; spotters, those with the Winchesters; and cover men, the ones with the shotguns. McAdams was clearly drawing up an assault plan, or "green light" as he called it.

"Can't you use any of these other men?" Gray asked.

McAdams didn't answer at first, then finally said, "Most of the guys you have here are from the vice squad or the K-9 corps. If we got them involved in an assault operation we'd be unnecessarily risking their lives and ours. In an operation like this it's not how many men you have, it's the training and discipline of the ones you're working with."

"If your men are so well trained and disciplined then why are half of them on strike?" Jimmy asked without really wanting to.

"I suspect because they're sick of being lied to by publicity-grabbing politicians," McAdams said, looking directly at Jimmy.

"Relax, sergeant," Gray said. "We've got a job to do here. Now what's your plan?"

"The big man here called it," McAdams said nodding toward Styles who, Jimmy knew, was also ready to take on the cocksure sergeant. "Once Blaisdell gets here, we send him out front. We have a shooter and a cover man in the alcove of the laundry next door to the grocery. We have the other two men go around the block to Webster Street to make sure none of his camel jockey cousins show up to help. I walk behind the crowd to Tanginka Liquors across the street and go up to the second floor apartment. When the asshole sticks his head in front of the window to talk with Blaisdell—pop, pop—two Winchester silverpoints in the cranium and . . ."

"Wait a minute, triggerman," Henry Styles said in his

deep baritone. "No way that man over at Tanginka is just gonna let you go walking around in his building. Billy Odoms is an ornery nigger. He don't like no one—black or white."

McAdams seemed undisturbed by Style's comments and simply went back to studying the decrepit buildings of the neighborhood. Two more bottles crashed against the rolling steel door that had been pulled shut over the store's entrance. Jimmy didn't share McAdams confidence, and neither did Captain Gray who kept looking back and forth between the angry crowd and the market. Kim, too, was restless. She was clearly depending on him to save the boys. Unfortunately, Jimmy knew they were only part of the problem.

"What about that brick building with the bakery on the bottom floor?" McAdams asked, nodding toward a large red building three doors down from Tanginka Liquors.

"That's over a hundred yards away," Gray observed.

"I can shoot the hind tit off a field mouse at a hundred and fifty," McAdams said matter-of-factly. "Do you think you can get me in *there* without any trouble?" he asked Styles.

"If JC wants I can. He's the one who calls the shots down here."

All eyes turned to Jimmy.

"One change," he said. "Let me do the talking. We don't have time to wait for the negotiator. Give me five minutes with him. If he won't release the boys, then we go to green."

"Fine with me," McAdams said. "How do you want to work it?"

"When I shoot my right cuff like this." He showed three inches of starched white beneath his tan summer suit. "Any time after that, man, it's your turn."

"What about the crowd?" Gray balked.

"As long as I'm standing out there nothing will happen. But if your man misses and something happens to those kids inside, I wouldn't want to be in any of your white skins."

Gray rubbed at the back of his neck as if already feeling anticipated bullet holes. McAdams signaled his men to move into the crowd, then disappeared into the van. When he came out he was holding another Winchester.

"If you served with the outfit I think you did, I don't have to tell you how to use this," he said, handing the rifle to Styles.

The ex-Ranger took the Winchester without smiling and methodically checked the scope and magazine. His bearded face took on a strange calm. Jimmy now remembered where he had seen McAdams's killer certainty before—in the face of Henry Styles. It was a quality that transcended color. McAdams had obviously seen it there too.

"Your man will have the Arab in his cross hairs right along with me. When you hear the first shot roll to your left. He's only got a handgun in there so there shouldn't be much danger."

"I'm not worried about me. Just make sure you don't let him hurt the two boys."

McAdams shrugged off Jimmy's show of heroism. He motioned Styles to follow him across the street. The big man hesitated in front of Jimmy. They had been too many years together for Styles not to know what was coming down.

"You don't want this one, man," he mumbled to Jimmy.

"I wish it was that easy."

"I counted four Muslim soldiers in the crowd."

"So did I."

Styles swept his teeth with his big pink tongue. He was trying to make sense of it all. Jimmy put his hand on Styles's huge back and walked him out of the command area.

"If it gets hairy I want you to take care of her for me. She doesn't understand."

"I'll watch her, man," he said, himself not understanding

anyone's taking this kind of risk for a woman. "Just roll like the cat told you."

"Sure, I'll roll."

When he came back to the van, Gray was yelling at his communications officer to keep pressing for reinforcements. Jimmy wondered who he was trying to kid. The sirens had stopped ten minutes ago.

"So tell me what a hostage negotiator is supposed to do." he said to the captain.

Gray stared at him. "I don't know why McAdams is even letting you do this. He's supposed to be the best, but I don't know—giving that mean looking guy a gun . . ."

Jimmy turned away and looked over to the market. The long summer shadows had just reached the sidewalk in front of it. There were cans and bottles strewn around the entrance. The word LIQUOR was printed in large, bold letters below the smaller ELLIS STREET MARKET sign.

He hadn't seen the Arab for the last few minutes. The son of a bitch had to be scared, but that didn't mean he would move. Arabs were crazy bastards.

"All I know is that they go to school in New York for a month," Gray was saying. "The department picks up the tab. It's supposed to be quite a trip."

"What are you talking about?" Jimmy asked.

"The hostage negotiator. That's all I know about them. They're specially trained in New York."

"Jimmy," Kim said. "I don't know. Maybe we should wait for the negotiator."

It was hard not to love her.

"I didn't ask you people to come down here. We can handle this without your help," Gray began testily.

"This is the ghetto, not a P.A.L. softball game, captain."

As if to punctuate his statement another brick hit the Ellis Street market.

"It's crazy, Jimmy, don't go out there," Kim cried.

"If I don't it's going to be too late for the boys."

"I won't let you."

"Hey, what happened to that hard-ass lady I love," he said holding her tight, using her trembling body to calm his own.

"If you're just doing this for me . . . I couldn't stand it if anything happened to you."

"I'm doing it because it's all I can do, baby. Understand?"

She was crying when she blinked her eyes that she did. He knew that she didn't as he wiped her cheeks clean with his.

"McAdams just gave the sign," Gray told him.

Jimmy tried to pull himself loose but Kim wouldn't let him go. And he didn't want to go. He'd lived forty-four years and never met a woman he really cared about like this.

Nigger's luck—that's what his mother called it when you had the number and the runner decided to go into business for himself.

"You want to use this?" Gray asked, holding up a portable megaphone.

Jimmy shook his head.

"I love you, baby," he said to Kim, taking her hands firmly from his shoulders.

Once he left the command area it was a different time and place entirely. His steps were careful, his hand movements deliberate. He walked down the east side of Fillmore. The market was to his left and the bakery to his right. The crowd, which fanned out behind him across the vacant lot kitty-korner to the market, had grown silent.

He was thinking faster than he was walking. All he had to go on was his own savvy. It had never failed him before, but before wasn't a half-crazy Arab with a .32 pointed at his head. Before wasn't four Muslim soldiers with their hands in their pockets waiting for him to make a wrong move.

The trick would be to gain the Arab's confidence without provoking the crowd. He was sure Abdafi wouldn't release the two boys unless he was guaranteed safe passage out of the area and protection for his store. What he wasn't sure of was whether or not the Arab knew such guarantees were easy for him to make but impossible to keep.

He was half way into the intersection when a voice yelled for him to stop. The voice was that of a frightened but rational young man.

"Mr. Abdafi, my name is Jimmy Cleveland. I'm acting as a spokesman for the city of San Francisco."

There was some movement inside the building. He thought he heard the Arab order the boys to lie down. Because of the western exposure he couldn't see past the storefront itself. The sunlight was swallowed up by the holes in the window. He strained to see in the darkness but couldn't.

"You're only making things worse for yourself, Mr. Abdafi. Justifiable homicide is not a crime, but kidnapping is. In California kidnappers can go to the gas chamber."

"If I let them go my store will be burned down," the Arab said from the darkness. "Everything I own is this store. My family will starve if it is destroyed."

"Your family will starve if you go to the gas chamber, too," Jimmy was surprised at how tough and persuasive he sounded. "Captain Gray of the San Francisco Police Department has given me his assurance that you and your store will be protected. At this moment, Mr. Abdafi, your survival is just as valuable to the well-being of this city as it is to your family. We can't afford to let this situation get out of hand."

"Why should I believe you? Faisal Abdafi is not a fool easily tricked by politicians."

"I don't think you have much of a choice, Mr. Abdafi. We aren't going to be able to hold back this crowd indefinitely. If it were up to them, you and your store would be ashes."

"I do not scare like a woman, Mr. Cleveland."

Jimmy wished he'd been to that school in New York. The

Arab was much more suspicious than he expected. He wondered if Abdafi had seen the tac squad disappear into the crowd. If he had, there was only one thing to do.

"I'm not out here to play games, Mr. Abdafi. You let the boys go right now and I'm sure the judge will understand. You make the police have to use force and your life in this country is finished—one way or the other."

"They come into my store," the Arab explained, buying time. "I don't want trouble. They laugh and try to steal my liquor. I ask them to leave but they keep taking more."

The Arab was getting excited as he talked. Jimmy thought he saw his head once through the wire mesh window. He was sure now that the store keeper was to the right of the steel door, probably near the cash register.

"This is America, Mr. Abdafi. You will get a chance to tell your story fully. If what you did was justified, then you have nothing to worry about."

"What's that jive, JC?" someone yelled behind him. Jimmy had hoped the crowd couldn't hear him.

"He killed a boy, man, he gonna die. Don't you rogue on the blood, JC. You'll die with him."

Jimmy considered turning to face the crowd but decided it was better that he maintain contact with the Arab.

"Mr. Abdafi, I'm telling you for the last time. Release the boys and come out with your hands up. I give you my word no harm will come to you if you come out now."

"You come in," the Arab yelled to him. It was an answer Jimmy should have expected—but he hadn't.

"What for?" he asked warily, knowing that he was still out of easy pistol range.

"We trade hostages. You for the two boys. That way I am sure you will keep your word."

He knew he had to accept the proposition. It was the only chance to get the boys free without firing a shot. Inside he could try to maneuver Abdafi into the window.

"I'll become your hostage on one condition . . . that you let the boys go while I'm still out here."

The Arab agreed and Jimmy began moving toward the grocery. His steps were uncertain. He could feel his heart beating out of control. He hoped McAdams and Styles were keeping it together better than he was.

"I'm not jivin', man, get that door open," he told the Arab.

He could hear the door being unlocked and the chain being loosened. The metal door slowly came up. As it opened he could see one of the boys standing just inside the entrance pulling on the chain. His eyes were practically popping out of their sockets. When he saw Jimmy he began pulling faster.

"That's all right, son, you be home soon," Jimmy told him.

The basketball shoes of the dead boy were visible just inside the door. They were under the newspaper rack. They were large feet for a boy of fourteen, and Jimmy reflected that Malcolm Dexter would have been tall enough to be a good ball player—if only he'd been smart enough.

With the door pulled up, Jimmy could see inside. The Arab, a head shorter but much stockier than the boy by the door, was standing where he had suspected, behind the counter near the cash register. Jimmy guessed the other boy was on the floor behind the counter. A large cardboard display advertising vodka was sitting in the window, blocking the view from outside.

"You have me in range now. So let the boys come out."

Just as the boy in the doorway started out the Arab reached over and grabbed him by the arm. Jimmy saw the revolver pointed at him now and understood instantly that he'd been had.

Casually he let his right arm stretch outward and upward until two inches of white cuff were visible. It wasn't hard to do when your arm was covered with sweat.

"That's right, nigger. Put your hands up and start walking this way. You make a move I don't like and I'll put a bullet in that fat belly."

The Arab had moved into the doorway and was holding the hand gun on him. His desperate eyes clung to Jimmy's.

By this time someone in the crowd realized what had happened. They began yelling at him to stay out of the store. He waited for the reports of the Winchesters. There was nothing.

"Start walking, nigger," the Arab yelled. "You tricked my brother but you won't trick me."

In his mind he knew he had to at least take one step, but his legs wouldn't allow him to.

"Jimmy, don't do it," Kim's voice cried out. He turned and saw her walking toward him.

He yelled at her to go back but she kept coming.

Out of the corner of his eye he saw two flashes from the window above the bakery. He wheeled back around in time to see the Arab thrown back against a stack of wine bottles, what was left of his skull landing near the feet of Malcolm Dexter. It had happened so quickly that the man hadn't even been able to pull the trigger.

The two boys, both spattered with blood, were out of the store before he had time to turn back to Kim. When he did she was almost on top of him. He reached out and grabbed her, burying himself in her smell and her softness. If he hadn't been holding on to something he would have fallen over.

He held her for what seemed a long time yet was only a few seconds. He could hear the boots of the flak-jacketed tac squad behind him as they secured the building, handcuffing the headless Arab and searching the market for any family or friends. The two boys waited behind them and Kim hugged each of them and cried some more.

He didn't see the conservatively dressed man until he was only ten feet from them, walking toward them with his hands at his sides. Jimmy didn't have to guess what the expressionless Muslim had in his hand. With all his strength he threw Kim and the two boys to the ground. Rolling away from them he made a lunge at the man who, by this time, had his arm raised.

There were two quick flashes followed by an explosion from across the street. Both Jimmy and the Muslim fell to the ground. The crowd, stunned by the abrupt and spectacular nature of the new violence, stood motionless as Kim crawled over to Jimmy's body.

27

FRANK parked his Camaro in front of a row of spectacular Russian Hill homes and sat with Schultz. Across the street was an elegant old thirteen story apartment building with an awning that read, "965 GREEN," the last building on the street before the pavement stopped dramatically at the edge of a hundred-foot cliff.

Frank had once made a delivery to the building when he worked for his uncle. He remembered taking the service elevator up five or six floors and stepping into someone's kitchen. He couldn't believe that a building would have separate elevators for service, or that a single apartment could take up an entire floor. When he delivered the package he'd asked the cook if he could look out one of the windows. He had been able to see everything from up there—the Golden Gate and Bay bridges, the Berkeley Hills, Mount Tamalpais, Alcatraz—all the way to the ocean. It was like being on top of the world.

"Not bad for a gook who runs a couple of junk shops," Schultz said.

"Do you think this is gonna work?"

"No, but I don't have a better idea. Other than going up there, holding a gun upside his head and asking him where the stuff is."

"I wonder if it would ever come to that?"

"You wonder if what would come to what?"

"Do you think you could ever off a guy yourself, be your own executioner? Say you know someone is a murderer. Someone like Ling who's responsible for probably hundreds of deaths a year but who the law can't touch."

"Are you shittin' me?"

"No, I'm serious. What if we never get Ling? We've known for over a year that he's the man, but the closest we've come to proving it is the heroin we found last night. What if we don't find Yee or any more heroin?"

"I thought you were supposed to be smart? You'd have to be out of your gourd to throw your life away on a guy like that. I've been a cop for nine years and the main thing I've learned on this job is no criminal is worth dying for."

"We could have died last night."

"Last night we were doing our job. We get paid to catch criminals just like we get paid to help old ladies across the street. Knocking a punk around is one thing, icing somebody because he's no good is something else. There are a whole lot of disgusting people around, a whole lot of murderers, and a whole lot of scumbags who make murder look humane. If you start taking them personally you'll end up having to put away half the human race."

"Are you tellin' me you don't take it personally? If you're that cynical, why did you come back to work?"

"Someone had to take care of you. Besides, Ted Thompson has bad breath. I couldn't stand having him come up to me on the picket line every ten minutes and telling me how much it meant to him and Clint that I was with them. I never was a team player."

"Hey—we got some action!" Frank said.

A Jaguar XJ–6 came out of the garage. Both men slouched lower in their seats.

"This is ridiculous," Barney said as the car drove past

them with a matronly silver-haired woman behind the wheel. "This street is too small. If one of Ling's men came through here they'd spot us in a second."

"What do you want to do?"

"Let's move to the other side of Jones, near that new highrise. If anybody spots us they'll think we're a couple of private dicks doing a divorce case. We won't be able to see the entrance but we can see any car that goes down the block."

Frank had started the car when a light blue delivery truck came out of the garage.

"Don't look over at him, Frank. Pretend you're just pulling out." Schultz told him quickly.

"You recognize it?"

The truck went passed them. Frank glanced up. The lettering on the side of the truck read GOLDEN GATE FISH MARKET—LICENSE #674328. It struck a chord with him too but he couldn't place it. He didn't dare look at the driver.

"That's the same truck that went into the tong headquarters the other night, I'd swear to it. Same driver too."

"Do you think he spotted you?"

"You never know which way those gooks are looking."

"Do you want to follow him?"

"No, I think we should sit here and wait for Ling to send Sid Yee and the heroin out with his doorman."

Frank spun the Camaro around and took off after the truck. By the time they got to the intersection at Leavenworth, it was gone. The only direction they couldn't see was to their right, down the north slope of the hill, so Frank turned the car sharply to the right.

The truck was already at the bottom of the block going across Union. From their position on top of the hill they could see Leavenworth all the way down to Fisherman's Wharf and across the water to Alcatraz.

"Hang back a little," Schultz said.

Frank rode the brake down the forty-five degree hill, until they went across Union and had to accelerate to avoid an oncoming car. The Camaro bounced off the hill before he was able to hit the brakes again.

"Just like 'Streets,' huh?" he joked weakly, but Schultz was concentrating on the truck, now crossing Filbert on its descent toward the bay.

"Where do you think he's going?" Frank asked.

"Not to Chinatown. I meant to run a check on that fish market last night, but we got busy. I should've done it this morning."

"Why don't you call it in?"

"No. I don't want to use the radio on this. Not yet."

In all the years they'd worked together Frank could never remember Barney using radio silence on anything. For all Schultz's cynicism he wanted Ling as bad as Frank did.

The light blue truck continued down Leavenworth until it reached Bay Street. They were two blocks behind it when it made a right turn on Bay.

"Take Chestnut, then we can pick him up at Columbus."

Frank dipped down Chestnut, past the Art Institute, then took a quick left onto Columbus. They were sitting at the stop light when the blue truck passed in front of them, heading east.

"Doesn't look like he's going to the Wharf either," Schultz observed. "This is getting interesting."

Frank, too, was beginning to be intrigued. A fish market truck, driven by a Chinese, leaves one of the poshest apartments in the city but doesn't return to either China-town or the Wharf.

They followed the truck at a distance of two hundred yards—there weren't enough cars on the street to risk getting closer. The truck went past the projects, past Akron and finally reached the Embarcadero.

"What the fuck?" Schultz swore as the truck turned left back toward the Wharf.

Frank turned the Camaro after him. He had no choice. They hadn't gone twenty yards when the truck turned again, this time into the entrance of the marshalling yard of the Pacific Shipping Company. The truck was stopped at the gate for clearance when they drove by.

Frank glanced up at the name again, then read the number of the pier—35—and remembered where he'd heard them before. He made a U-turn and drove back past the marshalling yard in time to see the blue truck disappear into the Pier 35 shed. Above the shed they could see the rigging of a freighter.

"I'll be a son of a bitch," he said softly when he had a chance to catch his breath.

"What?" Schultz asked.

"Remember that body we looked at Monday—Leroy Krebs, the one out on Pier seven?" Schultz nodded. "Andropolus ran a check on him. He found out he was a shipping clerk in Stockton who got canned because he was on the sauce. He also found out his previous job in San Francisco was in March of last year, for an outfit called East-West Lines. Last night he told me he'd just learned that East-West Lines had been bought by Pacific Shipping."

Schultz whistled softly through his front teeth as Frank parked in the gas station across the railroad track from the pier. "That's a lot of coincidence for one afternoon."

"Try out this scenario. Krebs came looking for work at East-West and discovers they've been bought out. He looks around and sees something about the operation that makes him suspicious. Don't ask me what . . . but he does some more looking, and asks some questions. Being a wino he doesn't have the sense to stay out of it. The more he finds

228

out, the more excited he becomes. Finally either someone who knows him talks, or he decides to use his information to get a job or some other kind of payoff, never suspecting that he's stumbled onto the biggest heroin operation in the United States. The tong has no other choice but to get rid of him, and they do it in a way that will discourage anybody else from getting any ideas."

Schultz wasn't buying it. "We don't know this shipping company has anything to do with anything. Let's just go on what we do have. A truck was in the wrong place at the wrong time. Now it's in the wrong place for the third time. What we have to do is get a look inside the truck, or better yet, inside that ship, because whatever was picked up at Ling's is on that ship right now."

"Want to call Brady and see if we can walk through a warrant?"

"The last time we tried to walk through a warrant it took six hours, and the magistrate was sitting. It's after five now and the city's in a state of emergency. We'd be lucky to get it by next Tuesday."

"Oh no." Frank shook his head. "We can't just barge in and do a probable cause search on this one. We blow this and Brady will have us sitting on the Pyramid."

"You gotta better idea?"

"Let's call Brady. He and Lipscombe can call in the DEA or Customs. They can post-date warrants better than we can. Use that pay phone over there."

"What are you going to do?"

"I'm going to have a little talk with the security guard."

Schultz felt very unsure about the idea but there was no time to argue. The break—the unexpected break Andropolus had talked about, when the lines fit together for no apparent reason—had come.

Frank crossed the street below the Pacific Shipping

Company and walked back up the Embarcadero, trying to look like any other tourist wandering along the San Francisco waterfront.

"How are ya?"

The dour security guard sized him up through the double grid cyclone gate.

"You lookin' for someone?"

"Naw. Me and my wife are stayin' down at the Ramada Inn at the Wharf. She went shopping over at Union Square and I thought I'd take a walk. I've always liked ports since I was in the Navy."

The guard's face brightened. He had guessed right.

"I was a navyman once myself, back in the days when you had to know how to swim to be a sailor, not work a computer."

"This is some operation you got here."

"Best on the coast is what they say. Those two gantries just been put in eight months ago," he said, motioning to the two huge cranes on either side of the dock. "You can load and unload an eight hundred-foot container ship in one day, and those babies you're lookin' at are forty feet long apiece."

Frank studied the silver containers and did his best to look impressed.

"That ship in port now. How long will it take to empty her?"

The guard laughed derisively.

"The *Mindanao?* If that old tub was full, I'd say about three days. With her, everything is done with ship's tackle like the old days. She and her sister ship, the *Luzon,* are the only break-bulk freighters left in the PSC fleet. Mr. Stevens junked the rest of 'em when he took over."

There was only one Mr. Stevens the guard could be talking about—only one who had the money to own a shipping line—Bryce Stevens, the hotel man.

"He must have a lot of money to put together an operation like this."

"Bryce Stevens has more money than God," the guard said reverently.

This bit of information didn't bother him although it seemed inconceivable that a man like Stevens could be involved in heroin smuggling.

He wanted to ask the guard about the truck but there was no way he could think of to work it in the conversation.

"I guess they got you working overtime because of the police strike, huh?"

"Double shift, twelve hours a day for the last four days. God damned cops, they never did shit anyway. Always comin' down here sniffing around for spare TV sets. I tell 'em they're welcome to whatever they can find laying around but if they start prying open the crates, I'm gonna have to shoot 'em."

The guard liked that and Frank did his best to like it too.

"You haven't had much trouble then?"

"Mister, you gotta be pretty strong or pretty stupid to try and rip off a whole container, if you know what I mean."

Frank said he did, but he was rapidly running out of small talk when the truck came out of the shed and headed back toward the gate. The guard turned around, saw the truck and unlatched the gate.

"God damned gook food," he muttered, his voice barely audible unless you were straining to hear it.

Pulling the gate open, he motioned Frank back out of the way. The truck came up to the entrance and the middle-aged Chinese driver nodded to the guard. The guard reluctantly returned the nod. Frank didn't recognize the driver who seemed more preoccupied with pulling out onto Embarcadero than checking out pedestrians on the waterfront.

He looked over at the phone booth. Schultz was gone. He wasn't in the car either.

The guard locked the gate and Frank came back to where he'd been standing.

"Gook food? What's that?" he asked innocently.

The guard grimaced.

"Three times a day they feed them raw squid and snails and God knows what else."

"Feed who?"

"The Chinese crew. Immigration won't let them come ashore because they go up to Chinatown and disappear. So we have to have the food brought in."

It was that simple. If he hadn't been sure before he was now. He was going to get on that ship if he and Schultz had to commandeer it in the harbor.

"Well, I'd better be moseying on back. It's getting near supper time and the wife will be hungry. Say, you got any good recommendations for food in this city? Someplace where we can get real bread and a steak without French sauce on it?"

"Can't help you there. My wife and I don't go out much. Besides, we live in Redwood City. It's too dangerous to live up here."

Frank began walking back toward Fisherman's Wharf. He wanted to get a look at the *Mindanao*. He'd never been on a ship in his life. When he'd first seen her sitting along the renovated pier his reaction was that she'd docked there by mistake. The paint on the black hull was peeling off, and the once white main deck was covered with rust and corrosion. She wasn't very big, maybe four hundred feet long and, if his eyes weren't decieving him, she was listing slightly.

"Kinda like putting a cat house in the middle of Disneyland," he heard Schultz say.

Barney was standing with one foot up on an old piling. He looked every bit the merchant marine he once was, or said he was. With Schultz you had to allow for creative imagination.

"How come you aren't following our friend?"

"Brady's got somebody on him. He did a check on the license and the truck's registered to the Golden Gate Fish Market on Pacific. But we don't want the truck. That old scow is where it's happening."

"How do you know?"

"Being the good policeman I am I went down to the Crow's Nest and picked up a copy of the Pacific Shipper. It has the arrivals and departures of every boat on the coast, plus their recent ports of lading. You didn't know I used to be in the Merchant Marine, did you?"

"Was that before or after your stock car career?"

Barney ignored Parker's crack and unfolded a piece of paper. "Here we go. Pacific Shipping Company. Inbound. Vessel *Mindanao*. It says the *Mindanao* left Hong Kong on July fourteenth, she arrived San Pedro August first and San Francisco August fourth."

"Yesterday."

"That means she leaves at high tide tonight for Vancouver."

"Did you tell the captain?"

"Not yet. What did you find out about the truck?"

"Enough to know that we have to search that ship before she leaves tonight."

28

UNLIKE most major cities, San Francisco had no sophisti-
cated civil defense command center, so the old lobbyist's
lounge in City Hall had been converted to that purpose. The
stately high-ceilinged room had been vacant for a number of
years, ever since the local TV stations had decided there
should be no more lobbyists allowed in City Hall, only
"municipal consultants," and the consultants didn't need a
lounge. To the mayor, the beautiful, empty room had always
represented the essence of political reform in the age of
electronic media: it looked and sounded good but meant
nothing.

He was sitting at a large walnut table in the middle of the
room. Ken Topham's chair was to his left. Topham and his
staff were responsible for communication with the various
residential and business districts within the city. Pinch
Murphy, as usual in full uniform, was standing next to the
large wall map directly in front of the mayor. On the map,
the city was divided into the nine police districts, and
Murphy's staff was responsible for communication with the
nine station houses and three emergency command posts.
Altogether there were some twenty men and more than
thirty phones in the room. Mayor Belardi's press secretary,

Eli Bergman, was keeping the press at bay in a room across the hall from the lounge.

When Murphy had given him the news twenty minutes ago, he hadn't been completely surprised. After hearing that Jimmy had gone into the ghetto to meet with the grocer he'd half expected he wouldn't come out. The memory of his discussion with him that afternoon was still fresh. There was a time in every man's life when a chance is given for redemption. Those who understand atonement will take that chance. His own actions during the past three days were not unlike his friend's. It made little difference whether their atonement was for spiritual or criminal transgressions, little difference that he was a Catholic and Cleveland a Baptist, that he was white and Cleveland black. A man does what he has to do to live with himself. Still, he was mourning Jimmy's loss.

"Gray says the Fillmore is unbelievably quiet. What happened to Cleveland really shook 'em up."

Pinch's voice had the intonation of a priest giving last rites. The mayor thought he detected a trace of scotch on Murphy's breath. He didn't blame him—it was going to be a long night.

His meeting with Clint Wallace had been an unmitigated disaster. The Police Officers Association president was implacable. The success of the strike had pushed him over the edge. He seriously intended to confront the National Guard when they crossed over the Bay Bridge later that evening. The prospect of the first armed confrontation between local and federal law-enforcement agencies since Little Rock didn't horrify the POA leader, it excited him.

Over the past six hours Murphy, Al Neilsen and other old-school cops had made big inroads into Wallace's support among the rank and file. Many of the strikers were beginning to realize they had been put in an indefensible position by a frustrated, overweight police sergeant with a talent for talk. Unfortunately there were still twenty or thirty cops who seemed ready to follow Wallace to the grave, and certainly to the Bay Bridge.

"What do you have from the Bayview?" The mayor had trouble hearing his own voice over the clamor. The phones had been ringing constantly for the past hour.

"Third Street is a stand off. Silver Avenue the same. Captain Hines says they're just waitin'. I think the Cleveland thing may have affected them too, but you can never tell with boons. They might just be waitin' to see if we're holding anyone back."

"Like who? The meter maids? What are we down to, ten percent?"

"I doubt that many. Including the inspectors, we don't have two hundred men who are working, and most of them are exhausted."

"A hundred police for seven hundred thousand people. That's really insane, Pinch."

They both knew there wasn't much time left. The Guard would be crossing the Bay Bridge at around six-thirty. It was five-thirty now. He was going to have to make his decision soon. Did he stand with Wallace and try to prevent the Guard from coming in, gambling that the city could hold on until the confidence vote at eight o'clock and that the vote would go the way he expected? Or did he sit tight in the command center and risk a confrontation between the Guard and the strikers, not to mention the Guard and the citizens?

Ken Topham came back into the room with an efficient looking young man in a three piece suit. There was no air conditioner in the lounge and the mayor had long since taken off his coat. The man, who looked vaguely familiar to him, walked over to the big map and studied the configuration of the pins.

"Who's that clown?" Belardi asked Topham.

"Nick Simmons. He's from the governor's office of emergency services."

"What's he doing here?"

"Keeping Moffat informed of every move we make. He tells me the governor is flying down to Treasure Island right this minute so he can come across the bridge with Hinshaw and the Guard."

It was a vision Belardi had seen from the beginning. Moffat in front of a column of National Guardsmen, coming into his city. . . . If there had been any question of what he would do, that question was now answered. He waved Pinch over to his side.

"Have you heard what Moffat and Zimmerman are planning to do?"

"The kid was just fillin' me in," Murphy answered. "They want me to be with them in case Wallace tries to stop them."

"What did you say?"

"What do you think?" he said with indignation, "Those are still my men with Wallace. I'd die before I let those jerks lead an army against them."

"What would you do, Ken? Would you let them come in?"

Ken Topham adjusted his glasses and thought for a second.

"A half hour ago I think I would have. But after hearing about what Jimmy Cleveland did, I'm not sure. I was wrong about Cleveland. I could be wrong about a lot of other people in this city. I don't think San Franciscans want the National Guard in their city. I don't think the police do."

"I *know* they don't," Murphy said. "If we can just hold on until the emergency meeting, I know they'll vote to come back to work."

"So let's keep holding. What do you have from the Mission?"

"Right now that's the worst area in the city. The command post captain tells me both the Filipinos and the Mexicans have taken to the streets. There's talk the Filipinos are going to go up to the Excelsior district and take on the Samoans."

"That's crazy." Topham said, "Samoans are three times as big as Filipinos."

"Those little flips are crazy," Murphy observed, "They get a few drinks in 'em and they'd take on a herd of elephants."

"Ken, maybe you should call Father Tanupoi and tell him to keep his boys under wraps. We don't want any of those bulls to get upset."

Topham was dialing the number before he finished the sentence. Murphy was called back to the police phone bank by his supervising captain. The mayor studied the map in front of him. The situation was critical, but so far, with the exception of the incident at the Arab market, there were no deaths. Public safety couldn't be guaranteed but no one had yet panicked. If the police could come back to work before the night was out he thought they would be all right. If. . . .

He used the map as reference, not for direction. Murphy and Topham would give him reports from their respective staffs and he would look at the wall. For him the lines on the map were three dimensional. He probably knew the city and its people as well as anyone alive. For each neighborhood, for each block, there were faces, stories, memories. Each intersection was a twenty-five-year file of information and experience.

Ironically, but not surprisingly, it was the poorer areas, the ones that consistently voted for police pay raises and benefits, that were now the hardest hit, while the middle and upper class property owners—the backbone of Zimmerman's support—were, so far, protected by their location. The mayor wondered if those indignant property owners understood how paradoxical their position was. They hired police to act as a buffer, to protect them from the poorer minority groups, then they turned around and put a shiv in the policeman's back over a property tax increase. It would almost be worth it if the cops let urban justice run its course. Street gangs, private armies, pimps and goons would replace uniformed police. The city would drown in its own blood.

"Kenny, what's the latest on that fire down on Third Street?" he asked, seeing another red dot go up on the map.

"Jumbo says they should have it before long. It's still a block away from the PG & E tank but they'll need lots of help evacuating if they can't control it soon."

"Pinch, what's the Harbor Patrol doing?"

"You know how hard it is to get them out of their cabin cruisers?" the chief moaned.

"Are you telling me this city is in a state of emergency and the harbor police are sitting in the bay watching it?" The mayor sought to control his anger. "You call Bill Wheeler right now and tell him to get his men ashore and over to that fire or they won't have jobs tomorrow morning. They're to use their own cars if they have to."

"Who's going to watch the waterfront?"

"I'll take care of that," the mayor told him.

As Murphy did an about face and snapped the order to his supervising captain, the mayor picked up the phone and dialed a familiar number—the office of an old ally, Mark Marcucci of the Longshoreman's Union.

"What the hell's going on?" the gravel voiced union leader demanded. "We've been trying to reach you all afternoon."

"I need your help. The city needs your help."

Like a lot of people in the city, Marcucci owed Sam Belardi plenty. Belardi would never have thought to call for himself, but he had no qualms about asking for the city.

"Name it," Marcucci responded.

239

"We need some of your foremen on the docks tonight to discourage any boosting. That'll free the Harbor Police to help out in other places."

"You got 'em," the longshoreman answered. "Anything else we can do?"

"Yeah. Tell Mo and the others on the council to back off of Wallace."

"We already have. Labor will never have anything to do with that bozo again. He's not interested in the working man, he wants to run the city. He actually told Mo that if the Labor Council voted to go out in a general support strike he'd help Mo with his contracts next fall. Can you imagine some flatfoot telling the Teamsters how to get a contract?"

"The man's an idiot but he's still dangerous. He's got a hard core of support. Listen, you and Mo have a certain amount of influence in the POA. If you could explain to the cops that from a professional labor man's viewpoint they're way off base with this thing. . . ."

"You can count on us, Sam."

When Belardi looked up again the young man in the three piece suit was blocking his view.

"The governor will be pleased to hear about the job your people are doing, especially under such adverse conditions," the man said. "I'm going to suggest to him that he and General Hinshaw join you here."

The mayor elected not to reply.

"They should be entering the city sometime after 6:30. What the governor would like both you and Chief Murphy to do is meet him as he's coming over the bridge. It would make for a very dramatic picture. Logistically the bridge offers a good vantage point of the city and, as I'm sure you know, most of the country is watching San Francisco."

The mayor turned to his administrator. Topham knew what was coming and was sliding down in his chair.

240

"What's your name again, son?" the mayor asked politely.

The young man repeated his name.

"Nick, I want you to do me a favor. I want to give Bill Moffat a message. I want you to tell him that he made a mistake when he called up the Guard but he'll be making a much bigger mistake if he tries to make a media event of this by personally leading the Guard into San Francisco. Can you handle that, Nick?"

The young man's jaw slackened momentarily, as if he were having trouble believing what he'd heard.

"Let me put it bluntly, Nick. If that imperious little prick you work for so much as sets foot in my city I'll personally kick his ne'er-do-well butt back to Sacramento."

"You mean you're going to try and stop the governor from coming over the bridge?" he asked.

"Now you got it, Nick."

"But Mr. Mayor, you'll be breaking the law. You could go to jail. State law supercedes local law in a situation like this."

"I'm a lawyer, Nick. I know all about precedents. Don't worry about me, worry about your boss. I hope he's smarter than he acts."

The badly-shaken young man looked to Topham for assistance and received none.

"Bryce will be on the phone in less than five minutes," was Topham's only comment after Simmons left.

Pinch Murphy was standing before him again. Captain Brady and Inspector Lipscombe were standing with him.

"Aren't you supposed to be down at your station?" the mayor asked Brady.

"We had to talk to you and we couldn't risk using the phone," the captain answered.

"What is it?"

241

Both policemen looked over at Topham.

"It's all right. He's with me," the mayor said impatiently.

"We know where the heroin is," Brady began in the middle. The mayor waited. "What we need is the judge's name on a search warrant."

"I've already cleared with the D.A.'s office," Lipscombe said.

"So why don't you go to the magistrate's office and get his signature?"

"We already have. Judge Ewing won't sign it."

"Let me have the affidavit on the warrant application," the mayor said.

"It clearly shows probable cause," Brady said, but, after serving as city attorney for eight years the mayor knew better. It had been his experience that one out of ten cops had a clear understanding of the law.

"The problem is we want to search a ship owned by the Pacific Shipping Company," Brady said bitterly.

The mayor looked up from the affidavit.

"What's the problem in that?" Murphy asked.

"Bryce Stevens owns Pacific Shipping," the mayor answered.

Pinch saw the problem. The mayor hastily read the affidavit of Officer Barney Schultz and saw almost immediately there was no way the factual showings constituted probable cause.

"Have you checked with Customs and Immigration?" he asked the two cops.

Lipscombe answered. "Customs say they routinely boarded the *Mindanao* yesterday morning and signed the papers for five thousand pounds of women's shoes, blouses and sandals from Hong Kong. Immigration says out of the twenty-three man crew, eighteen are Chinese nationals. They've restricted the crew to limited leave because of previous defections on past layovers. Another interesting fact is that Leroy Krebs, the first body we found in the bay this week, used to work as shipping clerk on Pier thirty-five when it was still East-West Lines. Frank Parker thinks he might have come back to the dock to apply for a job and noticed something out of the ordinary."

"But according to Schultz's affidavit the ship wasn't even in port then," Topham said.

It was Lipscombe's turn again.

"The *Mindanao* wasn't, but her sister ship, the *Luzon,* was. Immigration told us those are the only two Pacific Shipping steamers that make regular stops in Hong Kong and have Chinese crews. Evidently both ships are registered in Panama. All the other Pacific freighters are containerized and run under an American flag."

The mayor tried to remember what Stevens said about the old junks they'd scrapped when he took over East-West. He had wondered about it at the time but hadn't asked Stevens why they kept two of the four. It was interesting but it was still impossible—beyond impossible—to think that Bryce Stevens had anything to do with an international smuggling ring.

"Were you able to get anything on this Golden Gate Fish Market? Maybe they really are just delivering food."

"I sent two of my men by there twenty minutes ago. They said all they could find out was that it was run by Chinese."

"Kenny, send someone over to the Bureau of Records and see if we can get an owner on that market. I hope you have talked to the DEA."

"They say since we developed the case we have to come up with the authorization. I guess they didn't have to look up Bryce Stevens in the social register."

The mayor brought his hands across his eyes and pressed his fingertips gently to his temples. He was trying to clear his head, to give himself time to think. His lawyer's mind told him there was no way they had a case, yet his intuition told him they were on to something. It was more than the coincidence of the truck being at the tong building, then at Ling's apartment, then at the ship. It was more than the dead bum having once been employed by the East-West Lines.

He replayed his conversation with Stevens the day before in the marshalling yard. Bryce had mentioned a silent partner. A partner who he'd meant to check on but hadn't had time to. A partner who knew and liked the mayor but didn't want to be known just yet. . . . Stevens and R.Y. Ling had worked together many times on his campaign. He'd always suspected that their political comaraderie extend into the business world even though he'd never known the exact connection.

"What's the timing on this?"

"The *Mindanao* is due to sail at high tide. Which is eight P.M."

The mayor looked at his watch. It was quarter of six. "Give me twenty minutes . . . let me talk to Judge Ewing. I don't think you have enough for a warrant, but I think you're on the right track."

"What do you mean the right track? This is it!" Brady exploded, "We've got to get on that ship tonight and I don't give a damn whose company it belongs to."

Murphy and Lipscombe both tried to intercede but the mayor stopped them. His voice was emphatic.

"Captain, I've put up with your insinuations long enough. If you think I am, in any way, trying to protect R.Y. Ling, or for that matter, Bryce Stevens, you can go to the District Attorney with a formal charge. Short of that, I don't want to hear any more of your bullshit or you'll find yourself grooming horses for the Park Patrol. Understand?"

"Understood, Mr. Mayor." Brady was expressionless.

"Lipscombe," the mayor continued, "I want you to get in

244

touch with Customs and tell them to stand by. I mean I want them ready to tear that ship apart. Tell them to get the dogs, the frogmen, everything. If we board that mother I want to *find* something."

Brady and the narcotics inspector left the command center. Topham and Murphy waited for the mayor to say something.

"Kenny, call Mendel and see what we can work out. There's got to be a way we can get on that ship."

"I don't like it, Sam," Pinch Murphy told him, "There's no way in the world we can do a legal search of that ship on the strength of what we've got here. You know it and I know it."

"Bryce Stevens on line three," Topham announced.

The mayor pushed down the third button and picked up the receiver.

"Sam? Is that you, Sam?"

"Good evening, Bryce."

"Sam, what in hell is going on down there? I just talked to the governor and he tells me you're planning to block his entry into the city. Have you lost your mind?"

The mayor didn't need to answer.

"Look, Sam, there are niggers and Mexicans running wild in the streets. One of our councilmen has just been killed, I just heard. There's a war going on and we have to win it."

To them it was a war, the mayor thought to himself—old ladies carrying appliances out of Mission Street stores that they wouldn't know how to use, ten-year-old black kids grabbing enough candy to make them sick for a week. To Bryce and the governor that was rebellion. To him it was a tragedy.

"Bryce, I thought you and I went through this yesterday. I'll tell you the same thing I told the governor's errand boy five minutes ago. If Bill Moffat wants to lead an army into

San Francisco he's going to have to get by me to do it."

"The entire country is watching, Sam. He can't back down now."

"I don't give a goddamn who's watching, Bryce, Moffat is not coming over that bridge."

Stevens mumbled an epithet in frustrated anger. The mayor knew that for one of the few times in his life, Bryce Stevens was powerless. He hung up.

"Kenny, get Quinn Bucklin on the phone for me," the mayor said. "I don't care where he is, find him."

"You didn't say anything about the ship?"

The mayor glanced up at Pinch's question. He hadn't said anything but he hadn't forgotten. He'd seen too many cases of evidence suppressed by shrewd lawyers and just as shrewd clients negating consent searches. There would have to be another way. Maybe Bucklin would give them the answer.

It was then he remembered another time on another ship. Pinch had been worried that day too.

"I got it!" he said suddenly.

Both men looked at him.

"Read the affidavit. It says one of the policemen was told the truck was used to deliver food to the Chinese crew because they weren't allowed in port because of the previous immigration problems. That constitutes probable cause for a border search. Call Judge Ewing and ask him to look it up. I'm sure I'm right. Pinch, get hold of Brady and Lipscombe. Tell them they should be prepared to execute the warrant in thirty minutes."

29

FRANK and Barney were standing in the back of the assembly room as Brady and Lipscombe outlined the assault plan. The mood was very formal, very professional—none of the assembly room antics that usually greeted Lieutenant Burns when he read the watch orders.

Of the fourteen regular men in the narcotics division, ten were present, all except Lipscombe with beards or long hair or both. Some weren't much older than Frank. Unlike Homicide, you didn't have to be an inspector to work in Narcotics. In fact, three of the men in the room used to work in Central and Frank knew that none of them had yet passed the inspector's test.

Brady introduced a fellow in his mid-fifties. He was wearing the kind of seersucker suit that looks better crumpled than pressed. His name was Meadows, he worked for U.S. Customs, and he was supposed to give them a quick lesson on boarding a ship.

"The *Mindanao* is a typical C-3 cargo vessel built after the war—three holds forward, two aft. First, we'll concentrate on the superstructure. That's the cabin area in the middle of the ship. The deck on which we'll board is the shelter deck, or main deck. From there we go right up the ladder—the stairs—to the cabin deck where the crew is quartered, then up to the boat deck where the officers are, and finally up to the bridge.

"When we have the crew accounted for, we'll set up a holding area on the main deck up near the fo'c'sle. The important thing is to apprehend the crew as quickly as possible. We don't want to give anyone a chance to destroy evidence."

"What's the fo'c'sle?" Frank whispered.

"Don't worry about it." Schultz answered. "When we get aboard, just stay near me."

One of the narcotics men asked Meadows if they were to go after the captain as well.

"Well, none of the ship's officers are Chinese but that doesn't mean they aren't smugglers. Before I came over I checked our records on Captain Van Pelt, and I assure you he's no Admiral Nimitz. Yeah, bring him in too."

"If anyone gives you shit, put a gun in his ribs and call either me or Inspector Lipscombe," Brady added.

More questions were asked. There were always guys who asked questions. Frank wanted to get started. He was getting hot sitting around in his bullet-proof vest. His arm was beginning to act up. Mostly he was just anxious to get on that ship.

They drove down to the Embarcadero in three wagons and two patrol cars. Frank was in the first wagon and ahead of them was a patrol car carrying Brady, Lipscombe, the Customs agent Meadows, and an Immigration officer.

His fingers touched the twenty-shot clip of the AR-15 resting on his lap. He hadn't shot an AR-15 since the Academy. He remembered how surprised he'd been at the gun's lack of recoil. It was like shooting a .22 rifle. Unlike the M-16, which was full automatic and fired from five to ten bursts in a split second, the civilian model AR-15 only spit out single rounds as fast as the trigger was pulled. That was fine with him, though he knew of cops who fixed the sear and carried the damn rifle around in their trunks—waiting for the day a gang of blueberries would make the mistake of breaking up a tailgate party in the Candlestick parking lot. "Most of the cops are racist but only a few are killers," Schultz had said once, then added thoughtfully, "It's bad for our image."

The same security guard Frank had spoken to earlier watched the caravan pull up in front of the gate with a mixture of self-importance and confusion. Lipscombe handed him the warrant through the gate and he tried to read it quickly, which made it take that much longer. Brady grew impatient and climbed out of the driver's side of the car. The guard said something in protest and both Brady and Lipscombe shook their heads. The guard unhappily and reluctantly began unlocking the gate.

The cars all drove through and the guard hurried back to the security station to call his boss. Once inside the marshalling yard, their next job was to secure the ship from the rest of the dock. The five vehicles entered the north shed and fanned out across the length the pier. Startled warehousemen stopped what they were doing and watched.

Frank and Barney's wagon went to the center door of the five doors opening on the water. They climbed out of the wagon in silence, and took up positions opposite the single gangway. Within a minute fifteen rifles were pointed toward the deck of the ship. The dock crew, which had been busily loading the ship, stood motionless on the main deck, crates of cargo dangling from the boom cranes.

"Tell your loading crew to get off that ship fast," Brady ordered the stevedore foreman. "Just your crew, no one else."

The foreman told his crew to disembark. They didn't have to be told twice. Already some of the longshoremen were trotting down the gangway, some with their hands above their heads.

"What's going on down there? What is this?" a red-bearded man wearing a captain's hat said from the bridge. He had a European accent of some kind.

"Stay right where you are, captain, we're coming aboard," Brady told him.

"You can't board my ship without permission," the captain protested to Meadows. "This is a Panamanian registration."

"I don't care where you're registered, captain, you're docked in San Francisco," Meadows answered him, holding up the warrant.

Brady and Lipscombe led their fifteen men up the narrow metal gangway. Frank was in the middle of the column, behind Schultz. His first reaction to the main deck of the freighter was how uncomfortable it looked. It was nothing like pictures of ships he'd seen. There were dark gaping holes on the deck and many different kinds of machinery. Grease and oil soiled the deck. It smelled like a factory, not the sea.

As Frank stepped into the superstructure he heard the excited voices of the Chinese crew as they were rousted out of their cabins. The crew members put up little resistance as he, Schultz and three narcs marched them out to the fo'c'sle in single file. Frank counted fourteen. Lipscombe had said there were eighteen Chinese aboard. Their instructions were to hold them there until an interpreter came aboard from the Immigration Office.

"Come on, duck soup, keep moving," Schultz barked, prodding reluctant crewmen with the muzzle of his rifle.

There was nothing sinister about the crew. Their faces were flat and oval, with skin hard-finished from the sea and the sun. Their eyes were averted—the only Chinese Frank could ever remember looking him straight in the eye were the fei jai. They huddled together on the foredeck like cattle. None of them seemed to understand what was happening, only that rifles were pointed at them.

The captain could be heard arguing with Brady from the bridge—he was going to call the Panamanian consulate immediately, he would not allow his ship to be boarded illegally . . .

"Captain, I strongly suggest you start cooperating so we can begin the search," Brady told him.

The four ship's officers plus the captain, all wearing summer whites, appeared on the main deck and lined up in front of the crew. The red-haired captain probably weighed two hundred fifty pounds and was the most colorful in a white short-sleeved shirt and white short pants. He looked more like an out of work, overweight great white hunter than a ship's captain. He was still protesting the search in both English and his native tongue, which to Frank sounded like German.

Agent Meadows read from a clipboard which held the ship's manifest and roster. Meadows wondered aloud where the other four crew members were. The captain just folded his arms.

"Bos'n, do you know where the rest of your crew is?" Meadows asked a tall blond man with sharp features.

"Try the engine room," the boatswain answered.

"We've already been down there," Brady cut in impatiently. Frank obviously wasn't the only one who felt the pressure. Meadows politely told Brady he'd handle this part of the interrogation and proceeded to ask the rest of the officers if they knew where the missing crew members were. All three nervously looked to their captain. "No." None of them knew where the crew members might be.

The ship's officers were afraid, they knew more than they were telling. The captain and bos'n remained calm but the other officers looked uncomfortable. Frank again looked at the crew. They seemed oblivious to whatever intrigue was going on around them.

The interrogation of the officers was interrupted by the arrival of the Customs Office search crew—three German shepherds, or dope dogs as they were called, each accompanied by two uniformed Customs officers. The lone man not in uniform Frank assumed to be the interpreter.

One of the two Customs agents in the lead team was a very shapely blond woman. Schultz couldn't resist.

"How can that dog smell anything but pussy?"

Everyone on their end of the deck heard him. The narcs cracked up, including Lipscombe. Only Brady kept scowling.

"Captain, I want three of your men to accompany each inspection team," Meadows said. "Remember, there are still four unaccounted crew members. Team one will begin at the stern. Check everything. The afterpeak, steering gear, deep tank, every foot of the ship. Team two will start in the engine room and work its way through to the number three hold. Team three will start at this end, down in the forepeak and work its way up through the bos'n's stores."

"You say this is an immigration search!" the ship's captain spoke up vigorously. "Do you think you'll find a stowaway in our fresh water tank?"

"Chinese trout, Captain Van Pelt. The United States does not want any Chinese trout propagating in our streams," Meadows said.

Frank and Schultz were assigned to accompany team one which consisted of the blond, who, on close scrutiny had a face like a pomegranate, her partner and Rudolph, the dope dog.

Meadows and the Customs interpreter were just starting to interrogate the crew when they left. Frank wanted to hear what they said but fell in behind Schultz, stepping cautiously across the greasy deck, careful not to get too close to the open cargo hatches. He wasn't sure if he felt the ship rolling gently under him or if his equilibrium was being affected by four sleepless days and the three pints of blood he'd left in the Pacific Street apartment.

"This is the number three hold," Schultz explained as they walked past the fifteen by twenty foot hole in front of the superstructure. "The two holds behind the bridge are number four and five. That's where we're going."

Frank looked toward the back of the ship. The number four hold was open, but number five, on the other side of the boom crane, was covered.

"We're going down to the second deck," Schultz said, descending a steep metal stairway adjacent to the superstructure.

Frank followed Schultz and the inspection team down the narrow corridor that ran along the side of the ship's hull. The inside of the ship was cooler but more humid than on the main deck. They proceeded quietly, Rudolph sniffing both sides of the passageway. So far there were no signs of the missing crew or any contraband. Frank hoped he wasn't going to have to use the rifle. In the cramped quarters of the ship the bullets would go flying every which way.

When they got to something Schultz called the tonnage hatch, the team stopped.

"We can't all fit in steerage," the blond agent said as her partner turned the wheel and pulled open the hatch leading to the platform deck below.

Barney agreed. After some discussion it was decided that the narcotics man would accompany the Customs people below while he and Frank looked around the after storage area.

"We don't want to make it any harder on Rudy's nose than we have to," Schultz said, helping the shepherd down the ladder, "Some people claim cops have a distinct odor."

When the Customs team had disappeared through the hatch Schultz motioned for Frank to follow him.

"What is it?"

253

"The number five hold . . ."

"What about it?"

"I think the missing crew might be there."

"What are you talking about?"

"The way the ship is sitting in the water. It's out of trim. It's drawing too much water forward. I noticed it this morning but it wasn't until we got aboard and I saw that the dock crew was only loading in the four forward holds that I finally figured out why. The number five hold is empty."

"Maybe they just don't have enough cargo."

"When you're not running capacity you always balance— that's the first rule of a general cargo vessel."

"Schultz, there are times when you surprise me."

"Times when I surprise myself, Frankie," he laughed.

"So what do we do now?"

"We go down to the third deck and open up that hold and see what we can see."

"Don't you think we should get some help?"

"Do you?"

"It is kind of cramped down here," Frank answered.

He followed Schultz down a series of ladders deep into the old ship's innards. It was a pain in the ass carrying the rifle because he had to hold it with his bad arm, using his left arm to act as a grip on the handrail. The insides of the ship were clangorous and hollow, like the huge steel chamber it was.

Schultz held up a hand when they reached the third deck. Frank could feel the vibrations of the huge ship's machinery through the propeller casing beneath his feet. They stood silently before a heavy metal watertight door. There was no marking on it but Barney didn't have to tell him what it led to.

"We'll play it like it was a flop house in the Tenderloin— the only difference is we don't kick this one in. That sucker probably weighs a hundred and fifty pounds. You'd break your fuckin' leg off."

254

Frank took the right side while Barney slowly turned the handwheel, retracting the brass dogs which held the door closed. Frank felt his finger slide down on the trigger. The door clicked open and Schultz, too, raised his gun, holding the heavy door with one hand as he would the reins of a horse.

The door swung out towards Schultz and it was Frank who got the first view of the inside hold. The light was dim but Frank was able to make out two dark figures stooping over what appeared to be a naked body lying on the floor. As his eyes adjusted to the change of light he identified the two silhouettes as being Chinese and the body on the floor as a man. The Chinese looked up sharply when the light from the door flashed in.

"Police, don't move," Frank yelled, taking a step inside the door.

The two men stepped back from the body. It was then Frank saw blood drip from what looked like the blade of a knife. He knew who the naked man was without having to take another step.

Before he had time to move two shots sang past and slammed into the bulkhead behind him with a tremendous racket. He pulled the AR-15 muzzle to his left and fired three quick rounds in the direction of the shots before ducking back out into the passageway.

Schultz, still using one hand, yanked the door back on its hinges. "Where did they come from?" he asked Frank as they faced one another across the open space.

Parker's ears were still ringing.

"Your side, it seemed like only one gun."

"Did you get him?"

"I don't know what I got. There's someone on the floor in there. I think it's Yee."

"Is he dead?"

"He will be."

There was no more discussion. Both cops knew their next move, knew what it meant to keep Yee alive.

They went through the wide door together shooting at everything in sight. Frank took the right side of the hold, Barney the left. The sound was deafening as their fingers worked the rifle triggers like typewriter spacers.

It was over almost before it began—his rifle was barely warm. There had been a man on either side of the door standing guard. Both were now lying on the cold, wet deck of the hold. The two men who had been standing over the body were also on the deck but they weren't dead.

The only light came from a yellow bulb above the grid separating the hold between the second and third decks. The light cast an eerie checkered pattern of shadow on the floor of the cargo area.

Frank walked over and stepped on the hand of the man with the knife. The bloodstained blade came loose.

"Get up, asshole."

The man didn't move.

"I don't think they speak our language," Schultz said.

"That's all right, they seem fond of this position anyway," Frank said, cuffing both men's hands painfully behind their backs.

Schultz was standing over Sidney Yee.

"Poor bastard," Frank muttered.

The face was barely recognizable, so badly had he been beaten. Blood trickled from the places on both sides of his head where his ears had been. His hands and feet were bound behind him like an animal about to be put on the spit. There was no mystery about where Yee would have been going—a rice sack lay crumpled near his body.

"Lucky J not so lucky," Schultz said as Frank picked up the small gold chain by his feet. He rubbed the jade clean with his thumb. In the pale artificial light the stone looked almost black.

"I don't know, he's still alive."

"Not for long if we don't get him to a hospital. I better get up topside."

Frank was left alone in the hold with Yee. He knelt down next to him and cut the bonds from his hands and legs with the same knife which minutes earlier had taken off Yee's ears. Sidney grunted in appreciation but his agony was so great that his relief lasted no more than a few seconds, then he was again groaning and writhing from the pain.

Frank wondered if Yee could hear. There was a question he had to ask. Not about heroin, or about Ling.

"Can you hear me?" he asked gently. "Sidney, can you hear me?"

The naked man opened as much as he could of his left eye.

"Who killed Rita? Who killed Rita Chan?" Frank asked him.

The hideous swollen face tried to speak but couldn't. Frank asked him again.

"Who killed Rita?"

Yee's right hand moved slowly to his side. Frank looked down at Yee's leg. There was a tiny brand on Yee's thigh.

30

A sergeant with a strawberry for a nose looked out the window of his black and white at the press pass, then, rubbing the back of his size-eight head, looked at Harry.

"You sure you want to drive up there, Mr. Carl?" he asked warily. "This ain't no street fair."

"Sergeant, I know when to duck," Harry said out the window of his Ford.

"You're the only newsman to come up in this neighborhood," he said to himself as much as to Harry. He was plainly the kind of cop who worried. He didn't want to take responsibility for a big time reporter but, more than that, he didn't want Harry to get hurt.

"How many units do you have in this area?"

"Including me, three. Three cars for sixty square blocks."

"Maybe something will happen at the meeting tonight," he suggested.

The sergeant grunted. "When you've been a cop as long as I have, Mr. Carl, you know better than to expect logic from policemen."

Harry said the same was true of reporters and the two cars continued in different directions. Harry's Ford moved west up Page Street toward Mint Hill. There was still an hour before the POA meeting and he wanted to see what one of the so-called trouble areas looked like. After being castigated that morning by both the cities editor and Brit Jefferson, he had been told to stop picking on Bill Moffat. It seemed crazy for him to be risking his Ford, not to mention other prized extremities, for a story he would probably never write. But as they said about new tricks and old dogs. . . . It was too good a story.

Mint Hill, strangely enough, was named after the historic United States Mint which was on the south slope of the hill. It had once been a white working class neighborhood between the black Fillmore District and the chicano Mission District. Now the majority of residents were poor blacks, most of them having been pushed south by the redevelopment in the Fillmore. Jimmy Cleveland had once told him the Redevelopment Agency had a talent for creating ghettos faster than they tore them down. (Nobody played both sides of race street harder or better than Jimmy. Now some would say he played too hard and that's why he was dead. Some would say that but not Harry.)

The Ford crawled up the dirty, trash laden street, passing under the skyway at Octavia Street. It was still light but Mint Hill seemed beyond the reach of day and night. It was gray and quiet and smelled of burning rags.

A commotion on the next block caught his eye. "Jesus Christ," he murmured to himself as he approached the corner market, or what was left of it after the neighborhood kids had picked it apart. All that remained were the newspaper racks and the caged front door. The windows had been broken and the shelves were emptying fast.

The kids, some no older than eight or nine, were like an army of ants in an abandoned picnic basket. He'd been in Harlem and had seen worse in Asia but the scene at Larry's Market was more disconcerting to him. There was no rage, no hostility in the taciturn faces of the young black boys as they carted off boxes of candy, cigarettes and liquor. One young boy was struggling with a case of dog food. It was business as usual. They could have been on a loading dock.

He was reaching for his notepad when a bottle hit the passenger window. He flinched but the safety glass didn't shatter. The teenager who threw the bottle smiled and disappeared back into the market, probably for another. It didn't occur to Harry to be frightened, the scene was too surreal, too stark and mechanical for him to be afraid.

He looked up the street. Blinds and curtains were drawn. Lights were on in most of the homes. He found it hard to believe that parents could let their children run around on an evening like this. Were the parents afraid to stop them? Were they waiting for it to get dark enough to come out themselves? Or did they just not care? He couldn't get over how alien the street seemed. He was no racist, but he felt an unbidden wave of contempt for people who raised their children to loot a store so casually.

At the top of the hill he turned left on Webster toward the Fillmore. He passed another market, the Mint Hill Grocery. A middle-aged black woman, built like an oak wine cask, stood in front of the market with her huge arms folded defiantly across her breasts. She nodded to Harry as he drove past. Harry nodded back. Maybe there was still hope.

The woman in front of the store reminded him of Sam Belardi and of Jimmy Cleveland and of the sergeant with the strawberry nose. They were the story—not the police or the Chinatown gang killings or the presidential aspirations of Governor Moffat.

All day he'd been fighting Jefferson and other editors who wanted to go with the police angle. New York was drooling over pictures of striking cops drinking beer and waving pistols from the picket lines. Matt Fleming had fresh columns of statistics citing every crime committed in San Francisco over the past seventy-two hours, and, of course, research had come up with a list of police wages and benefits in ten major U.S. cities. That the SFPD wages and benefits were considerably better than New York and most other cities made the editorial board all the more anxious to run the greedy cop story. That afternoon Jefferson had given the green light for a cover story and the deadline was four P.M. Friday. It was a typical case of New York writing the story they wanted to see.

What his editors refused to realize was that the police strike was not the cause but only the symptom of a far more serious disease, of something whose true pathogenic signs were evident only when the city itself was examined. San Francisco, the nation's most beautiful city, the Paris of the Pacific, was being destroyed by the urban blight that had—less dramatically, perhaps—afflicted so many other cities over the last fifteen years. The city was being attacked from within, not only by its police but by its irate taxpayers, its hate-filled minorities, its cynical businessmen, its parasitical reporters and—finally and perhaps most brutally—by its political leaders.

The question wasn't the avarice of the police department, nor was it even the right of public safety employees to strike, but whether or not the city could be saved from itself. That's what men and women like Sam Belardi and Jimmy Cleveland and the lady in front of the grocery store were doing. But how could a national magazine, especially one based in New York, be expected to address itself to such a frightening question? The parallels were too close, the numbers too familiar. After all, Harry thought, what would happen if the patient died?

Suddenly he jerked the wheel right on Fell Street and headed toward the Bay Bridge.

31

FROM the skyway the mayor glanced over at the Ferry Building clock. It was twelve minutes after seven. Because of the POA roadblock, Governor Moffat and General Hinshaw had delayed their invasion until seven-fifteen. The governor's press secretary said General Hinshaw was planning a full-scale assault on the blockade—hence the delay. The mayor, however, suspected another less strategic motive—namely, Moffat's insistence that the television people have time to set up their equipment. Like all would-be conquerors he wanted to make an entrance befitting his ambition.

The delay would prove costly. Just how costly the mayor wasn't sure. A lot had to do with how he played the three kings he had just drawn to his low pair.

Spivac followed the flashing lights of the Highway Patrol car onto the Bay Bridge approach. The traffic was light; the CHP had rerouted both directions to the lower level of the bridge. The mayor remembered many summers before, when he used to ride the key system into the city on the lower level. Then it had been an adventure to come into San Francisco, one had an Oz-like sense of anticipation approaching the city skyline. Now a commuter could board a hundred-mile-per-hour train near his suburban home in

Concord, take the BART tube under the bay to his downtown office, and return home without ever seeing Coit Tower, the Ferry Building, the bridges and all the other landmarks that made this one of the most beautiful cities in the world.

He said a silent prayer as the limousine passed through the last Highway Patrol checkpoint before climbing the ramp onto the bridge. He was not the kind of man who usually thought in such terms, but he knew that the next fifteen minutes might well be the most important of his life. He prayed that his decision was the right one. He asked Constance's spirit to give him some of her strength and courage to defend this city. He asked God to be merciful if he couldn't make it.

He was alone in the back seat. Murphy and Topham hadn't been able to get away from the command center. The stalemate between order and chaos was about to be broken. The shock of Jimmy's death was wearing off and both the Bayview and Fillmore ghettos were brimming with violence. There were threats of reprisals by some of Cleveland's Redevelopment Agency cronies against the Muslim leader, Jammal Muhammad. There had been rumors of attacks on both the Park and Northern station houses. Judging from Pinch Murphy's reports, such attacks would meet little resistance. There were three men left in the Park station, and only two—the station commander and one lieutenant—at Northern. Perhaps the most significant and frightening statistic in an evening of horrifying numbers was the number of arrests made over the last few hours: zero. The city was beset by looters, yet no one had been arrested.

The huge silver-gray suspension cables began to lift the highway above the water. Ahead of them, halfway between the first and second towers, was an unreal sight: forty young to middle-aged police officers, dressed in Levis and T-shirts, all wearing bullet-proof vests, all armed, all looking or trying to look righteous, all standing or crouched behind the double row of cars and pickup trucks parked across the five otherwise deserted lanes of the upper level of the bridge. Behind the blockade was a phalanx of reporters. It was as if they were all waiting for King Kong to walk into the city.

"Michael, what kind of rifle is that cop in the Giant's cap holding?" The mayor recognized the AR-15s and the shotguns but not the larger gun.   Spivac made an admiring sound. "That's a .45 caliber Thompson machine gun. When those farmboys see that monster they'll shit bricks. That thing can get off six hundred and fifty rounds a minute."

"Where the hell did they get a gun like that?"

Spivac laughed. "Probably from the station house. It used to be the official police riot control gun up until five or six years ago when the City Council voted to take them out of the stations. Said they were too militaristic, didn't want our police force to become like a standing army."

The mayor thought of Wallace's ominous remark that afternoon: "They might get past us, but it's going to cost 'em ten men for every one of us." Later he'd asked Pinch if he thought Wallace's estimate was accurate. The chief told him it was. The City Council was afraid of a standing army but it was the City Council which had helped create one.

Spivac parked the car twenty yards behind the blockade, near the first tower. Both reporters and strikers strained to see who was in the car. No one was looking harder than Clint Wallace.

The big sloppy sergeant was standing next to the cab of a pickup truck. The door was open and it looked like he was talking into a CB radio mike, probably to a spotter stationed on top of Yerba Buena Island. Because of the bridge's construction it was impossible to visually follow the plane of the highway past the middle of the second span where the bridge was anchored by a huge cement block which rose some two hundred fifty feet out of the floor of the bay.

"Mr. Mayor! Mr. Mayor!"

Twenty reporters shouted his name. All three major networks and five or six local stations were there, along with reporters from every news organization in California. The governor's press office had done a good job.

"What are you going to do, Mr. Mayor? Are you going to stand with Wallace?"

The mayor gave a noncommital smile.

"Is it true that the governor and General Hinshaw are regarding this barricade as an act of open rebellion against enter the city and that only the President has the power to stop him . . ."

The questioner was Miranda Stone. The mayor had trouble ignoring her brittle good looks and hard brown eyes. It was only lately that he realized why. She reminded him of Ketty. The only difference was the freckles. Ketty Zimmerman was too rich to have freckles.

"Haven't you left for New York yet, Miss Stone? Before you go I want to give you a letter of introduction to the mayor. He's a good friend of mine, or at least he was."

The KSFT reporter, like one among many vultures, was caught up in the excitement of the kill and had no time for conversation. The questions became more and more frenzied.

"Is it true that governor and General Hinshaw are regarding this barricade as an act of open rebellion against the State of California?"

"We have reports that Wallace has lost the support of the rank and file in the POA and he'll be voted out later tonight. Will the strikers be granted full amnesty if they return to work and agree to submit their claims to a federal mediator?"

"Will that mediator be the secretary of labor? We have

reports out of Washington that the President has told Governor Moffat he will send the secretary out on the next plane if a tentative agreement can be reached."

Spivac abruptly led him away from the questions and the questioners and toward Clint Wallace.

"Ready, Mike?"

"Yes, sir, Mr. Mayor," Sheriff Spivac answered.

The mayor hadn't lost track of Clint Wallace's bulky form during the impromptu press conference nor had the sergeant lost track of him. Wallace was aware of the eight o'clock meeting in the Cooks and Stewards' Hall and both men knew the outcome of that meeting would be determined by the outcome of what took place on the bridge in the next few minutes.

The sergeant handed the CB mike to one of his aides and stepped forward to meet the mayor. Spivac stopped and the mayor walked the last few steps alone.

From where they stood the mayor was facing east, the direction from which the National Guard would come. There was a slight northerly breeze off the bay. For the first time in a week the mayor could feel a hint of moisture in the air.

"What are you doing here?" the sergeant asked gruffly, with no pretense of respect or formality. Clint Wallace was one of the least attractive and most unbalanced men he'd ever met.

"I thought you might need some help."

"I told you this afternoon, we don't want your kind of help."

"It looks like you could use it. You told me you were going to have three hundred men with you."

Wallace glanced behind him.

"We have enough to do the job," he said cockily.

"To do what job? To make forty fatherless families?"

"Listen, Belardi, I don't need some has-been politician telling me how to run my business. Now get the hell outta here before you and your bodyguard get hurt."

The sergeant turned to go back when the mayor preemptorily shouted his last name. Wallace was startled, startled enough to stop and turn around.

Belardi stepped forward to within a foot of the man's belly. He was so close he could hear Wallace trying to breathe. The mayor was betting that Wallace couldn't handle a face to face confrontation.

"San Francisco has put up with you long enough. Now, when the governor comes over this bridge I'm going out to meet him. Alone. We're going to have a brief discussion and then he's going to turn around and go back across the bay. I don't want you or any of your men to so much as sneeze while I'm talking to them. Do you understand?"

"You can't—"

"I can and I will do anything I have to to protect this city. For seventy-three hours our people have lived in the shadow of fear. Your shadow. Tonight it will be lifted, wiped out . . . If you don't think I'm serious I suggest you look at the bulge in Sheriff Spivac's parka. Underneath that parka is a .357 magnum revolver. If you or any of your men try to keep me from meeting the governor I've instructed the sheriff to shoot you in the stomach. I can assure you it will hurt you more than it will either of us."

Wallace's eyes stuck out in disbelief. Not a muscle moved in the mayor's face. When the sergeant couldn't even look over at Spivac the mayor knew he had him.

"They're coming, Sarge! He says they're coming out the tunnel right now!"

The cop next to the pickup was yelling. The rest of the men crouched down behind the double row of cars. His men were waiting for orders but Wallace still couldn't move.

267

"You better take your position with your men," the mayor told him. "Just be sure to stay on this side of the barricade."

Wallace quietly turned and walked back to his men. He'd helped bring the city to her knees, now he was on his . . . his props had gone out from under him . . . the shell was broken. . . .

The mayor stole a glance over the north railing of the bridge. He had no trouble locating Pier 35. Two helicopters were circling overhead. His eyes moved back slowly for a loving look at the city before him. He'd seen it a thousand times over but the sensation was the same. He had been a fool to think it could ever be different.

The suspicious cops watched him wend his way through the cars. They looked afraid but committed. Wallace's demagoguery had brought them there, he hoped Wallace's cowardice would help get them home.

"The mayor wants to talk to Governor Moffat," the POA leader explained to the waiting cops in his midwest drawl, "Hold your fire until he's safe back behind the barricade."

"It's too late for talk," one of the men yelled. He was holding a Thompson submachine gun and looked ready to use it.

"Tell that to your kids tonight, officer," the mayor snapped as he stepped out alone in front of the makeshift barricade.

There was no more yelling.

He walked toward the second tower. The evening sun threw an orange-pink light on the three magnificent towers before him. He could already hear the low grinding of truck gears beyond the rise and felt the steel girders vibrate under the wheels of the oncoming army.

He saw their helmets first, olive drab, standard issue. Then came the familiar Jeep grills, seven abreast, each carrying four khaki-uniformed soldiers. The men not driving were carrying M-1s and shotguns. Their young faces were orange in the strange light. The columns came steadily over the rise, each jeep followed by another.

"To protect lives and property" was the catch phrase of the National Guard's dual mission. Under ordinary circumstances their mandate covered federal property only, but Governor Moffat had seen to it that San Francisco's police strike had become "a major civil disturbance threatening the life and safety of every citizen."

William Moffat, the twenty-fourth governor of California, was sitting in the back seat of the lead jeep with Fred Zimmerman. Neither man wore a helmet and the governor's slick black hair didn't move in the open jeep. Moffat, who was two years younger, three shades paler and much more serious looking than Zimmerman, pursed his mouth when he saw who was waiting for him. Zimmerman turned his head and said something but the governor seemed to ignore him. General Hinshaw, in the front seat doing his best to look like George Patton outside of Salerno, also turned to address the governor. Moffat nodded his head once, then twice.

General Hinshaw raised his hand and the motorcade slowed to a halt. The lead jeep was less than ten yards from the mayor. That jeep was followed by about two hundred more, and they in turn were followed by convoy trucks. All seven columns extended back over the rise, continuing, he guessed, all the way back to the Yerba Buena tunnel. There were at least five thousand troops in the formations.

The guardsmen, who looked even younger close up, had their rifles pointed toward the policemen behind the mayor. He didn't look but was sure Wallace and his men had their heavy artillery pointed back.

It was General Hinshaw who broke the silence and ordered his men to shoulder their arms. The mayor turned to Wallace, who reluctantly gave the same order to his men.

"General Hinshaw, if you don't mind, I'd like to confer with the governor in private for a minute."

The general, who obviously did not welcome the presence of any civilians on the battlefield, stepped out of the jeep without answering. The governor was legally in command, as the mayor knew, and as such was the designated spokesman. Moffat and Zimmerman climbed down from the jeep and the three men stood facing the mayor no less than ten feet away.

"Mayro Belardi, as governor of the State of California, I order you to dismantle this barricade and let the National Guard troops proceed into the city."

The mayor had the impression that the governor was trying to reach the TV microphones twenty-five yards to the rear.

"Please, Governor Moffat, before you issue any executive orders I'd like a word with you in private."

The governor frowned—things were not going as he envisioned and his distress was obvious. The general, too, was impatient although the mayor suspected the sight of the Thompsons gave him more pause than it did his civilian counterparts.

"I don't have to read you the state constitution, Mayor Belardi. There is no question that your actions are in violation of . . ."

The mayor suddenly gripped the startled governor by the arm and led him to the railing of the bridge. Belardi was slightly taller than the governor and, though more than twenty years older, also stronger.

"What do you think you're doing?" the chief executive demanded softly, aware that a false move by either could catch them in a spray of bullets.

"I'm trying to save you an unnecessary trip across the bay," Belardi told him.

"God dammit, Belardi, if this is one of your ward heeler

tricks. I won't stand for it. Bryce told me you were losing it but he didn't say you were senile.

"See that last pier, governor? The one with the large gantry cranes and the helicopters flying overhead?"

Moffat looked down at the Ferry Building. He was unable to concentrate.

"No, governor, the last pier. All the way to the end just before you see Fisherman's Wharf," the mayor said, pointing with his finger.

The governor looked at the city as a tourist would. For him there were no memories, no emotions, to him it was a postcard.

"What about it?"

"That's Pier thirty-five, the Pacific Shipping Company dock. The rigging you see above the shed belongs to the PSC freighter, *Mindanao*. You're familiar with the Pacific Shipping Company, aren't you?"

"You know I am," the governor replied impatiently.

"Forty minutes ago the police found Sidney Yee, the Kum Hon leader, in the number five hold of the *Mindanao*. He had been tortured by four members of the crew and was about to be stuffed in a rice sack and thrown overboard. Ten minutes after Yee was found a dope dog sniffed out eighty-two pounds of heroin in the second deck storage area. The local DEA agent tells me he thinks it's the largest amount of heroin ever seized in the United States."

Moffat's chin involuntarily began to quiver. The mayor reflected on how much he was enjoying this conversation.

"Now you and I know—at least we can be reasonably sure—that Bryce had nothing to do with the smuggling operation. Unfortunately the public will think differently. I don't think I'm premature when I say that in light of the fact that Bryce Stevens was the finance chairman and chief fundraiser for every campaign you, Fred and I ever entered, that our political careers have come to an untimely end.

Untimely at least for you and Fred. Personally I was thinking of quitting anyway."

"You're lying. Bryce would never have anything to do with narcotics smuggling. That's preposterous."

He refused to look at Belardi when he spoke, but instead stared off to the west. His normally commanding voice sounded far away.

"There's something else I think you should know. Bryce has a silent partner with him in Pacific Shipping—R.Y. Ling, the president of the Son Lee Tong. The police tell me both the captain of the *Mindanao* and the Kum Hon leader Yee can implicate Ling in the smuggling ring. In fact they say Ling is the mastermind."

Moffat still kept staring off to the west and the mayor continued.

"I took the trouble of calling the secretary of state's office before coming up here to see you. I was lucky to catch him. He ran a computer check of your campaign contributors in the last election. Did you know R.Y. Ling's name appeared on twenty-five of your campaign committees?"

The governor of California finally closed his eyes to the beautiful evening panorama. The gesture, the mayor knew, was one of surrender.

32

"LINEUP in ten minutes," Lieutenant Burns yelled into the locker room.

"Jesus, I musta put on fifteen pounds," Mike De Angelo lamented to Frank as he tried to tuck his uniform shirt into his pants.

About forty other cops were doing variations on the same theme as the evening and night watches dressed for an emergency lineup. Those who had gone to the Association meeting said Clint Wallace had flipped out. He'd accused the mayor of threatening to kill him and had been booed off the stage. No one knew what Belardi had said to the governor. One man, who'd been on the bridge, said that when the mayor took Moffat over to the railing and pointed to something on the waterfront the governor looked as if he'd just pissed in his pants.

The vote had been nearly unanimous in favor of returning to work after the mayor promised the Association members full amnesty and a retroactive eight percent pay hike.

A few men muttered that they'd do it again, but everyone in the room knew that no matter how many more dollars a month they demanded, the political battle, the battle for public opinion, had been lost. Belardi told them they'd blown it with the people and now it was up to them to try and regain public confidence. Frank thought that at last many of the men he worked with realized they needed the public's good will and support as much as the people needed their guns. If that realization really took hold then the whole damn thing might have been worth it. If . . .

"So what did Janis say? Does Kathy want to see me?" he asked De Angelo for the second time.

"Of course she wants to see you. Janis said Kathy just wanted to get out of the city for awhile. I think she went over to Marin County."

"Marin County?"

"You know. The pot of gold over the Golden Gate Bridge. That place where all the trees grow in the shape of hot tubs."

"Yeah, I know what's over there. Coke dealers and retired ski instructors. Every sleazy bastard north of LA."

De Angelo laughed at Frank's outburst.

"Did she say Kathy would be coming home tonight?"

"Jesus, Frank, I don't know," Mike said, still smiling. "Why don't you call Janis if you're so uptight. All she told me was that Kathy called and wanted you to know she's all right."

Frank slammed his locker shut. He desperately wanted to see his wife. He was exhausted and confused. He was sick of shooting at yellow faces and staring at brands and trying to understand what it all meant. So much had happened and so little had been resolved. He wanted to get away from Central Station, from Chinatown. He wanted to be with his wife. He wanted to hold her and talk to her.

Marin County? She'd probably gone over to one of her friends' house. He knew that many students in her program lived in Marin. He couldn't remember if they were men or women. His lapse of memory made him slam the locker again.

"Parker, the captain wants you in his office," Burns said,

coming back down the stairs. "The rest of you in five minutes. Come on, get your butts in gear. We've got a lot of work to do tonight. There are a few people in this city who don't know your vacation is over."

"What's been coming down with you and Schultz? I heard you guys were in on a big raid earlier with the Feds." Mike asked him.

"I wish I knew," Parker said truthfully. He took a step toward the stairs then stopped. "See if Janis can find out where she is, huh, Mike? I've got to see her."

"Sure, Frank, sure," De Angelo said, still fooling with his riot equipment.

The captain's door was closed and Frank knocked. A hoarse voice ordered him to come in.

"You look worse than I do." Brady said, making a motion for Frank to sit down. There was a pause. He seemed to be trying to remember why he'd sent for him. Frank thought to himself that if he looked worse than his captain he must look awful.

"I just talked to your partner. I want both of you guys to go home and get some sleep. Let your friends Jones and Thompson clean up their own mess. It's basically a PR job anyway, and that's not your style."

Frank thought he was being complimented.

"How's the arm?"

"I'd forgotten all about it," he said, remembering the dull pain that had left his right arm numb.

"You and Schultz were very impressive today . . . "

"How does it look, captain? Are we going to get Ling?"

"If Sidney Yee lives . . . and will talk. If the captain of the *Mindanao* can be made to testify. If certain leads can be developed. . . ."

"You know they won't talk." Frank heard himself say in a strange voice.

275

Brady's tired eyes met his. Frank wondered when the captain had last slept. He also wondered if R. Y. Ling was going to remain a free man.

"When you're dealing with a man as wealthy and ruthless as Ling, nothing is certain, especially justice," Brady said. "The important thing is that we've blown his cover. The mayor has promised full cooperation, and now, with the Feds involved, the Son Lee Tong can be turned inside out."

"What you're saying, captain, is that it's out of our hands. Phil Andropolus gets shot in the back, an innocent girl is murdered, we find twenty million dollars worth of uncut heroin on a ship he probably owns and we can't even pick Ling up."

The captain stood up abruptly. His teeth were clenched. Frank thought Brady was going to hit him. Instead he turned and pulled out a drawer from the metal file cabinet behind him and took out a thick manila folder. The folder fell with a thud on the desk in front of Frank.

"You know what's in there, Parker?"

Frank had seen the file before but knew better than to answer his captain.

"Eight years I've been putting that together. Everything from help wanted ads in the East-West Times to report cards of thirteen-year-old gang recruits. Every time anyone in this station reported anything about the gangs or the Son Lee, I put it in here. I used to take the Chinatown Task Force reports home with me to study on the weekend. For eight years I've been watching, listening, waiting . . . peeling away the layers of rice paper one by one. In the beginning I didn't even know there was a man in Chinatown called Mancat Ling, can you imagine? I didn't know what a tong was. All I knew was that people in Chinatown were afraid and their fear was rooted in something more tangible than a distrust for police. Do you understand what I'm telling you?"

"I think so."

"You're right . . . the DEA *is* going to take over. To tell you the truth, I'd rather have the Feds handling the case than the people downtown. They've had enough chances. Law enforcement is just like any other business, the bigger the fish the heavier the line."

"Do you think there's a problem downtown?" Frank asked, remembering his own trouble with the narcotics squad.

"Let's put it this way. There's always the chance of a problem when you have a seventeen thousand dollar a year narcotics officer investigating a ten million dollar a year mobster."

Frank thought of telling Brady about the triad brands, about the blood types. Earlier he'd thought he might be able to solve Rita Chan's murder himself and then get the evidence to someone like Andropolus without becoming involved. But after seeing the mark on Sidney Yee's thigh he knew the case was too big for a white patrolman from the avenues. He knew there was more—a connection other than narcotics between the triad brands, Rita's death, the gang shootings and Ling himself—but he didn't know what the connection was or where to start looking for it. Maybe it would turn up in the Federal investigation. Maybe not.

"Time for the lineup, captain," Burns announced as he came into the room.

"Did you keep the reporters out?"

"The only people in this building are police personnel. But Al Landi wants to interview Parker and Schultz after the lineup."

"About what?"

"The Danny Pong shooting."

"Tell him to come to me. Frank and Barney aren't talking to anyone about anything. I already told Schultz."

Burns left the office and Brady put the file back in the cabinet. Brady put his hand on Frank's shoulder as they walked to the door.

"Look, Frank, I know how you feel. You're young, you're impatient, I don't blame you. If you weren't, you wouldn't be such a good street cop. But this kind of investigation takes time. There are just too damn many aspects of criminality involved, not only in this city, or only in this country, for that matter. I've waited to get Ling a lot longer than you have, and if I can wait a little longer so can you. All right?"

Frank had the same feeling he used to have when his father lectured him about getting good grades so then he could go to college so then he could make lots of money so then he could live happily ever after.

He left the captain's office feeling more frustrated than before. Now that he could go home he didn't want to. He didn't want to find Kathy not there. More isolation. He didn't want to have to telephone Janis De Angelo to ask where his own wife was. He was too tired and hyped up to sleep. He felt he had to keep moving. He didn't know where to go, except back to Chinatown.

"Hey, Parker," the desk sergeant yelled at him when he walked out front. "Did you get that phone message from the coroner's office?"

"What message?"

"It came in a few hours ago. It was from some doctor. Sounded like a faggot. He wants you to call him. Here's the number, says he'll be there late."

The sergeant held the slip of paper out with a limp wrist. Frank grabbed the paper and walked over to an unused desk. He dialed the number and asked for Dr. Fay.

"Officer Parker, I'm glad I could reach you," the assistant coroner said enthusiastically. Frank immediately regretted returning the call. "After we talked this morning I remem-

278

bered a new test just developed by the Los Angeles coroner, Thomas Noguchi. You know, the man who did the autopsies on the Manson victims?"

"What about it?"

"This test not only identifies a blood type, it can identify the sex as well. I ran the test on the sample we found under Miss Chan's fingernail and found it to be the blood of a woman."

"A woman? Are you sure?"

"I ran it three times. It took me most of the evening."

Suddenly it registered. He heard the words "Hong Kong girl like me."

Dr. Fay was suggesting they get together for lunch sometime next week. Frank said that would be fine and quickly hung up before the doctor could mention a date.

"You know where Schultz is?" he asked the desk sergeant.

"What am I, a secretary? I think he went across the street for a pop."

Frank went out the side door. He didn't want to run into his partner, nor did he want to see Captain Brady.

His Camaro was parked in the alley. The heat wave had broken and the air was cool and moist. He opened the trunk and took out an old football jersey and a pair of Levis. He took off his uniform shirt and pulled the City College jersey over his vest. The jersey was bulky enough so he could strap his Smith and Wesson to his stomach. He knew that what he was going to do could get him suspended, but he also knew this would be his only chance to act. Once the information about the blood type and brands came out in the investigation he would lose the edge. "Patterns appear and disappear," Andropolus said. If Brady wanted to wait six months to a year for official channels to solve Rita's murder that was his business.

The Mandarin Palace was on Washington Street between

Stockton and Powell, "Chinatown Heights" as the neighborhood was known. The streets were quiet and mournful. The gang killings of the previous days had visibly affected the community. As Frank had observed the summer before, the Chinese took the outbreaks of gang violence personally. The black and brown neighborhoods could go wild without the police but the Chinese would never loot their own stores. Enough shame had already been brought on the community. on the community.

He parked between the Mandarin Palace and the Chinese Baptist Mission. There was no time for reconnaisance; he had to find Patty Ho before the black and whites were back on the streets. The redolent street smell was the same as always. The door of the mission was open and he could hear hymns being sung from the basement. The Mandarin Palace was on the second floor but the street level glass door was locked. He pounded on the glass until the customary black shoes and dark baggy pants of the owner, Willie Toy, descended the red carpeted stairs. Although Toy knew him, Frank put his badge up against the window. Willie looked furtively up and down the street then opened the door a crack.

"Hi, Willie," he said pushing open the door.

"Police strike over," Willie said in mock relief, his black eyes still nervously watching the street. Frank suspected Willie was a member of the Son Lee Tong although he doubted he was an elder.

"Expecting someone, Willie?"

"Close early tonight," the Chinaman said evasively.

"I'm looking for Patty Ho. Is she still upstairs?"

"Patty no work here anymore," Willie said quickly.

"Maybe you can tell me where she lives."

"I don't know where Patty Ho live. She funny girl, come to work, go home, leave no address, no nothing."

"Don't give me that no nothing crap, Willie," he said,

grabbing Toy by the collar and lifting him up a few stairs, out of view of the street.

"You give me Patty Ho's address or this tie won't fit the neck of one of your Peking ducks," he said, choking Toy with his own necktie.

"This irregal," Toy coughed, at which Frank pulled even tighter. Willie's face began to turn the color of a bruised peach.

"Twenty-two Wetmore, she live twenty-two Wetmore, shingle house, number two."

Frank let go of the tie and Willie dropped to the steps. The address he gave was only a block away. He didn't think Willie would lie about something he could check so quickly.

He left his car where it was and hurriedly walked up Washington Street. There was a chance Willie or some Son Lee henchman would warn her so he didn't have much time. Wetmore Street was an alley halfway up the next block. He turned into it and immediately spotted the brown shingle apartment on the left side. The window sills had been replaced with aluminum siding, a telltale sign of Chinese ownership. He used his police "credit card" to open the door and walked into the lobby. There were the familiar Chinese sounds and smells, and fresh memories of other lobbies: Rita's, the Kum Hon hideaway. He felt nauseous, and he didn't know if it was because he was just tired or sick of Chinatown, sick of strange buildings and an even stranger culture.

Apartment 2 was on the first floor. He knocked once, then tried the door. Before he knocked again he heard a rattle of what he thought sounded like a fire escape being let down. He kicked the door in and ran to the window just in time to reach out and grab the wrist of Patty Ho. She screamed as he pulled her back inside the apartment. It wasn't easy. When she saw who it was, her pale, pushed-in face sank in relief.

281

"Expecting somebody, Patty?"

She shook her head, unable to speak. She was wearing a black housecoat and no shoes. Not the kind of outfit a young girl usually wandered around the alleys of Chinatown in.

He could see an empty suitcase lying on the bed. The one bedroom apartment was expensively furnished, much more so than Rita's, and the rug alone must have cost over two thousand dollars. The stereo speakers were the same brand as those at the Kum Hon hideaway.

"Earth, Wind and Fire . . . Lots of Chinese girls seem to like that group," he said, looking down at her stack of records.

"Me and Rita dance to it often," she said, brushing her shoulder length hair out of her face.

"It was on the record player when I walked into her apartment yesterday."

Patty's head bowed with renewed grief. He wondered how old she was. Twenty, maybe twenty-two. He couldn't see much of her body because of the housecoat, but her strength and the shape of her figure had not been lost on him.

"I heard from a friend that the group's name has some kind of symbolic meaning to the Chinese. It represents something to do with an ancient society, the Triad, I think it's called."

Patty's hand froze momentarily against her black hair, then she continued brushing.

"Do you know of that society, Patty?"

"Very old, I think."

"No, Patty, you more than think."

Without warning he grabbed her wrist again and spun her into him like a top. With his right hand he ripped her housecoat up to the hip. There, on the outside of her thigh just below the hip, was the inverted trine.

"*That's* what I'm talking about."

She relaxed in his hold. His hand, which had been on the outside of her coat, slipped onto her bare buttocks when he moved to support her. He wasn't immune to the temptation of the warm body close to him. He stepped back abruptly, forcing her to balance herself.

"What is it? What does the trine mean?"

"Go to hell."

"That isn't going to play, honey. You're in serious, serious trouble and I don't care who's after you—I've got you. I want to know who put that brand on you and why."

Her face retreated behind a mask of indifference. The mask of the fei jai he'd seen a hundred times. The mask he'd broken with his fist the night before.

"Look at your left forearm, Patty. Here, see those scratches? You got those yesterday when you held that pillow to Rita's mouth. That's right, you killed her and I can prove it. The skin under her fingernails is your skin. Sidney Yee and Danny Pong saw you coming out of Rita's apartment. That's why you set them up. Except you missed Yee. That's who you thought I was tonight, wasn't it, Patty?"

Her right hand automatically covered the scratches. The indifference had given way to fear, but Frank didn't think it was the law she was afraid of.

"Why?" he said, letting himself sound a little more sympathetic. "What I have to know is why you killed her. What could possibly make you kill your best friend?"

Her pale rose lips quivered. He noticed for the first time a small black mole under her left nostril.

"Sidney Yee is a bad mother fucker, isn't he, Patty? If he gets his hands on you he'll cut you more ways than a broken window."

She looked away.

"You know, I saw Sidney this evening. That's right, I saw

him less than three hours ago. We can't pick him up for anything now. Maybe it would be better if I just took you over to see him rather than take you down to jail. I know he'd want to see you, and it doesn't make any difference to me as long as justice is being done."

"No, please—"

"Then tell me why you killed Rita."

"I can't. I *can't* . . . they'll kill my family—"

"Who? Who will kill them?"

She threw herself on the floor, crying uncontrollably. She was nearing the breaking point. He knelt down on the carpet beside her.

"There's no other way, Patty. If it's the Son Lee, tell me. That's the only way you can save yourself."

Invoking the name of the tong had the desired effect. The sobs grew fainter.

"Tell me, Patty, or so help me God I'll let them have you."

The story came slowly.

"After you stop seeing Rita, she go crazy. She get very drunk many times. She say she will go to police. Tong spies hear about Rita. They tell me if my friend go to police I never see my family again. Yesterday when she call you I have to stop her."

Her body heaved at the memory of what had happened.

"How did it start? How did you get so involved?"

"They mark us when we leave Hong Kong. That only way we can come to America. Must have mark. They say they get us job and later we bring our family"—she made a cynical sound—"jobs are sing-song girl, looksie for gambling hall, sweat shop. If we want to get good job like waitress we have to pay tong one half."

"And if you don't pay, if you don't do as they say, they threaten your family?"

"More than threaten. One girl say she won't pay Son Lee more ransom. They send her ears of her father."

Frank remembered hearing about the Mafia using similar extortion methods thirty or forty years ago, but that such indentured servitude was still happening in America seemed incredible to him.

"Did you ever meet the president of the Son Lee? Did you ever meet Mancat Ling?"

She shook her head violently. The mere mention of the name seemed to terrify her.

"Have you ever heard any of the tong members mention his name?"

"Sidney Yee . . . Sidney tell Rita he talk to Mancat."

"Both Rita and Yee were property of the tong too?"

"Brother and sister."

"What?"

"Brother and sister. Sidney come from Hong Kong five year ago. He one of first with mark. He like working for tong, big man in Kum Hon gang. Then he send for Rita."

"No. They can't be. That's impossible."

He thought he had it all. A whole brutal, inhuman story—and suddenly he had nothing. The flat face looked up at him. The catharsis had given her new energy. When she stood up and walked into the bedroom Frank followed her, but not because she was a murderess.

Patty rummaged through her dresser, throwing beautiful silk kimonos and brocade dresses on the bed. She had been a well paid slave. When she found the packet she was looking for she broke off a rubber band and thumbed through it.

"Here," she announced, handing him a snapshot.

It showed a Chinese family—a mother, two sons and a daughter. Judging from the background—a sampan and water—he guessed it was taken in Hong Kong. It was a poor picture, but there, unmistakeably, was Rita at about twelve

285

or thirteen years old. Next to her, just as unmistakable, was the simian face of Sidney Yee. The sad little family of the refugee bank robber . . .

The nausea came back over him as he steadied himself against the dresser. Rita and Yee, brother and sister. It didn't make sense. It couldn't make sense and yet, in the maze that was Chinatown, he knew it didn't have to make sense to be true.

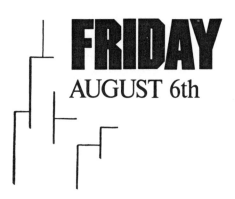

FRIDAY

AUGUST 6th

33

KATHY'S Volkswagen was in the driveway when he came home. It was late, three or four in the morning . . . he'd lost track of the hour. Twentieth Avenue was cold and wet. San Francisco summer had returned to form; the pavement shone dimly and the streetlight was a ball of yellow mist. The scene should have been familiar—and welcoming—but it wasn't. Maybe it was the hour, maybe it was Frank . . .

When he opened the front door he knew she was still up. The light was on in the kitchen and he could smell coffee. Kathy rarely drank coffee. He walked slowly toward the kitchen. Halfway down the hall he stopped. She had hung their wedding pictures back on the wall. He had never liked the pictures—her parents were too fat and his too old, and he looked like a nervous overgrown bumpkin in his rented tuxedo and regular boy's haircut. Only Kathy looked good. Born to be a bride, his mother had said. He remembered that.

"Frank? Is that you?"

She was sitting at the kitchen table, wearing a San Francisco State T-shirt. The word "Gators" was stretched out between her breasts. Her hair was scraggly and unkempt, her cheeks flushed. He didn't think she was drunk, but she definitely wasn't herself.

He laughed at the unlikely picture.

"What's so funny?"

"You."

She smiled tentatively then sipped from the cup of coffee in front of her. She drank coffee with the same awkwardness with which he smoked cigarettes. He bent over and kissed her on the cheek. She smelled like wine.

"You've had some phone calls. Reporters. Don't they ever sleep?"

"What did they want?"

"They wanted you. You must be a hero!"

He reached into the refrigerator and took out a cold beer with his left hand.

"Are you?"

"What?"

"A hero. Am I married to a hero?"

She laughed. It was a high-pitched laugh. The kind he'd expect from Rita Chan, but not Kathy . . .

"Barney called too. We had a nice chat. I think he was drunk."

"What did you talk about?"

"You. He says I should stay with you. That if I don't you'll become some kind of macho super-cop. The kind who take themselves too seriously and end up getting killed or getting crazy because cops are on the clock and criminals aren't."

"He should talk."

"That's another reason he wants me to stay with you. So you won't be like him."

"And what did you tell him?"

"That I'd think about it."

He took her crumpled note from his pants pocket and tried to conjure up the feelings he'd had earlier, to remember the urgency, the loneliness he'd felt when he'd read it.

"Did you really think I would leave you?" she asked.

"I didn't know what to think."

"I needed to get away from this house, from this city. I drove up the coast past Inverness. Then I went out to McClure's Beach. Remember when we used to go there with Mike and Janis?"

"Sure."

"There was no one there today . . . I mean yesterday. For the first time in I don't know how long I could really hear myself think. Then on the way back I stopped at Alice Pratt's in Larkspur and she invited me to stay for dinner. We taught the same workshop this spring."

The name wasn't unfamiliar to him, but the excitement in her voice was.

"She still can't believe I'm married to a cop."

"Why not?"

"I told her you were no ordinary cop. I think you'd like her. She lives with a man, Simon. He's in advertising. They have a spectacular hillside house above Madrone Canyon. He wants to meet you."

"Maybe we can all go out to dinner and I can shoot the waiter."

"Not funny, Frank."

"I'm sorry, honey. I'm very tired. Do you know what time it is?"

"Quarter to four in the morning," she said without looking at the clock. "I'm tired too but I wanted to see you. That's why I stayed up. I wanted to tell you about my wonderful day."

He took refuge behind his can of beer.

"When we were sitting on Alice's deck I could see the children playing in the park down below. They weren't like the kids you see playing here in the city. They seemed happier. It's not that they were white or rich or anything like that. What made them different was the soft light out there, the acres of green, the smell of the country . . . You could hear crickets and birds, their laughter. That's what I want for us. For our family."

He'd wanted to hear those words for a long time but now that she'd said them all he could do was take another sip from his beer.

"Alice says there are going to be four teaching jobs opening up in the Tamalpais school district next spring. I want to apply for one of them."

"You want to move out of the city then?"

"I talked with dad tonight. He said he could loan us the down payment on a house in the Larkspur-Corte Madera area. He said we'd need around twenty-five thousand dollars."

He stood there, waiting for something to seem real. He was twenty-eight years old. He made a little over fifteen thousand dollars as a patrolman and would make nearly eighteen thousand dollars if he passed the inspector's test in December. His wife was telling him that it was time to start raising a family and move to the suburbs. It was a progression he didn't question. Indeed, it was something he'd badly wanted. So why wasn't it taking?

"I know you don't want to leave the city, Frank, but I think once we go over there, once you sit on Alice's deck and breathe the evening air, then you'll see how country life can be."

"Marin County isn't the country, Kathy. The crime rate there is almost as high per capita as it is in the city. And that's without any spades."

"I wish you wouldn't use that word."

He already had his hand around the cold can when he suddenly realized he was too tired to drink any more.

"You'd only be twenty-five minutes from the station," she was saying as he put the can down on the table.

He tried to picture what life would be like in Marin. It

wasn't easy. He knew that a lot of cops lived in the suburbs, most of them in Marin. They were the kind of cops he didn't respect. A cop who didn't live in the city he worked in gave up something. He couldn't help it. Just like a cop who patrolled a community he didn't live in gave up something. Frank knew all about that. So did Woodruff Brady. . . .

His captain's long face had cracked with amusement when Frank had brought Patty Ho into the station a few hours before. "You don't trust anyone, do you, Parker?" he had chided Frank. "You're worse than I am." The two of them then took Patty into Brady's office. When Frank read Patty the Miranda warning, Brady was still smiling, but once she began her story the captain stopped being amused. The magnitude of the extortion and virtual bondage she described seemed to stun him. At one point Brady took his manila folder out of the filing cabinet but never once did he open it. What the Chinese girl was talking about had nothing—and everything—to do with his eight years of notetaking. Watching Brady's anguished expression Frank thought Brady could have been listening to a confession of his own wife's infidelities, not an account of R. Y. Ling's slave ring . . . .

"Frank, I'm talking to you."

He made an effort to concentrate on the plaintive face in front of him. He wished for both their sakes he could share her enthusiasm.

"What do you want me to say, Kathy?"

"You don't have to say anything. I just want you to try, that's all. Is it too much to ask that you try to meet some people who aren't part of your beat?"

"You know there's nothing I'd rather do than spend my free time playing tennis at the local raquet club. Then in the showers I can tell stories about nigger whores and drag queens with eight-inch pricks. Maybe they'd even let me fix their parking tickets."

"Damn you! Damn you, Frank! Can't you stop? For one second can't you stop being a cop?" she yelled. "Is it so impossible for you to relate to the world as a human being?"

"I wish—"

"No, you don't, Frank," she cried bitterly, "You don't wish. You don't have the imagination to wish. You complain to me that the men you work with are bigoted and greedy and lazy, but you aren't any different. You're as pitiful and paranoid as they are. Worse. Every day your world shrinks and you shrink with it. Barney was right, the only difference between you and the other two thousand policemen in San Francisco is you're going to be dead before you figure out that what you do isn't worth dying for."

Her outrage didn't affect him. Neither did Schultz's cynicism. He was too tired to get mad, too stale to argue. All he wanted to do was sleep.

He heard her crying softly in the kitchen while he brushed his teeth. Her wonderful day had been ruined. Strangely enough, he didn't seem to care. This time there was no guilt, no sadness.

His eyes looked swollen and the dark hair was down over his ears. Other than that he didn't look much different from the man he'd seen the last time he looked into this mirror. He knew he'd changed, though. In the last two days he'd killed three men—three boys, really. He didn't even know the names of two of them. He wished he could say that it bothered him, but it didn't. Maybe Kathy was right and he didn't have the imagination to wish, or enough compassion left to want to.

There was little question that his values, his perceptions . . . *he*, for God's sake, had undergone some kind of transformation over the past week. He'd noticed it again in Brady's office. While his captain had seemed confused, even betrayed by Patty's story, his own reaction had been the opposite. He had found himself intrigued, actually fascinated by her story the second time he heard it. Unlike Brady, he could accept the depth of Chinatown evil because for a while Rita had made him a part of it. He'd made himself part of it.

He put his .38 on the dresser, stripped down to his jockey shorts and crawled into the cold, clean bed. He tried to turn out the light but his arm was too stiff to move. He hoped Kathy wouldn't think his leaving the light on meant he wanted to talk.

"Committed" one reporter had called him—but that wasn't it. His superiors would say "highly professional" and put him up for a "meritorious," but that wasn't right either. It was simpler than that. It had to be simpler because the police department was bullshit and his marriage was all but ruined. It had to be simpler because he felt empty, and alone, even though he knew he was right. As right as he could be . . .

He closed his eyes and waited for exhaustion to become sleep.

34

SAN Francisco was asleep under a gray canopy of fog when the mayor came back from Bayview. He couldn't think of a better morning for the city to awake to. She'd had a long night. The fog would keep the summer sun off her burned and battered streets while its cool mist soothed her shaken citizens. He hoped her dreams were sweet. As far as he was concerned she could sleep in as late as she wanted. He wasn't tired.

He and Pinch had visited all three police command posts: Fillmore, Mission and Bayview. The captains and their men had been surprised and grateful to see them. The two men had shaken lots of hands and slapped many blue-shirted backs. The schism between the city and the police couldn't begin to close too soon. Pinch was to continue on a tour of the nine station houses while he returned to City Hall for an appointment with an old friend.

Commuter traffic was light on the skyway. Harry Carl had told him it would take a few days for the suburbanites to recover from the media shock treatment. The media itself had, of course, recovered nicely—as he and Harry had agreed, the collective conscience of the news establishment was notoriously resilient.

Already the *Chronicle* had made the transition from the

"City under Siege" headlines of the day before to an early edition editorial blasting him for his eight percent "surrender" to the striking police. The fact that San Francisco's two thousand officers had returned to duty and restored order to the embattled city streets in less than five hours didn't seem to impress the righteous eye of the morning daily. His favorite *Chronicle* columnist, in the only press-time column Sam could remember his writing in twenty years, said that the city had been kidnapped—the mayor had paid the ransom, now the kidnappers were patrolling the streets. Strong words for a man who hadn't set foot out of his Nob Hill townhouse, nor uttered a word against the police while the strike was still on.

The front page picture showed him with the governor "conferring" on the Bay Bridge. In a ten P.M. statement issued from the governor's mansion, the governor made it very clear that although it had been Mayor Belardi who had originally raised objections to the Guard's entering the city, it was William Moffat who made the final decision to keep them out. Politicians, the mayor reflected, were even more resilient than the news media.

They drove past the old Hamm's Brewery and behind the huge White Front store where the old Seals' Stadium used to be.

"Did you ever go out to Seals' Stadium, Mike?"

"No, Mr. Mayor, that was before my time."

"I was still in the City Attorney's office when the Giants played there. That was in 'fifty-eight when Horace first brought them out. But I'll tell you—it's the old Pacific Coast League and the Seals that bring back the memories. Nini Tornay, Bob DiPietro, those were my kind of ball players."

"Go to a game nowadays, it's not bad enough the Giants lose—you get mugged for the privilege," Spivac commented.

"That used to go on out at Seals' Stadium too. I remember

one guy in our office used to bring a bat with him. All the kids kept asking him where he got it, they thought it was bat day."

The mayor shook his head. There were a lot of memories.

"People forget the bad and remember the good," he went on. "You probably couldn't find ten people now who'd say the city is better than it was, say, thirty years ago. But the truth is, things aren't all that bad now—and they certainly weren't great then.

"Sure, the restaurants serve frozen crab, and there's only one sourdough bakery left, and the skyline looks like a broken erector set . . . and the people aren't particularly friendly—but you know, Mike, when I was a boy growing up in North Beach, no one talked to anyone unless they were from the same town back in the old country. My people were from Toscana and they'd cross the street to avoid the smell of a Neapolitan. As for fresh crab, it was fresh all right but only for two months out of the year, and even then it wasn't fit to eat some days because of spoilage.

"San Francisco used to be known as 'the city that knows how.' One, two phone calls to the right people and anything you wanted could be taken care of, from a visa extension to first-degree murder. Today you'd have trouble getting a parking ticket fixed without a grand jury investigation."

Spivak nodded and checked his rear view mirror, waiting for the mayor to go on.

"The city has changed, granted, but not necessarily for the worse. Everybody has a piece of the action now. I must have talked to twenty different community leaders last night. It was just like election night. But I tell you, they delivered. Damn right they did. If they hadn't, we'd have had one helluva breakdown, we'd still be fighting the fire. . . . She's still a considerable city, Mike. There's no place like her in the world. Don't let anyone tell you different. You hear me . . . ?"

298

Spivac coughed lightly.

"I guess I sound like one of the Chamber of Commerce shills who front for Bryce." The mayor laughed.

His driver didn't argue.

The limousine passed over Market Street. The next landmark was City Hall, and Spivac braked gently as they came down off the skyway.

"Sixty-three isn't that old," the mayor said suddenly, as if someone had said it was. "Look at the Chinese. Their leaders are just getting warmed up at around sixty. The Chinese and the Italians are alike—we're both late bloomers. Look at the Popes, for Christ sake." He smiled, and hoped he'd be forgiven for his slight blasphemy. "You can't even think about being Pope until you're seventy. Puccini wrote *Tosca* when he was eighty. Puccini was from Toscana too. He used to keep his power boat on a lake near Lucca where my father loved to fish. Every time he took the boat out my father said the fish disappeared but it was all right because it was Puccini. . . ."

"Your secretary wasn't at her desk so I let myself in."

Bryce Stevens was standing in Belardi's office when the mayor walked in. As usual he looked very fit, very debonair in a dark blue suit and white shirt, even though the mayor was sure he too had been up much of the night.

"She's home in bed. She was in the command center with me until six o'clock this morning."

"How's it looking?"

"Not much different from any other summer morning. The morning watch is on duty, commuters are going to work. The guests in your hotel are waking up to the sound of fog horns and cablecar bells."

"You must be feeling pretty good."

The mayor didn't answer.

299

"You almost single-handedly saved the city. It's a shame no one seems to appreciate it."

"I did my job. Others did more."

"You mean Cleveland?"

"No, not Jimmy. What he did was for another place. But there were all kinds of people, hundreds, thousands from every part of the city who held their ground, refused to be intimidated."

"I assume you're including the police in that number?"

"The police were manipulated into the strike by a few greedy men—the same way the taxpayers were hoaxed by Zimmerman. When the cops realized the real consequences of their actions they came back to work. Thank God they did. Maybe someday politicians will realize public safety is one thing that can't be politicized."

Stevens smiled. He'd always had the ability to make his smile hard-earned, but this morning the grin came cheap.

"Sam Belardi, the last of the old-time big-city mayors."

"I've got a press conference in half an hour, Bryce. What do you want?"

"A lawyer. A good lawyer who will be paid in money, not gold plaques," he said, gesturing to the wall. "I don't think those plaques are going to send your grandchildren to college."

"You've already got twenty lawyers."

"I've got twenty Ivy League tax dodgers. What I need is a man with political savvy. I want you to represent both me and Pacific Shipping. There's a good chance the Maritime Commission will try and shut us down because of what happened last night."

"I wouldn't blame them."

"Sam, you know damn well I didn't have anything to do with that heroin. It was Ling's operation all the way."

"I'm listening."

"He approached me about setting up a shipping company

about three years ago, just after your campaign. He said he had a friend who'd gotten to be a big wheel in Peking, and that this man was about to be named minister of trade. He said if we bought a shipping line, modernized it and proved we could compete with Sealand, Seatrain and the other big American lines, we'd have the inside track on trade with China. He was talking about an exclusive contract with the biggest country in the world, Sam. The kind of tonnage the shipping business hasn't seen since the closing of the Suez Canal. When East-West Lines came up for grabs, we moved. Ling and I each put up half the capital, about three million apiece, but it was agreed that my people would do the purchasing and run the company. Ling said he didn't want the local Chinese community to get wind of his involvement with a shipping line because they would figure out what he was up to. A lot of the older Chinese hate the Communists and it was important for him not to jeopardize his position in the community. His people would help line up some of the crews. It made sense and I agreed. I'd been wanting to go into something new with a big potential for a long time, and here was this guy handing me three million dollars and the kind of inside track you have to have in this business . . . I didn't have the slightest idea what the blue-eyed bastard was really up to until last night. The deal with his friend in Peking was supposed to be a year or two away because of some instabilities in the political situation there now. Hell, we're doing all right *without* the Chinese. No one was more surprised than I was when this little jerk from the Customs Office showed up at my home to tell me one of my ships was full of heroin. I wanted to junk the *Mindanao* and the *Luzon* a year ago, but Ling said we should hold onto them for tax purposes. My lawyers agreed with him, they said the depreciation left on those old barges was worth more than Tony Bennett for three weeks in the Phoenician Room—"

"Bryce, I can't help with this. It's a Federal case now. The DEA, Customs, Immigration, even the FBI are waiting in line for this one. The only man who can do you any good is in the White House, and the last time I checked, you and I weren't at the top of his guest list."

"Sam, I'll give you a retainer of one hundred thousand dollars to represent me and two hundred thousand more to handle the company's problems. We can serve Ling up to the authorities faster than the first course in a Chinese restaurant. Christ, you'd be doing a public service by helping put that bastard away."

"Provided I let your boy Moffat keep taking his bows, so he can pull the right strings for you after he's President?"

"You scared him to death last night with that secretary of state computer check bullshit. It took me two hours to convince him that Ling never contributed a cent to his campaign. He wouldn't believe me until we had the secretary of state go down and personally check through the contributions lists. Bill Moffat's cleaner than the Fuller brush man . . . I should know, I laundered him."

"Harry Carl once told me you had the integrity of a union pension fund. I'm not sure he was doing you credit."

"Since when did you start quoting reporters and worrying about integrity? I'm offering you a very sizeable amount of money to represent me as soon as you're out of here. Are you going to accept it or do I have to go somewhere else?"

"There's nowhere else you can go, Bryce. The government doesn't need you to get Ling. A cop named Frank Parker, the same kid who put us on to the *Mindanao*, brought in a Chinese girl who can tie the Son Lee Tong directly to an underground immigration ring. Turns out your partner and his associates were running more than narcotics into the country. They were also bringing in slaves from Hong Kong, and I mean slaves. They branded the coolies over there, then brought them here illegally. Then the tong threatened to kill their families back home if they didn't turn over a percentage of their earnings. In some cases, like the one last night, these people were actually ordered to murder for the tong—"

"My God, that's incredible. Do you actually think Ling was the head of this thing?"

"He's the president of the Son Lee. He's the man who gave you three million dollars and talked you into keeping the *Mindanao*. He's the man who came into my office last summer and told me there would be no more gang wars if the Chinatown Police Task Force was discontinued. I never asked questions because I didn't want to know the answers. He offered me votes and you money. We didn't want to know where or how. We just took what he offered and said it was from Chinatown. If it weren't for men like Captain Brady and Patrolmen Parker and Schultz we would never have found out a thing."

Stevens looked at his watch. He was a good enough businessman not to waste time philosophizing when the deal was dead. As a king-maker he was kaput. There was a good chance his business empire was also in jeopardy, but he refused to admit it—even to himself . . .

The mayor might have pitied his old associate, but to men like Sam Belardi and Bryce Stevens pity—given or taken— was anathema. You won some, you lost some . . .

The hotelman was about to leave when he stopped in front of the mayor's cabinet, the one with the pictures. He picked up a photo taken at Moffat's inauguration.

"You miss her very much, don't you?"

It was the first time Stevens had asked him about Connie since she died.

More than I ever dreamed, he thought, but wouldn't dignify Stevens by saying it out loud.

The two men watched each other in an awkward silence. For the first time since Belardi had met Stevens the hotelman was speechless. After twenty-five years their common ground had finally been used up.

"Go get yourself a good lawyer, Bryce, you're going to need one. As for Bill Moffat, tell him I took the trouble of taping our conversation on the bridge last night. That's right, it's all history. He might be clean, but he sure acted guilty."

"You son of a bitch."

Belardi nodded, and thought with satisfaction that politics was still a game of skill, not age.

After Stevens had left the office the mayor straightened the picture which had been moved. He noticed that his hand was shaking and he grabbed the bookcase to steady himself. The strain of the last five days was getting to him, but there was no time to rest. Not yet. He'd been in enough battles to know that the peace terms were often more crucial than the war itself. He knew that certain councilmen, led by Fred Zimmerman, would soon recover their nerve and sense of public outrage. There would be resolutions passed and City Charter amendments proposed to punish the police, to forbid future strikes. The POA had made a significant compromise in accepting four percent less than the traditional formula called for, yet their compromise would be held against them by the public. The *Chronicle* editorial already termed it "police blood money," even though of the seven innocent people killed during the strike, none were killed by police bullets. Jimmy Cleveland's death would become the rallying cry for politicians and citizens alike who had neither liked nor respected him while he was alive.
he was alive.

What Sam Belardi had to do now was continue what he'd been doing earlier that morning. He had to restore public confidence in the police. The best way to accomplish that was to restore the confidence of the police themselves. It had seemed to him during his visits to the command posts that many of the cops were as confused and angered as the citizens. They were relieved to be back at work but upset—some of them bitter—that the public reaction had been so unequivocably against them. They felt humiliated by the public's contempt, just as the citizens had felt humiliated by what seemed to them the cops' arrogance in striking.

In a few minutes he would go before the press and tell his city that there were no winners in a police strike . . . There could be no victory when public safety was the game . . . There was only loss. Loss of order, loss of respect, loss of property and inevitably, loss of life . . . .

His hand went back to the picture. He heard Kenny calling him from the outer office. He waited silently with his wife for Topham to come get him.